The Bushwackers

Strongheart had not even ridden more than ten miles north of Cheyenne, Wyoming, when Eagle, his magnificent black-and-white pinto, started snorting. Eagle's left ear started turning toward the hillock directly to the west of the trail, which ran north and south. Joshua put the spurs to the big horse and Eagle sprinted forward, and Strongheart heard the bullet crack behind his head as the big horse propelled him forward. Fifty feet on, he spun him around and drew his Colt .45 Peacemaker, firing a snap shot at the top of the bluff where the shot came from. He ran fast until he came to the end of the low ridge, and he quickly veered left into the prairie grass, bounding around the north end of the ridgeline.

Now, on the western side of the ridge, he saw two riders climbing into the saddles of two bay geldings. The cowboys took off south at a dead run, but it did not take long for the long legs of the sixteen-hands-tall pinto to start catching up.

The one on the right made a big mistake and foolishly drew his .44, turned in the saddle, and tried to make a snap shot back at Strongheart. Joshua did a quick draw and fired, his bullet catching the man under his bottom rib, and it went through his torso, tearing out the other side. He literally flew from the saddle and landed in a giant patch of prickly pear cactus. Obviously, he immediately started screaming in pain.

Strongheart yelled to the other, "You want to end up like him? Just keep running!"

THE INDIAN RING

Don Bendell

BERKLEY BOOKS, NEW YORK

BERKLEY
An imprint of Penguin Random House LLC
375 Hudson Street, New York, New York 10014

THE INDIAN RING

A Berkley Book / published by arrangement with the author

Copyright © 2016 by Don Bendell.
Penguin supports copyright. Copyright fuels creativity, encourages diverse voices,
promotes free speech, and creates a vibrant culture. Thank you for buying an authorized
edition of this book and for complying with copyright laws by not reproducing, scanning, or
distributing any part of it in any form without permission. You are supporting writers and
allowing Penguin to continue to publish books for every reader.

BERKLEY® and the "B" design are registered trademarks of Penguin Random House LLC.
For more information, visit penguin.com.

ISBN: 978-0-425-26655-7

PUBLISHING HISTORY
Berkley mass-market edition / January 2016

PRINTED IN THE UNITED STATES OF AMERICA

10 9 8 7 6 5 4 3 2 1

Cover illustration by Bruce Emmett.
Cover design by Lesley Worrell.

Penguin
Random
House

Experience has shown,
that even under the best forms of government
those entrusted with power have, in time,
and by slow operations, perverted it into tyranny.

—Thomas Jefferson

On February 2, 2010, I had a very freaky thing happen. Three years earlier, I had been recognized by the secretary of veterans affairs, R. James Nicholson, during a speech he delivered at the Denver VAMC, in which he stated that I was the perfect example of how healthy a disabled veteran could live by working out hard, not smoking or drinking, and by eating healthy.

However, three years after being recognized, I had a blood clot form, break loose, and hit a valve in my heart, and I had a heart attack. While visiting me the first week in the hospital, my wife of then almost three decades, Shirley Bendell, had a routine physical and was sent to an oncologist. Shirley was diagnosed with chronic myelogenous leukemia with lymphoid blast crisis, which puts you in the fatal final stages of leukemia, usually with only a few weeks to live. On top of that, she had a chromosome cell mutation that nobody had ever survived. For the next two years, Shirley went through ten rounds of chemotherapy, numerous trips to MD Anderson Cancer Center in Houston, a bone marrow/stem cell transplant, and many near-death experiences. On several occasions, doctors told me she would not make it through that day.

Shirley had a deep, abiding faith and tremendous toughness, and she had "prayer warriors" all over the country praying for her. She had been swimming a hundred laps at a time four days per week, lifting weights, doing Pilates, teaching martial arts, and training horses when she was diagnosed. At that time, she was sixty-three years old.

More than three years had passed since Shirley's bone marrow/stem cell transplant, and she was totally cancer free and, according to her doctors, a living, breathing, walking miracle. She was back doing Pilates, teaching martial arts, riding horses, and staying on the go. A year after her transplant, she and I danced all the twenty- and thirty-year-old couples into the floor at a banquet.

Shirley was by far and away, man or woman, the toughest person I have ever known, and at the same time, the sexiest person I have ever known. We were married for thirty-two and a half years, and during that time I fell more deeply in love with her every day.

She was only the third woman in history to be inducted into the International Karate and Kickboxing Hall of Fame, was a sixth-degree black belt master instructor in four martial arts, had been a recovering alcoholic and prescription drug addict for well over three decades, public about being a former victim of both gang rape and acquaintance rape, an actress, stuntwoman, producer, director, business executive, gymnast, mother, and grandmother, and she covered her head with a prayer shawl every single morning and read the Holy Bible, prayed fervently, and read devotionals daily. When Shirley danced, people on the dance floor often stopped and watched her. With eleven grandchildren, after her transplant, she was at an indoor arena running barrels and pole-bending on a horse, helping me brand and ear-tag cows and neuter bull calves, and teaching karate classes again.

However, 110 days post-transplant, Shirley developed a hideous complication called GVHD, or graph versus host disease. The new cells would travel from one organ to another throughout her body attacking the healthy cells. She was often in a lot of pain but never showed it to people, and on Valentine's Day, 2014, the disease finally won out. She conquered incurable leukemia, but not GVHD. With her sister and brother-in-law, my son, Josh, and me at her side, Shirley passed away and was finally out of pain and misery after a very courageous four-year battle. I was very sad but also very happy for her. She is now pain free living in a mansion for eternity.

For all those years, I was not only totally amazed at her, but I always got excited whenever she walked into the room. Just seeing her quite often took my breath away. Shirley Bendell, you were my soul mate, my best friend, my business partner, my mistress, my dancing and hunting partner, my fishing buddy, my saddle partner, and the love of my life. You insisted that I keep living life to the fullest and find love again. I did, but not a substitute for you. It is a totally different love than I had for you, and you would approve of her. In fact, you predicted exactly what she would be like. All you ever cared about was me and what was best for me. I will always love you and treasure our memories.

Shirley Ann (Ebert) Bendell (3/20/47–2/14/14),
I dedicate this book to you.

Your forever passionate servant,
Don

ACKNOWLEDGMENTS

I have to acknowledge my close friend Rudi H. Gresham. Rudi is a fellow former Green Beret officer and Vietnam veteran and has been a wonderful friend. Rudi is also one of the most colorful characters I have ever known. Although he has a bachelor's degree in chemistry, Rudi became a U.S. Army Special Forces (Green Beret) officer during the Vietnam War and was selected to become the aide de camp to Lieutenant General William Yarborough, who is called the father of the modern Green Berets. Lieutenant General Yarborough was the commanding general when John F. Kennedy made the green beret the official distinctive headgear of the U.S. Army Special Forces, and a statue showing that immortalizes both at Fort Bragg, North Carolina. He created Jump Wings for airborne soldiers and came up with other similarly important innovations. Rudi became like a foster son to the general and delivered the eulogy at William Yarborough's funeral. Rudi helped his friend Ronald Reagan get elected to the presidency and was credited by George W. Bush for helping him get elected, too. President Bush rewarded him with a presidential appointment as senior adviser to the secretary of VA, where he served throughout Bush's tenure and more. Rudi was given the Special Forces Association Operator of the Year award three times, and many, many other honors. He also owned a successful chain of radio stations in the South.

It is incredible how many veterans Rudi has helped behind the scenes over the years, especially Special Forces veterans. In many cases, they had no idea, and some still have no idea Rudi was pulling strings to help them out. Rudi and I worked on a political campaign together, and I got impatient and wrote an inner-campaign memo complaining about problems within the campaign. It was pretty critical, and I figured that it would get me fired. Rudi was my supervisor on the campaign and told them that if they fired me, they would have to fire him, too. He has done so many behind-the-scenes good things for veterans. He frequently quotes his friend the late Ronald Reagan: "There is no limit to what a man can do or where he can go if he does not mind who gets the credit."

He is married to the beautiful former Miss South Carolina Faye Breland Gresham, and they have three adult children.

Rudi, my friend, you always choose to be in the background making good things happen for others. This time it is about you. Thank you.

De Oppresso Liber,
Don

FOREWORD

I started American Indian fancy-dancing when I was just a young boy with the Minniconjou Indian Dancers in Akron, Ohio. We performed quite often and I won several competitions, even against Native American dancers. When my buddies and I played cowboys and Indians, I always wanted to be the Indian and studied American Indian lore all the time. I wore moccasins all through grade school and carried a beaded headband in my pocket and put it on when out of sight of my house. I started bow-hunting while still in elementary school. I had no Native American blood, but it was in my heart. I was like a cherry cupcake with vanilla frosting. I was white on the outside, but red on the inside.

I also grew up in a racially mixed neighborhood until middle school and always got along with everybody, never really understanding the reasoning behind or sense in racial prejudice. To me, it was stupid, pure and simple. By the time I was twenty years old, I was commissioned as second lieutenant in the U.S. Army, a product of Infantry Officers Candidate School, and after Jump School, I found myself at Fort

Bragg, North Carolina, earning a Green Beret. It was 1967, and I voluntarily took part in racial seminars for soldiers at Fort Bragg. I was the only white soldier standing with the black soldiers arguing for integration, and I was the only officer in the room.

This novel deals with the Indian Ring, one of the most unfortunate and shameful things that ever came out of Washington, D.C. It deals with racial prejudice, especially for the true Americans who were here when the white men first arrived. The Indian Ring was real and so was secretary of war under President Ulysses Grant, William W. Belknap, and so were the incidents involving him and his wives mentioned herein. Belknap was the head of the Indian Ring and was impeached by the U.S. House of Representatives after resigning in disgrace, but what about all those in the Indian Ring who were never brought to justice? The character Robert Hartwell is fictional, but could have been a real person. There were many in the Indian Ring who sought personal gain on the backs of the American Indian. That is what is so sad about our nation's history. There have been those throughout history who want power, fame, and riches; without caring a whit about those they hurt in the process. We should learn from our mistakes, not repeat them.

1

EAGLE

The warrior's eyes scanned the deep snow, and on the surface of the crusted, frosty blanket were the saucer-sized tracks he had been following all morning. He saw before him a wide fan-shaped track along the top of the snow, and his mind pictured the long tail of the two-hundred-pound male mountain lion, as it crouched here looking at three mule deer who had fled high up and were having trouble moving in the deep, silvery, natural straitjacket. The tall warrior knew what had occurred. The lion had watched the three nibbling deer browse for old vegetation after pawing it away through the snowy morass, while his tail slowly switched back and forth making the fan-shaped track as he prepared to attack.

Dark, intelligent eyes looked at the sign over high cheek-bones on the handsome chiseled face, and the brave could see a deep imprint on the snow's surface where the big cat had hunched down and sprung forward in a fatal charge. His eyes swept the snow in front of him in twenty-yard arcs going back and forth until he spotted the bright red crimson he had been looking for. Earlier, the warrior had constructed a pair of expedient snowshoes by bending spruce boughs into a large teardrop shape and lashing them together, weaving to create a back-and-forth webbing. These were lashed onto his feet, and he had easily glided along the top of the three-foot drifts following this large tom all the way up to this alpine spot. The nearest trees could only by seen by looking down thousands of feet below him. His horse was down there in the dark trees, grazing on lush green mountain gamma grasses. He had dabbed black ash from his campfire below his eyes to prevent snow blindness from the sun glare off the snowcapped peaks he was ascending in the magnificent Sangre de Cristo mountain range, which extended from southern Colorado down through New Mexico territory.

He moved to the splashes of bright red on the snow and saw the area where the lion had jumped on the back of the doe and broke her neck with one bite while gripping her sides with his retractable claws. He had apparently just started to feed and, sated, moved to a higher perch to watch the kill. The warrior knew he was above him somewhere, lying under a ledge watching over the prey while he rested.

A big tom like this would have an area he would patrol every ten to eleven days that would cover fifty to one hundred square miles. He would look for females in estrus, kill any male kittens he could find, and mark his territory. In the meantime, he would make kills like this once or twice per week and feed on it until the meat started to get a little tainted and move on, leaving it for other predators.

The warrior did not get too close to the kill as he did not want to scare the cougar away. Instead, he stood there, his eyes scouring the ridge above him, which rose up another five hundred feet or more to become part of Crestone Needle, a peak of 14,197 feet in height. Far below the white blanket he stood on, he could see the crystal-clear bowl of Colony Lake and the blanket of thick green evergreens. His eyes had been scouring every rock overhang and the big tom made a mistake. He twitched his long tail and the movement caught the warrior's eyes. The cat was bedded down no more than one hundred feet above him. He turned his head, knowing he was being watched intently, but his eyes scanned an approach route, and he moved off to his right over the ridge and out of sight. The wind was blowing from his left to the right, but he knew at over thirteen thousand feet up on these windswept peaks, the wind direction could change fifty times over the next hour.

He disappeared over the ridge and as soon as he was out of earshot, started climbing. He worried on this slope about an avalanche starting. He tried to figure an escape route as he climbed in case one started. However, he lucked out, and an hour later he was in the notch he had used as a navigation spot. If he worked carefully around this ledge, he should come within sight of the big cat fairly quickly.

Ten minutes later, moving slowly now on solid rock under the ledge, he stepped carefully in his winter moccasins. He had removed the snowshoes when he had gotten on the rock. He rounded a bend and the big cat was lying there asleep. The brave averted his eyes, knowing that animals and elite warriors have a sixth sense that alerts them if someone is staring at them. He affixed his gaze on a spot to the left of the cat's tail and proceeded slowly, cautiously. Twenty feet away, he stopped and raised his bow, nocking an arrow. Just then the cat raised its head and stared straight at him, and his ears laid back on his head. A long low hiss came from behind the bared fangs as the cornered animal readied to lunge itself at this intruder. The warrior released the arrow, and it entered the cat's chest low next to the left shoulder, and it penetrated its heart, went through the left lung, and exited the left hip near the hipbone. Blood streamed from the big cat as it screamed and bit at the exit wound, and it suddenly dropped down dead.

The warrior looked skyward, then at the big cat. Smiling and quoting Shakespeare's *Richard II*, Act III, scene 2 in perfect English the warrior said,

> *Nothing can we call our own but death*
> *And that small model of the barren earth*
> *Which serves as paste and cover to our bones.*

He grinned and added, "Sleep ye well, yon lion, and may I not waste your hide or meat, for the Great Spirit has indeed blessed me this day. Thank you, God. Amen."

Within an hour, his snowshoes replaced, and a field-dressed mountain lion hanging limply over his broad shoulders, half-white and half-Lakota Pinkerton Agent Joshua Strongheart started down the long ridge to the trees below timberline where his magnificent pinto gelding Eagle waited, as did a campfire just waiting to be lit.

The snow ended before he entered the big stand of lodgepole pines, so he removed the snowshoes and cast them aside after retrieving the leather thongs used to construct them.

When he arrived at his camp he immediately started the fire and placed some cougar steaks on a spit he made out of a green branch. He would eat a meal and then dress and cape out the lion, and stake the hide out in the sun and brain-tan it with the lion's brains.

After dinner, Joshua walked out onto a large rock outcropping jutting out from the trees. The terrain was very rocky in this area. He was down below Colony Lakes with his camp and now looked up at the peaks towering above him: Crestone Needle, Humboldt Peak, Crestone Peak, each sticking up through the white fluffy clouds that were hanging around fourteen thousand feet.

He thought about the woman he loved, the woman he'd lost. Her murder had been so horrible and so brutal, it had a tremendously negative effect on him, which still bothered him. A seven-foot-tall psychotic serial killer, a Lakota or Sioux, named We Wiyake, meaning Blood Feather, had killed her. Joshua Strongheart, after a year, still blamed himself for not protecting her. It made him decide he would never marry again. His work would become his life, but Strongheart was still grieving and spending much time like this in the high lonesome. He looked out over the Wet Mountain Valley and the Greenhorn Mountains on the eastern side of the emerald-colored valley. Tiny specks of ranches dotted the landscape, and to his left front he could see the growing town of Westcliffe.

Joshua Strongheart was one of the premier agents of the famous Pinkerton Detective Agency and was a favorite of Allan Pinkerton himself. Joshua's immediate supervisor was Lucky DeChamps, a Paris-born, very dedicated manager with the Pinkertons and Joshua Strongheart's strongest supporter and harshest critic when need be.

The tall Pinkerton agent's mother was a successful store owner in northern Montana who left him a healthy inheritance and his father was a Lakota (Sioux) warrior named Claw Marks, who fathered Joshua when he had a love affair with Joshua's mother, who was then fifteen years old. Feeling strongly that life would be too rough for her and his child, Claw Marks left her, telling her that the world would be too cruel for her and a half-red child if they stayed together as a couple. He died later heroically fighting a band of Crow warriors while serving as a rear guard for fleeing tribal

members. He told Strongheart's mother that he knew their
baby would turn out to be a boy, and said he wanted to leave
his knife for him. It was the size of a Bowie knife, very well
made, scalpel sharp, and was carried in a fringed beaded
and porcupine-quilled ornate sheath, with the instructions
that it was to be kept sharp, used effectively, and treated
with respect by his son. He was a member of the newly
formed Strongheart Society, so he told her to use Strongheart as their child's surname.

She married a very courageous, tall, slender lawman,
Dan Trooper, who was a harsh taskmaster for Joshua but
loved him like his own son. He left him his Colt .45 Peacemaker, one of the first made by Colt firearms, which had a
miniaturized copy of his sheriff's star on the pearl handle
of the gun. After spending years teaching Joshua how to
handle pistols and rifles, and how to fight with his bare
hands, he too left instructions that the weapon be kept clean
and well oiled and only used as a tool to protect others, for
self-defense, or sometimes for hunting.

Joshua had learned several years earlier that he simply
could not drink, that he had a problem with alcohol. Lucky
had paid his fine to get him out of jail, in fact, over an incident
that he did not even recall. He had severely injured several
men in a saloon fight, and was very fortunate that Lucky was
able to essentially bribe Strongheart out of the problem, but
his charge was to pay him back from his pay for months. In
actuality, Joshua could have paid from the generous inheritance his mother had left him, but he was very conscientious
about credit.

As he ate a delicious piece of meat, he thought about the
Spanish who had come through this area decades before and
reportedly left a giant cache of gold nearby on Marble Mountain in a place called Caverna de Oro, the Cavern of Gold.

After eating, Joshua worked on tanning the hide and kept sorting his thoughts. His job as a Pinkerton agent was an important one. The big half-breed did not know it, but his business would end up becoming the model for the U.S. Secret Service. He had to be on top of things, and he knew he was not. He knew that he often sorted things out up where the eagles soar and people's voices could not be heard. Before dark, he moved to the shore of Colony Lake and fished for cutthroat trout, and kept several nice ones. He returned to camp and cooked them up for dinner, then slept early.

It was two hours before daylight when Eagle's soft whinny brought him wide awake. Joshua looked at Eagle's ears and they were pointing toward the winding trail he took to ride up to this loft. His powerful black nostrils were clearly flaring in and out. Rifle in hand, Strongheart ran over to the large rocks overlooking the trail as it rose from far below. The wind was carrying a scent up the ridge from someone or something out of sight thousands of feet below, but Strongheart could see nothing, nobody, no animals.

The small patrol had camped for the night one thousand feet below Strongheart. They were well back into a grove of aspen trees and one man sat on guard while the other five slept.

The sun started to peak through the aspens above as it rose over the Greenhorn mountain range across the valley to the east. Shards of light pierced the forest veil like arrows seeking unseen targets in the dark green morass of leaves. The guard had fallen asleep right before dawn and right after he built the fire to be ready for warming his waking fellow cavalrymen. The corporal in charge chewed him out for sleeping on guard while relieving his bladder. The men stirred and started to move toward the fire and suddenly saw the tall Indian half hidden in the forest shadows. There was no hiding the sixteen-hands-tall black-and-white pinto horse he sat upon. All the men froze staring at the business end of Strongheart's Colt Peacemaker. He had dealt with deserters before so he was not taking any chances.

"Howdy, boys," he said with a smile.

"Mr. Strongheart?" the corporal said, relieving Joshua's concern.

He holstered his pistol, clearly seeing the relief drain from several faces.

"What brings the cavalry up here in the mountains, Corporal?" Joshua asked.

"We were sent, Mr. Strongheart, to find you, sir." the cavalryman replied, "You are supposed to report to your boss with the Pinkerton Agency. They said it is top priority."

"Well thank you for all the effort, gentlemen," Joshua said. "How about breakfast?"

The corporal said, "Sure, Mr. Strongheart. We were just gonna fix hardtack, beans, and sourdough. Will, get the fire going better."

Strongheart said, "Instead of that, how about some fresh cougar meat and wild turkey eggs?"

"Cougar meat," one of the soldiers said, "Ah'm gonna git sick."

The corporal said, "Lion is the best wild meat there is. I'll take some, Mr. Strongheart."

Joshua looked at the naysayer while he dismounted and started getting the food out of his saddlebags, and said, "Stop and think about it, partner. Most of their diet is deer. They only feed on a fresh-killed deer a few days, and then leave it for other predators, and find another one to kill."

The young trooper said, "No thanks, Mr. Strongheart. Every bite I would be picturing eating mah paw's barn cats. Ewww."

The other men chuckled but all except the one tried it and loved it.

Strongheart, accompanied by the patrol, rode into Canon City two days later. They left on the train, and he rode immediately to the Western Union office.

The telegram from Lucky said one thing, "Must talk STOP Meet in Denver STOP."

2

THE ASSIGNMENT

It was two days later that Strongheart sat down across from his boss in a small café, drinking coffee.

"Are you ready to get back to work?" Lucky said.

"Of course, boss," Joshua said, "You pay me to be ready."

"*Sacré bleu*," Lucky replied, "I want to know if you are ready to work, not that you are willing to. You have been through a great deal, my friend, but I have an important assignment if you are ready."

Strongheart said, "All I have is my work, Lucky."

"President Grant wants us to discreetly investigate criminals in his own administration," Lucky began, "Secretary of War William W. Belknap and someone who seems to be a strong ally of his: Robert M. Hartwell, who we believe leads a large syndicate of very corrupt individuals."

"The Indian Ring," Joshua replied.

Lucky smiled, "Ha ha, you have been keeping up with things. Yes, the Indian Ring. We want a complete investigation of it. Belknap, as you know well, found out, resigned his post in disgrace, and was actually impeached by the House.

Hartwell is the true leader now. Strongheart, *zee*, the president said that Belknap is highly visible, and he may have to end up dealing with him even more politically, but Hartwell is not as visible, and the president does not care much about his fate."

Strongheart simply grinned while sipping coffee. He understood the message and was thankful.

Lucky said, "We want you now to go to your father's people and speak with them. We have had many reports that the Lakota as well as the Cheyenne and Arapaho are banding together because of the Indian Ring. So many white men have been invading the Black Hills in search of gold, the buffalo are being slaughtered, they geeve the tribes cheap blankets and sell zee ones the government issues, and so many things."

Joshua took a sip of coffee and said, "Tell me about Crook."

Lucky motioned for the waiter and said, "We better order a meal."

A waiter came over, they both ordered food, and then Lucky started to explain the situation that was fast developing. Twenty-four hundred soldiers were going to try to force the Lakota, Cheyenne, and Arapaho back onto their reservations, including the band of Joshua's father. Brigadier General George Crook had become the commander of the Big Horn/Yellowstone Expedition on May 28, 1876. It was now approaching mid-June. The day after he took command, he led a force out from Fort Fetterman with fifteen companies from the 2nd and 3rd Cavalries, five more companies from the 5th and 9th Infantries, more than a hundred wagons, pulled by more than 250 mules, and they were being joined by 261 Shoshone and Crow, who were also referred to as the Absaroka and were bitter enemies of the Lakota, Cheyenne, and Arapaho.

Lucky explained that Crook gave orders for all the men

to travel very light but to carry a lot of ammunition. When the column reached Goose Creek, the wagons and all the teamsters would bivouac there, and the infantry would mount up on mules and join the cavalry that way. Up until then, he gave orders for a quick march.

Crook had already made a major error in March when he'd attempted to force the Lakota and Cheyenne back on their reservations. The general had actually delegated to Colonel J. J. Reynolds to continue the pursuit of a large number of Lakota and Cheyenne after Crook and his troops got stopped before they even got to the Yellowstone River by a blinding blizzard. Reynolds found a village with many guns and much ammunition and a remuda of close to 1,500 horses.

Strongheart listened intently as Lucky explained that Colonel Reynolds attacked the large Cheyenne village with just one of the three 2nd Cavalry companies he commanded, leaving the other two behind. He attacked the camp and seized or destroyed much of the guns and ammunition, as well as the large herd of horses, but the surviving Cheyenne defenders started fighting more viciously to protect themselves and the village. Reynolds failed to bring reinforcements in to help him out.

Strongheart spoke, "Where the white man has really underestimated the fleeing of Cheyenne and Lakota warriors is a major misconception on his part. Those tribes and some of the other tribes are realists and they know that white men are many and just keep coming. However the male populations of the tribes keeps dwindling. Often, in attacks like that the warriors run and are pursued by the army. Most commanders feel that they are afraid, but they are not. It is tactical, Lucky. They only want to fight when they are certain of winning, because they must preserve their numbers."

Lucky smiled, saying, "Well those Cheyenne did not give

up. They kept up attacks until Reynolds's men were exhausted. That night the cavalry troopers all fell asleep they were so tired. The Cheyenne sneaked in and got back all their captured horses."

Joshua grinned.

Lucky went on, "I understand that Crook ees—I mean, is—very angry and is court-martialing Colonel Reynolds." He took a long sip of coffee and went on, "We have been very frustrated because Hartwell always seems to be one step ahead of us."

Joshua said, "Then they probably have a spy somewhere in your line of communication."

Lucky replied, "*Oui*, that has been a major topic of discussion with us. Mr. Pinkerton feels that strongly and ees worried that maybe it ees someone in our organization."

Strongheart said, "Why don't you put the word out today within the Pinkerton Agency that I am going to meet with the Lakota and will be leaving Denver tomorrow to speak with them because they have important news about the Indian Ring that they will only tell me. If there is a spy, maybe he will have someone try to stop me."

Sarcastically, Lucky replied, "Maybe we could just paint a large target on your back?"

"I didn't say I was planning on getting shot, Lucky," Joshua responded, "I will watch my backtrail. If there is a spy, this might flush him out."

"You must give me your word you will be very careful," Lucky replied.

Joshua chuckled, "I am a Pinkerton Agent, not a school marm or a suffragette. I didn't take this job, Lucky, because I wanted to run a museum or a library."

Lucky laughed heartily and raised his coffee cup in a toast.

3

THE BUSHWHACKERS

Strongheart had not even ridden more than ten miles north of Cheyenne, Wyoming, when Eagle, his magnificent black-and-white pinto started snorting. Eagle's left ear started turning toward the hillock directly to the west of the trail, which ran north and south. Joshua put the spurs to the big horse and Eagle sprinted forward, and Strongheart heard the bullet crack behind his head as the big horse propelled him forward. Fifty feet on, he spun him around and drew his Colt .45 Peacemaker, firing a snap shot at the top of the bluff where the shot had come from. He ran fast until he came to the end of the low ridge, and he quickly veered left into the prairie grass, bounding around the north end of the ridgeline.

Now, on the western side of the ridge, he saw two riders climbing into the saddles of two bay geldings. The cowboys took off south at a dead run, but it did not take long for the long legs of the sixteen-hands-tall pinto to start catching up.

The one on the right made a big mistake and foolishly drew his .44, turned in the saddle, and tried to make a snap shot back at Strongheart. Joshua did a quick draw and fired, his bullet catching the man under his bottom rib and going through his torso, tearing out the other side. He literally flew from the saddle and landed in a giant patch of prickly pear cactus. Obviously, he immediately started screaming in pain.

Strongheart yelled to the other, "You want to end up like him? Just keep running!"

The bushwhacker only thought this over for ten seconds before sliding to a stop. He spun his horse around and his hand immediately started hovering over his own .44. Strongheart slid Eagle to a stop less than ten feet away now, and they could hear the other behind Joshua moaning in the patch of cactus. Joshua knew that the man was seriously thinking about drawing.

Strongheart said, "Mister, in his play *Julius Caesar*, Shakespeare said, 'Until the day of his death, no man can be sure of his courage.' Now the question is, do you want today to be the day of your death? If you do, just yank that smoke wagon and try going to work. I'll make a believer of you."

The ambusher's hands went up in the air still holding his reins.

"I ain't no hero nohow, Mr. Strongheart," he drawled with a thick Southern accent. "Please don't plug me, suh. Kin we check on Jim-Bob?"

Strongheart said, "Yeah, climb down and let's walk back to him."

Strongheart took the man's reins and led the other horse and flipped Eagle's reins over his neck. The big paint followed him as trained. If he dropped the reins on the ground, the horse would ground-rein in place and not move, but when he put them over Eagle's neck, the horse would follow him like a puppy dog.

Jim-Bob was screaming in pain. He was black. Joshua

signaled the other outlaw to sit cross-legged where he could watch him, and he knelt down by the man, checking his wounds.

Jim-Bob, also with a Southern accent, said, "Please help me, Mr. Strongheart. It hurts so bad."

Strongheart said, "Jim-Bob, I can't help you. You are dying. If we move you it will just give you more pain. Just lie still and make peace."

Jim-Bob said, "Slim, it hurts. Can y'all just put a round betwixt mah eyes, please?"

Then he stared off at the sky, saying, "Ma, I fed the master's dog, but he done kicked me again anyhow."

He died just like that.

"Dadgum!" Slim exclaimed, "Ol' Jim-Bob has gone under. We rode the owl hoot trail together nigh on three year."

"Not a very wise trail to follow," Strongheart said.

Slim shrugged his shoulders and replied, "Reckon not. Guess Ah'll be followin' my ole pard ta hell now. They're gonna stretch my neck I figger."

Joshua replied. "That does not have to be true, Slim. Maybe they will give you a break if you are willing to testify in court about who hired you."

"Ah'm a dead man, anyway, Ah s'pose," he said. "Thet man thet hired me probably'll plug me afore y'all kin hang me or even git me ta court. I could tell he was a tough hombre."

"Got a name?" Joshua asked.

"No, suh," Slim said, "But he showed me a Pinkerton badge and said killin' you was official business."

"Where did he hire you and what did he pay you?" Joshua came back.

Slim said, "He given us each fifty bucks and fifty more after'n you was dead, if'n we come back ta Cheyenne and collect it."

"Where is the man and who is he?"

"He rides him a roan Appaloosa, which ya kin always find tied outside the Hitching Rack Saloon," Slim replied.

Strongheart said, "Why'd he pick you two?"

The outlaw responded, "We was ridin' the grub line and seen him there gamblin' a time or three. He said someone he was playing blackjack with tole him we would do any type of job and keep our mouths shut."

Strongheart said, "What does he look like?"

Slim chuckled. "A dandy, suh. He dresses like one a them city boys who fancies hisself a shootist. Wears a pair a Russian .44s with fancy ivory handles and tied-down cross-draw holsters, black tie, black suit, boots. Ya know what I mean. He has a long-droopin' mustache an' his hair is kinda reddish and real, real long. Hangs all over his shoulders."

"Sounds like George Armstrong Custer," Joshua mused.

"Yeah, old General Custer. I seen him a few months back," Slim came back. "Fancy dresser fer shore. Ridin' a big ole purty red Thoroughbred."

He had apparently seen Custer riding one of his two chestnut Thoroughbreds, Vic or Dandy. He rode both interchangeably.

Strongheart corrected him, "Custer is not a general though. He is a lieutenant colonel. He was a brevet general in the Civil War."

Getting very serious, Slim got a grim look on his face, saying, "Mr. Strongheart, what about me?"

Joshua said, "Well, we'll head back to Cheyenne. I'll turn you in, but my boss will want to talk with you. I'll tell him you have been cooperating and can maybe help us some more."

"Wal," Slim said. "Ah'm plumb sorry I tried ta plug ya, suh. Ya think they're gonna stretch mah neck?"

Strongheart said, "No, the Pinkerton Agency has a lot of influence, a whole lot. As long as you are trying to help us with information, my boss will keep you from getting strung up. We need to saddle up and get moving."

"What about Jim-Bob?" Slim asked,

Strongheart said, "What about him? He tried to bushwhack me. Just like you. By the time I get you to Cheyenne, I'll need to spend a night there, and head out in the morning, So, you boys cost me at least a day. I'm not burying him. Coyotes need to eat, too, you know."

"Yes, suh," Slim said humbly. "Ah'm plumb sorry, again."

Joshua said, "You and I don't have any shovels, but if you want to put his body under the cut bank over there and kick dirt in on it, I'll let you do that and say some words over him."

Slim thought for a second, then said, "Naw, hell with him. He's gone. Ah feel bad enough 'bout the trouble we caused ya."

Strongheart saddled up and told Slim to do the same. They left Jim-Bob's body lying in the prickly pear. Joshua would tell the sheriff about it in Cheyenne.

They rode due east to the road and Strongheart put a pile of three rocks on top of each other so the sheriff or undertaker would know where to turn north to find the body if they were going to pick it up. He had already put Jim-Bob's guns as well as Slim's on Eagle.

4

MORE SHOOTING

Slim was locked up in the jail in Cheyenne, and Lucky was on his way from Chicago with a team to interrogate him. Strongheart walked into the Hitching Rack Saloon shortly after dark. He immediately saw a man at the poker table who fit Slim's description, which was very accurate. Lucky had already sent him a telegram stating that he was not a Pinkerton based on the description, and Joshua knew he would have remembered a man who looked like this.

As soon as the man saw Strongheart, he rose to his feet. He wore a pearl-handled Colt Navy in a cross-draw holster and his left hand went behind his back, telling Strongheart he had a gun hidden there, too.

"Mister," Joshua said, "personally, I would love for you to try to pull that belly gun and try to get busy with it, or even that cross-draw. I don't like someone hiring men to dry-gulch me. However, I really need to know why you hired them and also why you have been posing as a Pinkerton, so kindly move your hands away from both guns. Let's just talk."

Strongheart saw the man think about it briefly, but

suddenly his eyes opened wide with that deer-in-the-torchlight look, and he knew instinctively he had to move. Joshua's hand streaked down and up in a flash, and he saw both revolvers appear in the man's hands, as his own Peacemaker stabbed flame. The bullet left a large crimson splash in the center left of the imposter's chest, as his heart literally exploded from the bullet. His body folded up like a rag doll, and he dropped in a heap without moving a foot.

With the discipline of a practiced gunfighter, Strongheart quickly ejected his empty shell and replaced it with a bullet from his gun belt. A man stood up to his left, and Strongheart whirled drawing.

The man, a big, burly, redheaded teamster put his hands up palms facing out and laughed nervously, "Easy, mister, easy. I was just gonna tell ya that was a righteous shooting. Ya gave that man every chance in the world not to draw."

Strongheart reholstered his six-shooter, saying, "Sorry, sir. Thank you. Would you hang around until the police or marshal get here and explain what you saw?"

"Shore," the big man said extending his hand.

They shook.

"You'll be the Pinkerton Strongheart, eh?"

Joshua said, "Yes, I am. How did you know?"

The man chuckled and held his hand out with a sweep showing Strongheart's presence.

He said, "Look at ya. I heard about ya plenty and looking at ya it shore as hell ain't hard ta guess who ya are."

Joshua was embarrassed.

A deputy marshal came in and got the accounts from several eyewitnesses including the teamster. He knew Joshua from the Pinkertons and knew of him by his reputation. He and Joshua went through the man's pockets looking for evidence but found none.

Then Joshua asked the teamster, "Did you see this man come in here with anybody?"

The freighter said, "I shore did. I come in the same time, and he rode up with a feller in a fancy business suit, and he was riding the prettiest big old black Thoroughbred you ever seen. Long legs and he had a fancy Mexican black saddle. He took off before you come in. Not too long before."

Joshua said, "Did you see which way he rode off?"

"Nope," the teamster replied. "Sorry. I tell you what, though. That Thoroughbred is seventeen hands tall if he is an inch. Find him and you'll find the man. That horse was some beauty. Had a white blaze but no stockings or socks. All black."

"That helps, mister," Joshua said. "Much obliged."

As soon as the deputy released him, Strongheart took off looking for a beautiful black Thoroughbred and the man who owned it. He started riding through the nighttime streets of Denver thinking that next morning he would make the rounds of blacksmiths and livery stables and ask about such a horse. The grass was greening and bears were out of hibernation. Strongheart was looking forward to and hoping for a wonderful summer ahead.

Little did he know that June would be one of the bloodiest months he would ever witness.

He went into a saloon when he found a tall black Thoroughbred tied up outside and looked around.

He went up to the bartender and quietly asked, "Do you know who owns that big black Thoroughbred outside?"

"Shore enuff, Injun," the big, gruff barkeep answered. "That big boy belongs to ole Alejandro Cabal, over there playing poker. The skinny little Mex runt ya see. Why? Ya wanna buy him?"

"No," Strongheart responded with a grin. "Just wondered. Handsome horse."

He looked at a very small Hispanic-looking man in the corner engrossed in a card game. He knew that was not the varmint he sought. Joshua thanked the bartender and walked out. Climbing into the saddle he headed north away from the saloon and just happened to notice two men saddling up nearby and walking behind him up the street. He kicked Eagle into a trot and glanced back, noticing that the two shadowy figures followed suit.

Strongheart suddenly turned right down a side street then left into a narrower street filled with closed businesses. The two riders soon turned the same corner behind him, and Joshua kicked Eagle into a canter, making a couple turns back onto the main busy street he left. Numerous saloons and bawdy houses dotted both sides of the street and there were plenty of sounds of music, laughter, and shouts from most buildings.

The two men held back a safe distance, but there was no denial in Joshua's mind. He knew they were up to no good, and then he noticed a third rider joined them. The next street over also was a busy street and ran parallel to Cherry Creek. He kicked Eagle into a trot and went down the street, glancing into each saloon door until he saw what he wanted.

He finally saw a saloon with two large bat-wing doors and could see it was a large saloon with a rear entrance on the road that paralleled Cherry Creek. Joshua quickly spun Eagle around and launched him toward the saloon entrance. He drew his pistol and fired in the air, and all the men at the bar saw him darting toward the doors and quickly jumped back away from the long mahogany bar. Lying low over Eagle's neck Strongheart went through the doorway at breakneck speed and galloped the depth of the saloon and tore out the doors at the far end, went to his right, crossed the road, and jumped a hedge down into Cherry Creek, turned left and ran full speed for a mile.

The three ambushers did not know what to do, as Joshua's move caught them so suddenly. They finally sped down the street, around the corner, and they ran north, the direction he'd angled when he'd exited the bar. It took them an hour before they unraveled his trail south on Cherry Creek, but many more hours before they found out he'd left Cherry Creek and doubled back heading north.

Strongheart rode well into the night putting Denver and Auraria behind him. He knew that these three characters obviously hired to assassinate him would also know he was headed north into Montana territory to meet with the Lakota. Joshua, however, would plan his own meeting with them.

He could have taken the railroad, but Strongheart knew that these men would keep coming if somebody wanted him dead that badly. They also needed an intelligence report on this obvious conspiracy, so he decided he had to capture at least one of them alive. He was well into Wyoming territory when he picked his place to confront the trio, an area with cottonwoods and other large trees off to the north of the trail. It was in a sort of natural bowl about an eighth of a mile east of the north-south trail with lush grasses for horses to graze, plenty of trees for firewood and shelter, a fast-running stream, and out of the prairie wind, so Joshua knew he would find the remains of many campfires, which he did.

The investigator, simply using common sense, knew these three riders would make camp in this small grove. Strongheart quickly rode through the grove of trees making his plan. He then moved downstream and set up his own camp, got what supplies he needed from his saddlebags, and went back to the camp area, leaving Eagle there grazing near the creek. He simply knew the three ambushers would not be able to resist the camp area.

It was not an hour before the three appeared, stopped out on the road and, like he suspected, immediately rode toward the trees. Strongheart stayed back in the trees, watching. They picked one of the first campfires, which even had some firewood stacked near it. They watered their horses and let them graze on the lush green grass along the stream bank.

Charlie Lombardi immigrated to New York City when he was a small boy from Sicily, Italy. His family was very traditional and tight knit. Mano Nera, the Black Hand, was a secret organization that began in Naples in the seventeen-fifties. Charlie's father was in the process, with some friends, of reviving it in the eastern United States as a secret extortion organization, which would eventually evolve into the modern-day Cosa Nostra, commonly referred to as the mafia. His father had gotten a strong start with his friends, extorting protection money from any family and business he could detect a weakness in. That was the environment Charlie grew up in and was a big part of his character now.

He fell in with Texas Tom Hardcastle and George "Oink" Johnson. Texas Tom should have been named Texas Tom Hardcase instead of Hardcastle. Texas Tom grew up near Austin, Texas, and was an experienced cowhand. His only problem was the devil he turned into every time he pulled a cork on a jug. He was a big, strong man and had literally killed a man with his hands in a saloon fight, been charged with murder, and escaped the hangman's noose by escaping from jail in a small Nebraska town. He started riding the owl hoot trail and had done one murder for hire and held up two stagecoaches.

Oink Johnson was also called Tightskin behind his back, because he was so large and bulky his skin seemed like it was stretched over a large frame. He had no neck, was short, but bull strong and had short-cropped red hair and a long red beard. Oink got his nickname because of the way he laughed. He sounded like a pig grunting when he really got a laugh going. Oink was rattlesnake mean and sadistic. He had robbed and killed and was also a rapist. This was unusual, because outlaws had been known to turn on their own if they molested women. There were so few women in the West, so most men were very protective of womanhood in general.

By dark, the three had large steaks grilling over a large fire, and a skillet with sliced potatoes and onions. Strongheart could hear his stomach growling as he smelled the fresh steaks they had picked up from a butcher in Denver. Joshua lay in the foliage just a little outside of the circle of light from the fire. He had trained himself years before to ignore hunger, thirst, heat, cold, and insect bites when in such a situation, whether stalking man or animal. He had several more hours to wait, but in that time he would watch the three and listen to see how they interacted with each other.

Joshua Strongheart lay in the shadows for several hours, watching the men share a bottle of whiskey and swap lies. He listened to their conversation and determined that Oink was the overt intimidator and mouth of the group, but Charlie Lombardi was the brains, the quiet shrewd one who spoke little, but he was definitely the leader of the trio. Based on this, Joshua formulated his plan.

After midnight, all three were asleep and snoring soundly. He crept forward silently and made it first to Oink. He removed the man's pistol from the holster and ejected the bullets into his hand, then replaced the gun in the holster.

He slowly crawled over to Texas Tom and started to do

the same with him. However that cowpuncher had better instincts. He came wide awake clawing for his gun, and Strongheart's Peacemaker ended that as it came crashing down on his left temple, producing an instant goose egg, and knocking him out.

Strongheart looked over at Charlie, and he did not stir, nor did Oink. He undid Texas Tom's gun belt and removed it. Then, he tied the limp assassin's hands behind his back.

Now, he crawled toward Charlie. He slowly inched forward on his belly. The Pinkerton was now only five feet away.

Suddenly, Texas Tom, who had come to, yelled from behind him, "Charlie, look out! It's Strongheart!"

Charlie Lombardi sat bolt upright drawing his pair of .44s, giving Joshua no choice. His hand streaked down and up with his Colt .45 spewing flame. Two rounds that could be covered with a silver dollar slammed into Lombardi's chest, both hitting his heart. He immediately slumped into a motionless pile of rags. Strongheart heard a gun click behind him, and he spun around as Oink tried fanning his empty gun with nothing but empty clicks. Strongheart raised his own gun, and Oink dropped his.

Joshua pulled six bullets from his pocket and said, "Looking for these?"

The man spat on the ground, glaring at the half-breed.

Joshua said, "Toss it over here."

Begrudgingly, Oink threw the pistol to the Pinkerton, who caught it and tucked it into the back of his waistband.

Oink said, "Yer a lot taller 'n' me, Strongheart. You kin talk tough with a gun in your hand. What about with just yer fists?"

"No," Joshua grinned broadly at the bushwhacker. "I like it a lot better with a gun in my hand. Sit down by the fire."

Strongheart added some wood and set the coffeepot on

the coals. Then, he tied Oink's hands behind his back and whistled. Seconds later, Eagle came galloping up. Joshua unsaddled him and let him start grazing nearby. He retrieved his breakfast fixings out of his saddlebags and started making himself breakfast while speaking to the two would-be assassins.

"So you three were hired to bushwhack me, right?" Strongheart said, while making breakfast.

Texas Tom said, "Yep. Good money, too."

Oink snarled, "Shut yer durned mouth, ya fool!"

Strongheart said, "Why should he be quiet? He might be saving himself a lot of jail time."

Oink said, "So what? All y'all can do is hang us."

"What does that mean?" Strongheart asked.

Oink looked at Texas Tom and said, "Don't say nothin' else!"

Texas Tom said, "Yer crazy! Strongheart, if I spill the beans, can ya make sure the judge takes it easy on me?"

Oink said, "Ya better not say one more word."

Strongheart pulled his Peacemaker out and held it like a hammer saying, "That is good advice. Want a long nap?"

Oink sulked.

Texas Tom said, "We got hired ta follow ya and kill ya by a powerful feller who works fer a really big government feller. We ain't the only ones hired, neither. The word is out: Kill Strongheart."

Strongheart started downing his breakfast and coffee. Listening and thinking.

Joshua said, "This man that hired you. He have a name?"

Oink just glared at Texas Tom and growled.

Texas Tom said, "Yes, sir. His name is Robert M. Hartwell. Tiny man but important. Got lots a money. Gambles a lot and likes him the women."

Oink said, "Now ya done it, ya idjit. We're dead fer sure now."

Ignoring Oink, Joshua said, "How do you know he's powerful?"

Texas Tom said, "He works fer the durned government. Clothes show it, too. Expensive clothes, and he always has gun hands around him."

Giving in to their fate now, Oink joined in. "He's a really tiny feller, but jest the way people treat him ya can tell he's powerful."

"He rides him a big old black Thoroughbred," added Texas Tom.

This news hit Joshua square between the eyes. He had seen this Thoroughbred back in Denver, but the bartender in the saloon had lied to him about the owner, identifying a Mexican in the corner as the owner.

5

RETURN TO DENVER

Three days later, Lucky and two other Pinkertons met Strongheart back in Denver. Oink and Texas Tom were being held in jail.

Lucky rode a livery stable horse, as the pair rode to the saloon where Strongheart had been given the wrong information. They went inside and the same saloon keeper was there. Joshua walked up to him, reached across the bar, and grabbed him by his lapel, dragging the two hundred pounder across the bar with one hand and a lot of adrenaline pumping. He stood the man up and slapped him across the face.

Strongheart said quietly through clenched teeth, "You told me the correct name of the big black Thoroughbred a few days back but lied about the owner. How much is he paying you?"

The bartender looked nervously from side to side and whispered, "Can we go outside and talk?"

The other bartender had both hands below at the back of the bar and Strongheart drew his pistol in a blur, saying, "Get your hands off that scattergun, mister, if you value your life."

The bartender said, "It's okay, Slim. I'm taking a break for a few."

The man's hands came up on the bar, and he shook his head while Joshua marched the man outside with Lucky following.

"What's your name?" Strongheart asked.

"Luck," the man replied.

Joshua replied, "Well, we will change it to Hard Luck if you do not answer my questions. How much is he paying you?"

"Nothing, mister," Luck said. "He was upstairs that night with one of the women, and two or maybe three of his gang or whatever you call them were right there within earshot. I didn't wanna get killed."

Strongheart let go of his lapel and said, "Keep talking."

Luck went on, "His name is Robert Hartwell, and he worked with William Belknap, the secretary of war. I think he was one of his top men."

Luck continued enthusiastically, "He always has bodyguards around him, and they are all gun slicks. Last year, one of our regulars was killed. He had a freighting outfit with a government contract. He used to carry supplies out of Denver to Injun agencies up north, down south toward Fort Union, and out east. He told me he didn't go west outta Denver cause of the mountains. Anyway, he had a load of blankets, which he swapped for some cheaper ones. I heard him making the deal in the saloon. When I say load, I mean a couple warehouses full, not just one wagonload."

Lucky said, "What happened then?"

"After he and the feller he was dealing with shook hands, he turned to me and asked me how much I heard," the bartender said. "I should have said 'Nothing,' but I was loco I guess and told him 'All of it.' Can we go somewhere and talk private? I don't want to get seen talking to you, Mr. Strongheart."

Joshua said, "Sure, you have a back room?"

Luck said, "Yeah, the poker room is empty tonight. Let's go back there."

The men made their way through the smoky saloon, sitting down at a large felt-topped poker table in the back room.

Luck went on, "He had two of his gun hands with him, and nodded at them. They grabbed my arms and put my hands on the bar. Then, all of a sudden—have you ever seen one of those push-button knives?"

Joshua said, "I carry one."

Luck went on. "Well, this little feller pulled one out of his pocket, clicked it open, and come down stabbing my left hand, and pinned it to the bar. Did I ever start yelping. Look at my hand."

He put his left hand out setting it on the green felt table-top, and there was a nasty scar in the palm. Turning it over, he revealed the entry wound in the back of the hand where the blade went through.

The bartender went on, "Mr. Strongheart, he told me the names of my three kids and my wife. He told me I would make me some extra money each month by just keeping my mouth shut, but if not, my whole family would be kilt."

"Where does he stay in Denver?" Strongheart said.

Luck said, "He stays in a hotel . . ."

Crash!

Luck's luck ran out. The bullet hole appeared in the middle of Luck's forehead and three other shots, out of many, hit his torso before it fell to the floor. Lucky dropped to the floor drawing his .44.

Strongheart, already firing into the darkness, said, "Take the front door, boss!"

He sprinted toward the now-shattered window and dove headfirst into the darkness, firing as he went. He heard thundering hoofbeats as several horses ran into the darkness, and he fired after them. Strongheart headed back to the front door of the saloon and went in. Lucky was heading back into the poker room and pushing gawkers out of the way. Joshua and Lucky quickly looked the scene over for additional clues but saw none.

They went back out into the saloon and Lucky approached the other bartender and started questioning him. In the meantime, Joshua spotted a cowpuncher sitting with his back to the corner and at a table, and noticed he was watching the door. Strongheart walked over to the table and grabbed a chair.

"Mind if I sit?" he said.

The cowpuncher said, "Help yourself. Name is Rowdy Gaits, and yer Strongheart, the Pinkerton."

They shook as Joshua said, "Guilty. You been a lawman, haven't you?"

Gaits said, "Yep. Punching cows now, but worn a tin star most of my grown-up life."

Strongheart said, "Figured that. I saw how you were watching the door and crowd. After we took that bartender in the back, did you see anybody who might have told the bushwhackers?"

"No, sir," Rowdy replied. "One feller left the saloon after you went back, but he looked like a man who would spend an hour finding his horse outside."

Joshua chuckled, stood, and shook again, saying, "Well, that is easy enough to understand. Thanks. Nice to meet you."

Rowdy said, "Been an honor. I have heard many good things about you."

Joshua returned to Lucky just as two deputy town

marshals came in, and they shook hands with Lucky and Strongheart.

Lucky said to Joshua, "You talk to these gentlemen, and I will head to the jail. Those two men you brought in are obviously in danger."

Joshua escorted the two deputies into the poker room, and they surveyed the damage and the body. Joshua detailed the shooting for them. Then, they went out into the saloon, and he bought them each beers and had lemonade himself, while they filled out a report.

A half hour later, Strongheart left and headed for the jail. Lucky was there speaking with a deputy. Joshua sat down.

"It has been quiet so far," Lucky said. "You weel—will—handle them anyway, Joshua."

Strongheart shook his head looking out the window.

"Lucky," Joshua said, "you remember when I got shot up so bad in that gunfight down in Florence, Colorado?"

"Do I remember?" Lucky replied. "You lingered near death forever. You had many holes in you, my young friend."

Strongheart said, "Two things. One, I did not care right then. I was just angry. Two, I knew that I have trained with pistols, rifles, my knife, for years, for many hours. Most of them were young men, most who probably could never even afford one. I knew they would feel very confident in their superior numbers, so taking them on was not really amazing."

"I disagree, Strongheart. Everybody does. You fought an army and won single-handedly," Lucky exclaimed.

"Yes, but they were not really an army," the tall Pinkerton replied. "They were a gang of untrained men who had not ever practiced much with guns. Only one man, their leader, could shoot."

He looked out the window and walked back to the table.

"These men that Hartwell has can kill me easy in a fight,"

Joshua said, "These men are trained, experienced shootists. Gunfighters who have shot while being shot at before. It will be a totally different fight. I have to get an edge."

Lucky said, "What?"

Strongheart was frightened. He hated being scared, but he also knew that it was natural. He had a large group of trained gunfighters who were being paid good money to kill him. He also knew that fear would help keep him alive, on edge, prepared. He had to figure out how to handle them though.

He looked at his boss and confessed, "I don't know, but I will think of something."

"Whatever you do, Joshua," Lucky teased, "please do not get shot up again. Do you know how much time I wasted having to visit you in the hospital here in Denver?"

Strongheart grinned and just then the window of the sheriff's office exploded with flying glass and Lucky was slammed backward into the wall, a bright red splotch of blood on his chest. He was unconscious already.

Joshua looked at the two deputies and said, "Get the bleeding stopped and get a doctor quick!"

He jumped through the shattered window, gun drawn, one eye closed, so his eyes would quickly adjust to the darkness outside when he opened them. He hit the sidewalk on his feet and kept going forward into the dirt street in a shoulder roll as two bullets cracked above his head. Joshua fired, rolled to his left, fanned his Peacemaker, rolled to his right, and fired again, then quickly reloaded. He was firing where the flashes appeared in a window across the street. He heard what sounded like a body falling hard, and he dashed across the road and into the hotel, up the steps, and kicked in the door of the room where the shots originated.

He found two men, one moaning on the floor with an upper chest/shoulder wound and a second lying flat on his back with a bullet hole directly above his right eye. That man had a Sharps .45–70 Government rifle lying next to his body.

He turned his attention to the wounded man and immediately knew the man had to have a broken collarbone and probably a broken right shoulder. He kept his eyes focused on the sniper's eyes and his left hand. Both men had expensive suits on and wore holsters indicating they were experienced gunfighters.

Strongheart said, "Mister, I know you are a shootist, so that tells me you have a hideout belly gun. My question is, do you want to die trying to pull it?"

The gun hand grimaced in pain and said, "Yer right, Strongheart. It is tucked into my right boot. Just then, his left hand whipped out from under his coat holding a Navy .36 and Joshua's Peacemaker spit fire. The man felt a bullet slam into his chest and then a second one. Everything went black and he felt the life leave his body, and then he felt nothing.

A deputy ran in the door, gun drawn, and Strongheart winked at him, saying, "I wish I could have questioned him."

The deputy asked, "Hideout gun?"

"Yep," Strongheart said. "He tried to go for it, but was a bit slow. How is my boss?"

"Bad," the deputy answered. "They are rushing a doctor to him. Go ahead. I will take care of this."

Strongheart ran back to the office and was very saddened to see his boss and close friend Lucky lifeless on the floor. A doctor was hovered over him listening with a stethoscope. Joshua could see two bullet holes in his chest, large ones.

He asked, "Doctor, will he live?"

Not looking up, the doctor said, "I don't know. I am not hearing any bubbling from his lungs and both bullets missed his heart. You are Mr. Strongheart?"

"Yes, Doc," Joshua replied.

The doctor responded, "I have heard a good bit about you from other doctors and nurses, all good."

"What will you do with him?"

The doctor said, "I have an ambulance coming as soon as they hitch up the team. We will transport him to the same hospital you stayed in so long. I would prefer, Mr. Strongheart, that you not come there tonight. We will be working on him all night, I believe."

Joshua said, "He got shot because he was around me. When you can talk to him, tell him I filed a report with Chicago, which I will go do now, and tell him I killed both men that plugged him. Please also tell him I am going on to my assignment. That is what will stop this bushwhacking."

The doctor said, "I will. In fact, deputy, if you will please transcribe all that for me, so I get it correctly."

The deputy in the corner of the office went to the desk and pulled out paper, ink, and pen, saying, "Will do, Doctor."

Suddenly, Lucky opened his eyes and said, "Joshua?"

Strongheart knelt down by his boss and friend.

He said, "Yes, Lucky?"

Lucky said, "I heard you. I will be fine. Go get the rest of them. Shut down the Indian Ring."

Joshua said, "You have my word."

6

SUN DANCE

It was several days later when Pinkerton Agent Joshua Strongheart on majestic Eagle pranced through the various tribal circles of the giant encampment along the shores of the Rosebud Creek in Montana territory. Literally thousands of Lakota, Cheyenne, and Arapaho milled about in various activities. Strongheart had been stopped several times but many knew who he was by reputation, and he was always a welcome visitor. He arrived at his late father's tribal circle and dismounted.

Within two hours, Joshua found himself in a large lodge smoking a pipe with his uncle Praying Bear, the mighty Hunkpapa Lakota medicine man Sitting Bull, Oglala Lakota war chief Crazy Horse, Cheyenne chief Gall, Lakota chief Rain-in-the-Face, who swore he would someday cut out the heart of Custer's brother, Medal of Honor recipient Tom Custer, and eat it, and other famous chiefs.

Sitting Bull drew thoughtfully on the long-stemmed pipe waving smoke over his head with one hand, blew out a long stream of blue smoke, which mated with the rising mist over the large fire, and watched it ascend upward and out the smoke hole of the bull-hide lodge.

He said, "We all know that Wanji Wambli, who the *wasi-cun* call Joshua Strongheart, comes to us with news from the *wasicun*. When a warrior prepares for the sun dance ceremony, he takes one or two summers. Wanji Wambli fought and took the medicine of the mighty We Wiyake. He has prepared, so before we speak we will sun dance together. A tree has been prepared. That is all I have to say."

There it was. Strongheart was elated yet disheartened simultaneously. It was such an honor to be invited to participate in a once-in-a-lifetime opportunity.

On the other hand, he was in a rush to try to stop the decimation of the Plains tribes because of the Indian Ring. Joshua wanted to hurry and make things happen, and get to the bottom of Hartwell and Belknap's scheme, however the venerable holy man Sitting Bull invited him to participate in the sun dance ceremony before he could even address his concerns to anybody. It was the Lakota way: First things first, don't rush into conversations.

His uncle, the chief of his father's tribe or familial circle, provided Strongheart with a teepee, and he went there to rest, start fasting, and prepare himself for the grueling ordeal ahead.

It was the middle of the night and there was a scratching on the buffalo-hide lodge. He grabbed his Colt Peacemaker and held it under his buffalo-hide bedcover.

"Yes," he said softly.

She entered.

This woman was beautiful, remarkably beautiful. Lila Wiya Waste, which meant "beautiful woman," was his cousin who secretly loved Joshua. Her husband had been killed by a she-grizzly with two cubs. In the past, Lila and her mother had nobody to bring meat to their lodge, but

Joshua Strongheart would come to her village and help her get meat for the lodge, because he was her closest relative. She remembered fondly how Joshua told her not to just marry again but to wait on a warrior who was worthy of her.

She stared at Strongheart over the glowing embers of his dying fire. His eyes were entrancing, and then she reached up and undid the leather thongs holding her dress. It fell around her ankles revealing a muscular, well-proportioned female physique. She was ravishing and now she stood before Joshua naked in the firelight, dancing light from the flames highlighting her sensuality even more.

Strongheart stood and looked at her longingly, many thoughts flashing through his mind.

Joshua slowly reached down and grabbed her buckskin dress and raised it up over her shoulders. Disappointment showed on her face.

"Lila," he said, "We are cousins. I am like your older brother, your protector. But I am also a man, and any man would want you very much. You have such great beauty and so much more to offer a man. But, my cousin, I loved Belle very much. I found her after We Wiyake butchered her, and I see it many times each day. I will always feel like she died because of me. We Wiyake wanted to steal my medicine, so he took the one thing I truly loved, her. When I love, that fills my heart, and I cannot ride two horses at once. In the same way, I cannot love two women at once, and I still see Belle everywhere I look each day, and in my dreams at night. You honor me very much, my beautiful cousin, but this cannot be. I will always love you, but you are my family."

Tears rolled down her cheeks, and she spoke quietly, "I can never love another man, either, because, Joshua, I have always loved you, and I always will."

He stood and she did, too. He stepped forward and held her in a warm embrace, but not a romantic one. She laid her head on his muscular chest and Lila sobbed while he stroked her hair slowly. She stopped crying, and he pushed her back a step and wiped her tears with the back of his index finger.

He said, "You will find a great man someday when the time is right, if you let God, the Great Spirit, prepare that man just for you."

He kissed her on the forehead and said, "I must sleep and prepare myself for the sun dance."

Lila smiled bravely and left the teepee. Strongheart lay down and could not sleep. He pictured her beauty over and over, and the man in him felt frustrated thinking how easily he could have just taken her and not looked back. Then he would picture Belle in all her beauty and would feel ashamed of himself.

Finally, Joshua steeled his mind for the task ahead. He knew he would soon be going through an ordeal when Sitting Bull summoned him.

Sun dance is a traditional Lakota ceremony representing life and rebirth, and it occurs during the summer solstice. The dancing and piercing begins at the full moon during the last four days of the four-week ceremony. Normally, a person is invited to participate but must spend a year in preparation for the sun dance. There are many sweat lodges and some warriors go on vision quests, usually in the mountains. Because of the ordeal Strongheart had been through hunting down the seven-foot-tall crazed killer, We Wiyake, or Blood Feather, who had killed Joshua's fiancée as well as many Lakota and whites, Sitting Bull had let Strongheart know that he had already been through more than a year of preparation.

The previous day was called Tree Day and a selected brave went out with several assistants and looked for a cottonwood tree that would be just right for the ceremony. The cottonwood was considered a sacred tree because its shape was said to have inspired the shape and construction of the very first Lakota teepees. The scout had searched along the banks of the Greasy Grass, or as the whites called it, the Little Big Horn, and had found one a quarter mile downstream from the giant encampment. The area was prepared for the dance and rest of the ceremony.

The next morning there was scratching on Joshua's lodge, and his father's best friend, Yellow Horse, came to him with an eagle fan and eagle-bone whistle. Joshua was to go to a sweat lodge and was led downstream to the ceremony site, where he entered the lodge.

Outside the sweat, he saw the stoic Oglala Lakota war chief Crazy Horse, who wore a red-tailed hawk feather tied down on the back of his hair and a pebble behind his left ear. He also always wore a sheep's-wool anklet over his left ankle to hide the bullet scar from years before. Everybody felt Crazy Horse was blessed by the Great Spirit and could not be touched by bullets, and he did not want to spoil their image of him. He was noted for being very aggressive and courageous in battle, but with the Plains tribes, being close to or blessed by the Great Spirit drew higher accolades than courage in battle.

In the sweat lodge were several dancers including the mighty medicine man Sitting Bull, who spoke no words. This was not the right time for Joshua to speak to him about anything, as the sun dance ceremony was a very private personal occasion. Each man was alone with his own thoughts, and Strongheart decided he would take full advantage. After all he had been through, he needed this time of great introspection.

When the sweat concluded, the scout who found the tree

led the dancers and others to the selected cottonwood. Everyone gathered around the tree in small groups at the four compass points and offered prayers. A piece of braided leather rope was tied to the top of the tree by the scout who climbed to the top. Then Crazy Horse, because of his many battle honors, came forward and counted coup on the tree. Three other select warriors came forward to cut the tree down, taking turns chopping. In the meantime, Sitting Bull, Joshua Strongheart, and the other dancers were given blankets to catch the tree in as it was lowered by the rope. Blankets were placed on the ground anywhere the tree might touch as it was carried to the ceremonial circle.

The dancers were instructed to carry the tree into the circle from the west, and it was again laid down on a series of blankets, with no part of it touching the ground. Next, the dancers tied bundles of sage and, in some cases, tobacco, to the top of the tree. Then like a Christmas tree, the sun dance tree was raised up and the trunk was carefully placed in the hole in the center of the ceremonial site, which had already been dug out by younger warriors.

For three days, Strongheart, still fasting and only drinking that sage tea and water, did the sweats and meditation in the morning, then danced all day, taking breaks to go off and pray and ask for a vision. The men and women of the village and the sun dancers would start dancing each morning and would dance in a clockwise motion with warrior men on the inside and women on the outside.

Then, on the third day, which Lakota actually call "piercing day," the *heyoka* would start dancing. These were clowns, people with mental illnesses, or any who have shown themselves to be very spiritual people. This was to motivate the sun dancers as all of these three groups were considered very sacred and spiritual. Only the *heyoka* would

wear black-and-white and dance in a circle going the opposite way of the rest of the people. The *heyoka* clowns would
also do silly or ridiculous things trying to get the sun dancers
to laugh even as the latter were expected to maintain a very
serious meditative demeanor.

In the afternoon, the sun dancers were stopped and those
who elected to be pierced, which was a much greater honor than
simply dancing, were all made to lie down. Piercing was, by
far, the most sacred part of the sun dance ceremony of the
Lakota, which was the only nation to practice it. They saw it as
making a personal sacrifice for the good of all red brothers.

One by one, holy men from each tribal circle went to
each sun dancer and cut two holes in that dancer's chest
slightly above the nipples on the pectoral muscles. In Joshua
Strongheart's case, instead of a sharp knife, a ceremonial
golden eagle talon was used, which did make Joshua feel
even more special. Then wooden or bone pegs were inserted
into the holes as that sun dancer was blessed and prayed
over by the medicine man. Before they all stood again, Sitting Bull sat up and cut himself up and down his arms and
sides, making fifty additional cuts on his body to show he
was really willing to sacrifice for mankind.

The sun dancers were told to approach the tree and the
medicine men attached braided leather thongs from the top
of the sacred tree to the pegs sticking through the flesh on
each man's pectorals. The most senior medicine man there,
a leathery and very wrinkled old man, instructed the dancers
to dance up to the tree, then back until the pegs pulled their
flesh out. They were told to do this three times, then on the
third try, they were to dance backward and when the flesh
started stretching, they were to thrust themselves backward
with all their weight and strength tearing the pegs through
their flesh. Strongheart noticed that the much older Sitting

Bull was bleeding profusely, so the Pinkerton decided he would endure whatever happened. He did. Some dancers did not tear their flesh when they tried, but Joshua made his rip free and he fell on his back and look skyward, barely conscious as his father's village medicine man came forward, cut the remaining pieces of flesh with a sharp knife, and placed them in the ceremonial fire.

7

THE VISION

At first there was blackness, but then somewhere in that darkness Joshua Strongheart could hear the sounds of the drums and the chants of the singers. He could see a purple mountain range in the distance and a small dot in the cloudless sky flew toward him. It took a long time to get near him but it kept getting larger, and he saw it was a bald eagle. As it flew closer, he saw a human face on the eagle, and it was his beloved Annabelle Ebert. She had never looked more radiant or beautiful than now. She was in human form wearing a shiny gold dress, and she was mounted atop Gabe, his red-and-white overo paint, which had also been killed by We Wiyake.

Belle rode right up to him and smiled the whole time. So did Joshua.

He spoke first, saying, "I love you, Belle. I always will, I can never love another. I am so sorry I got you killed."

Then he felt tears spilling down his cheeks but they started turning to ice. He realized he was back above timberline in the Sangre de Cristo mountains, where he had gone to meditate and grieve.

Strongheart started saying, "I'm so sorry," over and over.

Belle spoke very sharply and emphatically, "Joshua! Hush up right now. You did not get me killed. Blood Feather did."

Joshua cried, "I am leaving the Pinkerton Agency. My job got you killed."

Belle started laughing, and he got irritated. Why was she laughing?

Belle said, "You silly man. Do you suppose I would have fallen in love with you if you were working as a desk clerk at the St. Cloud Hotel, or running a freight line out of Pueblo?"

"What?" Joshua replied. "Is this a dream? It seems so real."

Belle said, "It is a dream, my love, but I am real. I am not there now, but I am real, Joshua."

He cried tears of relief and saw that her skin was unblemished, and she had no wounds anywhere, like she did the last time he saw her.

Gabe whinnied as if to let him know he was real, too. Suddenly, Gabe was gone, and they were in her café in Canon City sitting at their private table in the kitchen.

Belle came closer and smiled warmly.

She said, "Joshua Strongheart, I fell in love with a gentle kind man, who is a mighty warrior, too. My first husband was a cavalry officer. I never would have married a hotel desk clerk. If you were not a Pinkerton agent, you would be a sheriff, or frontier scout, or Sioux war chief. You can love again, and you must be good at your job, for that is what made me love you, too. You are a hero and cannot help that."

She started to back away, and he wanted her to stay, but now she was back on Gabe.

He said, "Wait."

Belle smiled and said, "There was never anything to forgive, Joshua. You must live and smile and be my hero."

He heard the beat of the drums and felt warmth on his face. She was gone just like that, and he realized he was dreaming. He tried very hard to bring Belle back but his body wanted to make his eyes open. He looked up at the blue sky and realized the sun was positioning itself to decide where to drop down and find a hiding place behind the distant mountains to the west. There was activity all around him, and he saw the medicine man from his father's circle sitting cross-legged smiling at him as well as Yellow Horse, his father's friend.

Joshua sat up and his chest ached. He looked down at dried blood all over his chest.

The medicine man puffed thoughtfully on his pipe, stating, "You had a vision."

It was not a question but a statement of fact.

Strongheart said, "Yes, I did. A strong one."

The medicine man said, "Sitting Bull had a vision, too, and wants us to eat with him when the sun goes into its lodge and smoke. He will speak."

The meat in Sitting Bull's teepee was steak from a pronghorn antelope and it was delicious. He also was given coffee and a dish made out of sliced apples and grapes. He had cleaned in the river and bandaged his chest, putting a poultice on the wounds, which was very soothing. He could see Sitting Bull was cleaned and patched up, too, very much unlike the bloody mess he had been earlier.

As they smoked, a man painting a winter count on a piece of stretched hide was painting symbols of Sitting Bull's vision as he related it.

The Hunkpapa shaman puffed on the pipe and blew a tendril of blue out, the smoke slowing to a snail's pace and curling into a lazy climb upward toward the teepee airhole.

Sitting Bull waved smoke over his head and face with his other hand and then spoke, "I had a vision."

Everybody in the teepee stared at the popular medicine man with intense interest and hung on to every word.

"The *wasicun* came to our lodges firing their rifles. Many warriors braved up and many coups were counted. There were many circles of lodges along the water and bluecoats falling upside down into our encampment like grasshoppers falling from the sky. They were lying all around the circles with their heads pointed in toward the center."

Joshua heard the rest of his words but thought about the statement "their heads were pointed in toward the center," and that they fell headfirst out of the sky. That meant that many white men were killed in his vision.

Religiously, Joshua Strongheart was a Christian and raised in church by his mother and stepfather, but he never judged or demeaned his father's spiritual beliefs. He always wanted to be open-minded, and he truly wondered if Sitting Bull had had some kind of premonition. Sitting Bull was actually named *Tatanka-Iyotanka*, which meant "a buffalo bull sitting down on its haunches." He had been chosen before the sun dance by the united tribes to be chief of all the Lakota while defying the *wasicun*. He was noted for many courageous deeds in battle, including walking out between battle lines of Lakota and cavalry soldiers during a lull in one battle where he sat down and ate lunch just to intimidate the "long knives." What was most important to Joshua Strongheart, Sitting Bull earlier had been made the chief of the elite warrior society that transcended tribes within the Lakota nation referred to as the Stronghearts. Joshua's father was one of its first members, and it was where his white man's name was derived from. His mother gave him the first name Joshua from the Bible, and always read the verse to him Joshua 1:5: "There shall not any man be able to stand before thee all the days of thy life: as I was with Moses, so I will be with thee: I will not fail thee, nor forsake thee."

These last months, more than a year actually, since Annabelle Ebert was butchered, Joshua had really been soul-searching, questioning his own religious beliefs. He also was really leaning toward leaving the Pinkerton Detective Agency, blaming his occupation for what had happened to Belle. The vision he had had during the sun dance gave him a new clarity of purpose. He would pursue his career as a Pinkerton with a vengeance.

Yes, he met with a lot of prejudice in his travels, but Strongheart also knew that most white people back east assumed all cowboys out west were white men. However, many were actually Indians who had learned to live in white society, former black slaves, and Mexicans who preferred it north of the border. Truth be told only one third of all American cowboys in those days was white. He had been treated well by the Pinkerton Agency and there would be opportunity for him there. Belle, in his dream or vision or whatever it was, was correct. He was a man of action and would become very bored in a normal job after the life he had lived.

Now, Sitting Bull shooed everybody but Joshua from the lodge. He smiled at the half-breed and offered him the long-stemmed pipe. Joshua took a long puff and as the smoke wafted out of his mouth he waved it over his head. The two smoked for a full ten minutes before a word was spoken.

Sitting Bull said, "Wanji Wambli has been asked by the *wasicun* chiefs to speak to his father's people, to your people, and tell us we are bad Indians and we must go back to our reservations."

Strongheart chuckled, then replied, "No, Sitting Bull, there are some bad *wasicun* as there are Lakota whose hearts are bad, too. They hate and see with angry hearts, not their eyes and their minds."

He puffed on the pipe to let those words sink in.

"There are white men among the chiefs who steal from the nations, from all nations. They take blankets that Washington buys for the Lakota, the Apache, the Cherokee, and more." Strongheart went on, "They sell the new good blankets and take a little money to buy old bad blankets and give these to the red people."

Sitting Bull smoked thoughtfully then said, "Why do they kill so many buffalo?"

"To kill you and all our people," Joshua replied. "They feel if the buffalo dies, the Lakota and all plains tribes will die."

Sitting Bull puffed again several times, then said, "This could be true, but if all buffalo are taken away, we will ask Mother Earth to give us new animals for our meat, hides for our lodges, and clothes. The Great Spirit did not give the buffalo to the Lakota to hunt them. He gave the buffalo to the Lakota to feed and clothe them."

Joshua thought about this simple, logical, positive thinking when faced with the enormity of the problem, and he understood he was in the presence of a great man and a true leader.

He said, "Yes, they want me to speak peace with you, but they want me to find these bad white-eyes and catch them."

Sitting Bull said, "And then what?"

Strongheart said, "They will go to jail, or they will die by my guns."

Sitting Bull grinned and then chuckled softly, "The *wasicun* and their jail."

Strongheart went on, "The *wasicun* call them the Indian Ring. We know now William Belknap, one of the white chiefs in Washington is the chief of the Indian Ring, and he is no longer any type of chief. He had a subchief named Hartwell who has been the real chief of the Indian Ring. They want to eliminate the buffalo, thinking it will kill the plains tribes. Many greedy men are getting much money by stealing your blankets and supplies and replacing them with cheaper ones and other things like that."

Sitting Bull said, "The leaders of the Long Knives are foolish, too. They think the Lakota, the Chyela (Cheyenne), and the Arapaho are cowards because we flee when they attack our villages. They do not understand we leave so we do not lose warriors that we must have to fight. Now, many have come together, and we will not leave if the Long Knives come. We will fight and many Long Knives will die. We are Lakota. We will die fighting not freezing and starving on the reservation."

Strongheart said, "My chief, they want me to tell you not to fight, but I do understand. White men have found gold in the Black Hills and come here all the time. That is sacred ground, but they do not care. The Indian Ring likes this, encourages it, but hear me, my chief: Not all *wasicun* hate the red man. Some do, but many do not."

"I know this, young friend," Sitting Bull replied. "But when they come to kill us or put us back on the reservations, our arrows will not ask who hates us and who likes us."

They both smoked for several minutes without speaking.

Then, the chief said, "You must kill these men. This Indian Ring."

"I cannot kill them all, but I will kill the Indian Ring," Strongheart replied. "It must die before more of our brothers and sisters die."

Sitting Bull rose and blew smoke toward the smoke hole, watching its egress.

He said, "Many more will die. We made peace and we made a treaty. The *wasicun* broke that treaty. They must fight us now. The thief does not say, 'He is a good man and I have stolen from him.' The thief hates him instead. You should leave soon. We will break the camp tomorrow and go to the valley of the Greasy Grass. I think the Long Knives will come soon and many will die. I saw this."

"I wish all men could live together," Strongheart sighed.

Sitting Bull smiled, saying, "Maybe, someday the eagle and the rabbit will lay down together and have many babies."

Joshua chuckled at that one.

He said, "I will leave tomorrow."

8

AMBUSH

Joshua rode a steel horse and kept hearing a clicking sound. He looked down and the horse did not have legs. It was built like Eagle, but it had narrow gauge railroad car wheels and the horse was rolling along swiftly in an easterly direction. This was very obvious because he kept noticing the sun as a big ball behind him. His eyes started fluttering, and he realized the clicking was the sound of a campfire with the sticks crackling in the fire. It was also the sun behind him, as his back was toward the fire. He rolled over facing the fire as his eyes came open, and he saw a man sitting there on a long log drinking coffee. His head ached like an abscessed wisdom tooth, and most especially when he turned over. His hand went down to his Colt, but it was gone, and he saw it and his holster lying next to his head. He relaxed but started wondering what was happening.

Then he realized who the man was. It was his friend Chris Colt, chief of scouts for Lieutenant Colonel George Armstrong Custer of the 7th Cavalry.

Colt sipped his steaming coffee and said, "Welcome back, Joshua. You want some coffee?"

Strongheart moaned while he sat up and reached up to his head, feeling a large bandage tied around it. He was confused, very confused. He tried to answer and felt himself slipping back into unconsciousness.

The sun was hot and bright as his eyes came open. It was daylight, and he remembered waking up and seeing Chris Colt, but he was gone now. Strongheart felt better and stronger. There was still a fire and a coffeepot on the fire. He got up, took care of his needs after a long sleep, and returned to the fire, pouring himself a cup of coffee. He was in a glade of cottonwood trees along a clear stream, the camp was out of reach of wind and wandering eyes, and the leaves of the cottonwoods clearly filtered the smoke so a smoke column could not be easily seen at a distance.

Leaning against his saddle he saw Eagle grazing in the green grass along the creek. His fiancée, Belle, had left him a pocket watch, and he pulled it out and saw that it had stopped. Looking at the sky he knew it was mid-morning. Now Strongheart was even more frustrated. For his watch to stop, he must have been out for a long period of time.

He felt hungry and looked for food. Near the fire were some hardtack biscuits ready to be heated up and a slab of bacon. There was also some sweet corn sitting in a pan of water near the fire. It had apparently already been boiled.

Joshua, without thinking or feeling confused, moved to his pistol and drew it from the holster. Something told him to do so, a sense, a warrior's sense of knowing. Then he heard a twig and soon hoofbeats. He saw his friend Chris Colt riding up along the creek bank on a large black-and-white overo paint horse, similar in appearance to Gabe, the red-and-white paint horse killed by We Wiyake.

He saw a field-dressed young buck deer draped over the back of Chris's saddle. Colt smiled and nodded.

"How's your head, Strongheart?" Colt asked.

Joshua said, "Aching like a toe would if you dropped an anvil on it, and like it's filled with oatmeal and molasses. Where are we, Colt? I have a million questions."

Colt dismounted, stripped the saddle and bridle off and his horse, War Bonnet, trotted over to Eagle, who gave a low whinny. The two grazed side by side.

Chris carried the small buck to a tree nearby and tied off its forelegs to two branches, using leather thongs. He had already removed the intestines, genitalia, and the scent hocks on the inside of the back knees, right after he'd shot the buck. Colt immediately went behind it and cut the back straps off and then rinsed them in the creek. Strongheart's mouth watered.

An hour later, the two men finished their food and started drinking coffee.

Chris Colt said, "What was the last thing you remember?"

Strongheart got frustrated, as he felt confused. Then, he remembered.

"I went through the sun dance ceremony," he said touching his sore pectoral muscles without thinking, "along with Sitting Bull. After we had a talk. Where are we, Chris? What happened?"

Colt said, "Well, Custer and I got crossways with each other and to make it short, I am no longer his chief of scouts. Sitting Bull moved the big camp from the Rosebud to the Little Big Horn and I was traveling toward the Rosebud and got about halfway between the two places. They're about eighty miles apart. I saw this figure in the distance traveling southwest on a black-and-white paint. It was you, but I could tell you were being followed at a distance by two hombres."

Strongheart said, "So, we are about halfway between Rosebud and the Little Big Horn?"

Colt said, "Yep, but a little farther south. I figure you were maybe headed toward the railroad."

Joshua said, "I'm having a hard time figuring out anything. You know my boss, Lucky DeChamps. He got shot and is in a hospital in Denver. Maybe I was on my way to see if he is still alive. He better be. Did I get shot?"

Colt said, "Yep, you bounced a bullet off your noggin. Got your hair parted."

Strongheart said, "What happened?"

Colt said, "I saw them running over to the backside of a ridge that curved with the gulch you were in. They reappeared ahead of you and were way out of range of my gun. They got down and one held the horses, and the shooter was aiming at you with what looked like a Sharps rifle maybe. It was a big one."

Strongheart whistled and Colt went on, "You were way out of range for my long gun, so I aimed right at you, hoping the bullet would hit somewhere, like a rock, where you might hear it. Your horse gave a little jump right before he shot and you flew out of the saddle."

Joshua said, "What happened to the dry-gulchers?"

"They saw me running toward them and got the hell out of there like someone set their horses' tails on fire," Chris said. "And I had a choice, chase them or try to save you."

"You think they are out of the area?"

Colt laughed. "I'd say so. All that happened four days ago."

"Four days!" Strongheart said. "I've been out for four days?"

Chris just chuckled.

Joshua got serious. "Thanks, Chris. I owe you big stakes."

Colt said, "You owe me nothing. Is the meal helping?"

"Yeah, a lot," Joshua said. "Why are you heading for the Lakota anyway?"

Chris Colt poured both another cup of coffee and replied, "I have become friends with Crazy Horse, and I have to try to get there to stop what's happening. Custer is marching toward Sitting Bull's new camp on the Little Big Horn."

Strongheart said, "Sitting Bull and his men are in the thousands, and they are not running, Colt."

Colt said, "I know that. I wanted to warn Crazy Horse, and try to get them to move the camp, just in the hope we can stop a slaughter. Custer is hell-bent on fame and glory because he wants to be president, and he is going to get his men killed."

He added, "I need to tell you what happened at Rose Bud Creek since you left."

While Strongheart slowly regained his strength and ate again, Chris Colt explained what had happened at Rosebud Creek after Joshua left and got dry-gulched.

As Joshua well knew, January 1, 1876, all Indians who had not joined reservations were declared "hostile." The commanding officer in charge of the campaign to return members of the Plains tribes to reservations or kill or imprison them was General George Crook, with a complement of twelve companies, ten companies of cavalry and two companies of infantry, and two main commanders: Lieutenant Colonel George Armstrong Custer and Brigadier General Alfred H. Terry, who was the overall commander of that column. On March 1, the main column left from Fort Lincoln. They were besieged by blizzards from the get-go.

Initially, the Crook's Crow and Shoshone scouts spotted Sioux and Cheyenne along the Powder River. Colonel Joseph Reynolds had them follow some Lakota and then attacked their village on the bluffs over the Powder River. Reynolds had to retreat, however, because of heavy long-range rifle fire by Lakota warriors. When he rejoined Crook, the general returned the command to base and promptly court-martialed Reynolds for his failure.

The Lakota victory at Powder River really motivated the warriors and increased participation as more warriors joined Sitting Bull. That was why so many were at the giant encampment when Joshua went through the sun dance and more were joining each day, with Cheyenne and Arapaho joining the swelling Lakota ranks. By the end of May, Crook set out with his column again with more than a thousand cavalry and infantrymen and more than fifty officers, as well as 262 Crow and Shoshone scouts. Crook's force was just one of three columns planning on serving as attacking and blocking forces to squeeze the warriors into unwinnable battles. Crook neared Sitting Bull's encampment at about the same time Joshua Strongheart joined the giant circle.

Crook had stopped and fortified his forces at the Tongue River. At that point, Sitting Bull had not had his vision yet and he, Joshua, and several more were preparing for the sun dance. Sitting Bull sent a warrior volunteer with a coup staff with white cloth tied to it. He took a message from Sitting Bull warning Crook not to come any closer to the Lakota forces and their allies. The warrior said that Sitting Bull said to tell the general if he advanced, he would have a big fight on his hands. General Crook ignored the warning and pushed on, wanting a fight anyway.

On the morning of the 17th of June, the day after Strongheart left Sitting Bull, Cook's soldiers were taking a meal break along the Rosebud Creek, and were attacked by Cheyenne and Sioux being led by Crazy Horse. The first attack was repulsed, not by the cavalry but by Crook's scouts, the Lakota's enemies, the Shoshone and Crow scouts who fought hard trying to impress Crook and his men. Crook was still being naïve about the Lakota, however, thinking they would flee if he attacked in force. He did not know how many thousands of Lakota, Cheyenne, and Arapaho had assembled and banded together. On Crooks orders, Captain Anson Mills led his Cavalry companies up Rosebud Creek and attacked the Lakota satellite camp that Crook believed lay just ahead.

Crook was shocked when the warriors attacked his column in the area Mills's unit had been in instead of fleeing. Crook then sent a courier to fetch Mills, who actually ran into the rear of another Lakota force and surprised them from behind, putting them in the midst of two forces, Mills's and Crook's. The Lakota, however, ran around Crook's force and made an escape, so Crook was already claiming he had won the Battle of the Rosebud. Strategically, he'd gotten whipped, as his men had shot more than twenty-five thousand rounds of ammunition and only killed thirteen Lakota, but he lost twenty-eight men, and had well over four dozen wounded. Crook was forced to return to his base camp on Goose Creek. Crazy Horse and Sitting Bull headed toward the Little Big Horn River to place their new giant encampment.

Chris Colt said, "I have to get to the new encampment and see if I can stop the slaughter. That idiot Custer will certainly get many brave men killed."

Strongheart said, "I am a big boy, my friend. I have to head out after the ones who shot me. I'll have a headache but thanks to you, I'm alive."

Chris said, "I followed them a little, and I bet they are heading toward the railroad south and west of here. When you track people, you kind of figure out where they are going, and not just see their tracks."

"Denver!" Joshua said, "I bet they took off after my boss, Lucky, figuring they got me. I have to saddle up, Chris."

"Me, too," Colt replied, "I have to talk to Crazy Horse. Good luck."

"You, too," Strongheart said, "Thanks, my friend."

Both men saddled quickly, gave each other waves, and rode off in opposite directions.

9

ANOTHER TRIP TO DENVER

Eagle was a very fast-trotting and smooth-trotting horse. Strongheart could actually say *slow trot* or *fast trot*, and the horse would respond to the voice command. He had another gait that Joshua called a floating trot, which the horse did to show off. He would toss his mane and tail from side to side and do a fast stiff-legged trot. Right now, he was eating up miles doing a fast trot, as Colt wanted to hit the north-south line, which would take him to Denver.

John Garden had been an engineer for several years and loved the railroad, but he hated this long uphill stretch. His long train slowed to a crawl going up the long haul. He was thinking about this when he saw the column of smoke and large fire right on the middle of the tracks. He started braking at first, thinking it might be hostiles. Then he saw the big black-and-white pinto and the cowboy wearing a bandage wrapped around his head and holding up a badge. He stopped and Joshua rode up to the engine sliding Eagle to a stop.

Garden said, "What in tarnation!"

Joshua interrupted, "Sorry to halt you, mister, but I have

an emergency. My name is Joshua Strongheart, and I am a Pinkerton agent. Are you headed to Denver?"

John said, "Yep, why?"

"My horse and I need a car, please. I can pay you whatever the price," Strongheart said.

Garden climbed down out of the engine and walked in front of Eagle saying over his shoulder, "Shore enough, Mr. Strongheart. I got an empty boxcar full of straw. Just got to rig some kind of ramp to get your horse up in it. You look Injun. Are ya?"

Joshua smiled. "Half. My father was Sioux and my mother was white. Grew up here in Montana territory, a good ways west of here."

John said, "Well, son, to be a half-breed and a Pinkerton agent, I would say you must be a man to ride the river with."

Strongheart grinned listening to this straightforward railroad man. He was very short with graying red hair, but Strongheart could tell he was all man. One of those characters he enjoyed meeting who you knew could be counted on.

They made it to the car and the brakeman met them, shaking hands with Joshua and telling Garden he had heard of Strongheart.

Strongheart used dry straw to give Eagle a rubdown in the boxcar. He wanted to stay busy because he really wished the train would move faster. Joshua was certain these killers would be after Lucky to kill him. They obviously were very desperate to stop anybody trying to investigate or shut down the Indian Ring. Millions were being made and millions more would be.

The morning sun had just started streaking in the window when Lucky opened his eyes to the clicking of the hammer of the six-shooter. Allan Pinkerton opened his eyes, too. He had slept all night in the chair near Lucky's bed and was now looking into the business end of pistols held in the hands of two very rough-looking hombres. One was tall and thin with a jagged scar running the length of his face, and the other was very large and very tall.

The large one said, "Shoot 'em, Skinny Tom."

Tom said, "Naw, not yet we won't. You two are gonna tell us where we kin find any others that know about yer investigation. We kilt yer half-breed already."

Lucky started to respond and Allan Pinkerton cut in, "Do you gents know who I am?"

"Who are you?" asked the large one, "Yer another one a them Pinkertons thet is supposed to be so hotshot. I know thet."

Allan said, "I am Pinkerton, Allan Pinkerton, and I am the one you want to talk to. Not him. He knows nothing about this investigation, but I know everything about it. You want to take me somewhere away from here, and we will talk."

Skinny Tom said, "Nice try, boss man, but we shot your boy here whilst he was powwowing with the half-breed. He is real involved."

"Yeah, and Robert Hartwell wants all of ya dead," the large one said.

Skinny Tom said, "Hush up, Rufus. Why'd'ya say Hartwell's name, ya big lummox?"

Rufus said, "Don't matter none. We're gonna kill these two, and they know it."

Skinny Tom said, "Rufus, you finish off this Frenchyman in the bed here, and ole Pinkerton's gonna start squawking. Cover yer gun with the pillow, so it ain't so loud."

Rufus pulled out a long hunting knife and approached Lucky menacingly. Lucky spit in the man's face and stuck out his chin defiantly. He raged and raised the knife.

Boom!!!! He looked down, clawing at the giant gaping

bloody hole in his chest, and he heard the knife hit the floor, and he realized he was looking at pieces of his lung and sternum around the edge of the large hole, the exit wound from Strongheart's Colt .45 round that had torn through his back. His legs folded as everything went black, and he was dead before his body hit the floor.

Skinny Tom spun with his pistol only to see his right thumb disappear in a splash of blood, as Pinkerton's shot from his Navy .36 in his shoulder holster tore off his thumb and the hammer of his .44. He screamed and grabbed his hand, as nurses and a doctor came around the hallway, but Strongheart waved them back.

Lucky and Allan Pinkerton looked at Strongheart standing in the doorway, gun in his hand.

He nodded and smiled and chuckled when Lucky said, "What took you so long, dead man?"

Skinny Tom said, "We kilt you. I seen the bullet hit yore head and knock ya off'n yer horse!"

Strongheart chuckled sadistically. "I'm a Pinkerton. We don't die so easy, in case you hadn't noticed."

He caught sight of Allan Pinkerton straightening his shoulders a little more, his chest sticking out.

"Now, before the police get here and worry about your rights, you are going to give us some answers, some important ones," Strongheart said.

Skinny Tom said, "You can go ta hell, blanket nigger! I ain't sayin' nothin'!"

Strongheart fired from the hip and the man's index finger on the same hand disappeared, and Skinny Tom clutched at his hand, screaming.

Joshua grinned, saying, "Pretty please? You still have eight more fingers, ten toes, and more body parts I can shoot off. I have a lot of bullets."

"Okay, okay, I'll talk," Skinny Tom cried out. "Jest fix my hand!"

Allan Pinkerton winked at Strongheart, while Lucky lay in bed, grinning.

Joshua hollered over his shoulder, "Doctor, we need assistance!"

Skinny Tom fainted as the doctor and two nurses rushed in the door. They immediately started tending to the assassin's wounds.

In less than an hour, his whole hand was bandaged, and he was lying in his own hospital bed, but cuffed to the rails. Allan Pinkerton had a stenographer, and once Skinny Tom started spilling the beans, he held nothing back.

Strongheart and Allan were questioning Skinny Tom when Lucky, in a robe and slippers, slowly walked into the room.

Strongheart said, "You need to be in bed, boss."

Lucky said, "No, I do not. I have been walking some since yesterday."

Strongheart shook his head, "I knew you were too ornery to die."

Pinkerton said, "Somebody has got to keep watch on you. Might as well be Lucky. What's this about them killing you?"

Strongheart said, "They nicked my head and my friend Custer's Chief of Scouts Chris Colt found me. He chased these bushwhackers away and nursed me a little."

The doctor walked in and Allan said, "Doctor, my employee here also has a head wound, and I would like him checked out."

Joshua started to protest but Pinkerton put his hand up, and Joshua stopped.

10

HARTWELL

Robert M. Hartwell was born in 1840 in Baltimore, Maryland. His father was a Baptist minister and his mother was a housewife. Robert was very intelligent and an excellent student in school. His one drawback was that he was stunted at birth and was extremely short and slender his whole life.

He was bullied and teased in school growing up because of his slight stature. The worst of the lot were the Baxter bullies. All the kids called them that behind their backs because it aptly described them. Both boys were very large and very mean.

Robert devised a scheme and stopped in at a general store, which had a huge selection of guns, on his way home. This was something Robert frequently did. He stared in particular at two matched derringers, .45-caliber Philadelphia derringers. They were displayed with a leather bag of ammunition and were in a felt-lined cherrywood box. One day, Robert went behind the downtown buildings and set fire to a millinery down the street from the general store. Soon, a bucket brigade was formed and everyone ran to watch. He ran into the store, unseen, stole the guns and ammo, went out the back door, and headed home, his heart pounding.

He was small but his arms were strong from splitting wood for the fireplace and cooking stove, so he soon developed the ability to absorb the recoil of both guns. He could only practice so much, because he could not come up with more power and ball for the guns.

The Baxter bullies had a farm just outside town overlooking one of the many wooded creeks in the area. Besides being mean, the two loved fishing. One summer morning, they arrived at the fishing hole with some grubs and red worms they had saved up for this day. Their plan was to catch a lot of sunfish and bluegills, and maybe a crappie or two. They sat down in their favorite spots along the creek bank, and Robert came out of hiding. Spotting him, one stood while the other remained seated. Robert grinned evilly and drew both derringers out, shooting both boys in the face pointblank. He stared at their faces in death for a few moments and then ran, undetected. Mrs. Baxter heard the distant gunshots, then thought it might be the neighbor shooting groundhogs. People were mystified at the shocking murders of the Baxter boys but the murders remained unsolved.

Robert was pretty much guiltless about the whole affair, even burning down the store just to create a diversion. What he wanted to accomplish was all that was important to him. This success would set a pattern in his life.

He learned that the woman who owned the millinery store lost everything. The store burned to the ground, but in young Hartwell's mind, she was simply another Baxter bully to be used and cast aside for his needs. At the funeral of the two boys, it seemed like half the town showed up and many tears flowed. Instead of feeling remorse, this emboldened him. Not even a teenager yet, Robert was a complete sociopath.

Worse yet, he knew that he could get away with whatever he chose to do in order to pursue whatever goal he was after.

As time passed, Robert did not grow in stature, but he grew alarmingly in ruthlessness. By the time he was full grown, he had murdered several more boys, two grown men, and one woman. In each case, it was to rob those people of large sums of money, with which he used to buy a wardrobe of respectability, or so it was in his mind.

He started acquiring gun hands and heavies, always the most ruthless, insisting that they wear expensive suits. Something psychologically made him do this, thinking it somehow made him more respectable. Little did he know that decades later, men like Alphonse Capone and Meyer Lansky would be born to a similar life, and would become known as gangsters. Hartwell always wore tailored suits and rode expensive Thoroughbred horses.

One of the defining moments of his life came in his mid-twenties. He had consorted with many bawdy-house women since his mid-teens, but he accidentally found a woman who took his breath away. She was only a few inches taller than he, which was unusual as most women were much taller. She had strawberry-colored hair and owned a large restaurant in Saint Louis, and she had inherited a very large estate from her wealthy parents in New York. Isabella did not trust banks or attorneys at all, because of her late father's outspoken opinions.

She made the mistake of letting Robert see her tens of thousands of dollars in cash stored in her large safe, leaving him on the horns of a dilemma. There really was not much of a moral struggle in his mind. She was a woman he cared for, yes, but this was cash that would help him further his quest for his version of power, riches, and fame. He killed her and burned her down with her house. His sacrifice was one of his nice suits, which was singed in fire. He even put a minor burn on his arm when he acted like he was trying to get into the inferno to save her when townspeople rushed up.

Now, his black horse stabled in a stock car, Robert Hartwell was on his way back to Washington, D.C., to meet with Belknap. Through his own extensive network, he knew that the Pinkertons had Skinny Tom in custody, and he knew the man's character. He would definitely talk. In fact, Hartwell knew that he would sing like a canary. An all-out plan would need to be developed to wipe out, bribe, or blackmail the Pinkerton leadership, and Joshua Strongheart definitely would have to be killed. Hartwell wanted to get to Washington and meet with his former boss, William Belknap, and figure out the best way to do this. The ambush attempts were obviously not working at all. They also had to meet with other members of the Indian Ring to figure out how to make even more millions at the hands of the tribes who had signed treaties. They would also discuss their brand-new victory. Presidential hopeful Lieutenant Colonel George Armstrong Custer and a battalion from his 7th Cavalry regiment had just been wiped out, to a man, by a combined force of Lakota, Cheyenne, and Arapaho warriors. The only living friendly to survive was the badly wounded horse of Captain Myles Keogh, a horse named Comanche. It would be treated and live many more years in the lap of equine luxury. Major Reno and Lieutenant Colonel Benteen and their battalions were also attacked but survived in battles farther down the valley of the Little Big Horn River. This was what Hartwell had hoped for, a major red victory, which would fan the flames of hatred and anger toward the red man and only help further the goals of the Indian Ring.

The Indian Ring had already initiated and created a market for buffalo robes and had tourists even shooting bison from trains for sport, with teams of hide hunters slaughtering them by the dozens each day. Each incursion killed hundreds of thousands of bison. This was the staple of the major plains tribes such as the Lakota, Cheyenne, and Arapaho. The reasoning was, if the buffalo vanished, so would the Plains tribes. Gold had been discovered in the Black Hills, but it was a sacred ground for the Lakota and prospectors were flooding into the Black Hills.

Ephraim Johnson was far and away the largest and strongest man that Robert Hartwell had ever seen in his life. He was taller and broader than anybody they ever encountered, and he was Hartwell's toughest and most trusted henchman. If he grabbed a table, a log, a chair, or anything, it moved.

The train started slowing down and soon was at a crawl, so Hartwell summoned Ephraim to check it out. Ten minutes later, he returned to the tin man's private car.

He said, "Boss, there is thousands a buffalo blocking the tracks, thousands!"

Hartwell grinned, standing and fetching a Sharps .45–70 long-range buffalo rifle.

He said, "Grab weapons, boys! We're going to shoot bison!"

As he walked through the next passenger car, Hartwell, laughing, yelled out, "Come on, gentlemen. Thousands of buffalo out here for us to shoot at, grab your weapons."

Men rose throughout the car and followed Hartwell's gang out the back door and soon shots rang out from all over the now-still train.

Almost blocking out the sun with his body mass, Ephraim led them forward to a flat car and Hartwell and his men took firing positions, and soon the large hairy beasts' bodies were lying everywhere in perfect position to start rotting in the prairie sun.

Robert Hartwell smiled seeing the crimson carnage all about them. This was becoming a major strategy of the Indian Ring: getting people to kill as many bison as possible, with ridiculous strategies such as this, and manipulating the commercial market for buffalo robes. The Plains tribes were so dependent on the large herds of bison all over the frontier prairies, the Indian Ring felt that they could see the demise of the troublesome Plains tribes commensurate with the destruction of the bison. This would open up the Black Hills much more for the exploration and prospecting of gold all over the Lakota/Cheyenne/Arapaho sacred hunting grounds and there were many under-the-table deals with mining companies connected with such exploration. Having Custer killed at the hands of the red hostiles was very fortuitous, because he was very popular in some quarters as he had presidential aspirations. He felt that his former boss in Washington would have many plums for his pie from investors in trading posts all over the West, when he got there because of the Ring's recent successes. Custer's death was his biggest key.

11

THE BATTLE

Joshua Strongheart was grim-faced and determined as he left the hospital. He was going to Washington to find Robert Hartwell and probably kill him and all his men. This was a strange challenge, as he had never been back east where civilization was more structured, more established, more settled.

The tall half-breed was saddling Eagle when the arrow hit the wall of the livery stable high above his head. He looked up and saw it was a Minniconjou Lakota arrow, a signal to him. Someone had come to the land of the *wasicun* to speak with him.

Joshua saddled up and rode into the darkness in the direction the arrow had flown from. He was near the edge of the massive town, which had been growing since 1860 when it had maybe five thousand residents and within a few years its population would reach greater than one hundred thousand.

He heard a bird whistle from the trees that ran along the creek that poured into centralized Cherry Creek. Joshua swung Eagle toward the sound and the big paint stuck his ears forward, seeing the person with his large eyes and smelling them with his flaring nostrils long before Strongheart would see them. As he dismounted, the shadowy figure ran forward and threw small arms around him. It was Joshua's beautiful cousin Lila Wiya Waste. Joshua could not help himself. He wanted to take her to the ground right there and make love to her the rest of the night. She was truly beautiful and truly loved this tall half-breed relative of hers. She reached up with both arms and pulled his lips down to hers. Strongheart kissed his cousin passionately and thoughts swirled in his head. He pictured Belle that he had loved so much and missed her touch and kisses so. He pulled away and pushed Lila back. Neither of them spoke, just stared into the other's shadowed face.

She said, "Wanji Wambli, we must talk. Follow me."

They mounted up and rode northwest, leaving Denver's lights behind them and riding into the foothills, which gave way to the snowcapped peaks that were clearly visible during the day. An hour later, Lila pulled into a tight grove of trees and boulders with a small creek running through it. There was a second pony grazing there, which gave a welcoming whinny when they rode up. They dismounted, unsaddled, and Joshua rubbed Eagle down with some dry grass.

In minutes, Lila had a nice fire going, which she had already built earlier. It was clear to him she had camped here several days already. Neither spoke while Strongheart put on a pot and made coffee. He turned to see his beautiful cousin totally naked, the light on the fire dancing on the many curves of her body. Joshua poured two cups of coffee and handed one to her.

He said slowly, "My beautiful cousin, please pull your dress back up."

She reached down, staring at him all the while, her chest heaving in and out rhythmically, and pulled the elkskin dress up, tying it over each shapely shoulder.

Joshua kept seeing the image of her nakedness, and he wondered why he had to be so principled. He wanted to hold her, caress her so badly.

He said, "Your name is Beautiful Woman, because you are. I was wrong to kiss you and will not do it again."

She interrupted, "Why Joshua? You are in my heart, where you have lived for many summers."

He said, "You are my cousin. You are almost like my sister."

"No," she said, tears filling her eyes.

"Hear me," he said firmly. "I must speak on this. Lila, I have thought many days about Belle and how much I loved her. The *wasicun* had a great storyteller and his words, all his tales, have lived well beyond his death. He told a story of great love called Romeo and Juliet, and he wrote:

'Death, that hath suck'd the honey of thy breath,
Hath had no power yet upon thy beauty;
Thou art not conquer'd; beauty's ensign yet
Is crimson in thy lips, and in thy cheeks,
And death's pale flag is not advanced there.'

"That was Romeo speaking to his lover Juliet, lying dead before him. He was basically telling her that she was still beautiful, even in death, and that is what I have remembered of Belle. I saw her in death, and she was butchered by We Wiyake, but in my mind here, I see her only as the beautiful woman I loved."

Lila put her hand up and sipped her coffee.

She said, "I have brought you much news, but this is what I wanted to speak to you about. Yes, I have always loved you, Joshua, but my heart tells me to speak to you because I love you. I know you loved Belle so, and you miss her like you would miss the air if your breath was taken away from you. I must ask you a question. Have you not almost been killed by the mighty bear?"

Strongheart said, "Yes."

She said, "And my husband was killed by the mighty bear long ago, and your father, my uncle, was almost killed by the mighty bear saving your mother. Is this not right?"

"Yes," he said wondering what she was getting at.

"Then, why did you follow me to this place? Are there not bears here?"

"Yes," he replied.

"Why do you ride alone all over the country where the mighty bear lives? Why do you camp at night alone, by yourself, when you know the bear will smell your food and come?" she asked.

Joshua said, "Just because a few bears have hurt me or hurt people I know or killed some, I cannot live my life afraid of them. I just have to be careful, that's all."

He thought about his words as Lila grinned at him.

She said, "You loved Belle with all your heart. You wanted to marry her and to have little children. You wanted to spend your nights with her under your buffalo robe and your days with her at your side."

"Yes," he said.

Lila went on, "But she was stolen from you by the Evil One. Her life was snatched away like that," as she snapped her fingers.

The beauty went on, "Your heart was ripped from your chest and you looked to the Great Mystery and cried out, 'Why?'"

Joshua got choked up.

His cousin continued, "So, now you are not afraid of the mighty bear whose claws and teeth tore your flesh, but you are afraid of love, which has no teeth. It has no claws. I always thought that the mighty Wanji Wambli feared nothing."

Her words hit Joshua like a punch in the stomach, and he wanted to vomit.

He headed for the darkness, saying over his shoulder, "I have to go pass my water, Lila."

Deep in the trees, Strongheart started sobbing and pounded the cottonwood tree before him. He wept and wept like he had never wept before. He looked skyward and wept even more, but these were cleansing tears. His beautiful cousin he had taught so many things to had just given him the answer that had been eating away at his heart. He dried his tears and washed his face in the stream and dried it.

Then, he returned to their campsite. Lila was sitting by the fire drinking coffee. She poured him a fresh cup, and he nodded, sipping on the hot brew. He loved the taste.

Finally, Joshua spoke, "Sweet Lila, my cousin, I told you of our great storyteller William Shakespeare. He also said, 'A fool thinks himself to be wise, but a wise man knows himself to be a fool.' I thought I knew how to handle Belle's death, but I did not until you gave me words of wisdom. Shakespeare also said, 'Life every man holds dear; but the dear man holds honor far more precious dear than life.'"

He sipped his coffee thoughtfully and said, "What that means is me acting like a true warrior, a true man, is more important than death itself. I can no longer run from loving again, because then I would not be Joshua Strongheart. I would no longer be Wanji Wambli, One Eagle. I should then be named One Rabbit."

Lila took a long sip of coffee and said, "I love you, Joshua."

He said, "I love you, too, Lila and you must understand, I desire you very much, too, but our love can never be."

"Why?" she said, tears flooding her eyes, "I do not care

that you are my cousin. I cannot look at other men. I only think of you and see them as little boys standing behind you, waiting for your shadow to fall on them."

Strongheart said, "Lila, I am red and white. I love to hunt the wapiti with my bow, and sit around a good fire telling stories and making trades, but I also love to read Shakespeare and go to cities, eat in restaurants, and more. I love my job very much. I will not live in the red world the rest of my life, and you would not be happy living as a white woman would. My father was right when he left my mother. It is hard when you have a heart that is red and a heart that is white, but if you lived in the world of the *wasicun*, it would be even harder for you. You gave me words of great wisdom. Now, we must use that same wisdom to think on this matter, and in your heart you know I am right."

She started sobbing, and Strongheart moved over to her and embraced her, letting her lay her face on his large chest and cry. He stroked her hair softly and thought about doing that so often with Belle. He held her for a good half hour, until she was done crying. She looked up into his dark eyes.

"Joshua," she said, "Kiss me one last time as Lila, not as your cousin, so I can always remember it."

Without hesitation, he lowered his lips to hers and kissed her, longing for more, but not allowing himself to give way to the passion. He kissed her the way he knew he must for this would be the last such kiss. Their lips parted, and she smiled at his handsome face, but her bosom was heaving up and down like a runner after a long race.

"Yes, in my heart, I know," she said simply.

Lila moved back to the log where she had been sitting and poured more coffee, drinking it and smiling bravely. She had processed it in her mind and heart that quickly. She then got up and walked to her parfleche, where she retrieved a large rolled-up piece of dried leather. Strongheart was curious but quiet while he poured her and himself more coffee, as she unrolled the leather piece.

They sat by the fire, and looked at the crude map of the Little Big Horn River valley and the giant encampment of Lakota, Cheyenne, and Arapaho. Circles of simple depictions of teepees were all along the river, each representing a tribe or clan. Green paint showed him trees, mainly along the river, and there were arrows and places where soldiers in blue coats lay, apparently dead.

Lila explained, "The elders were going to send a chief to speak with you, but I asked them many times to send me,"

Joshua was growing alarmed and wanted to understand.

Lila said, "Long Hair Custer is dead and all his men."

Joshua was in shock and immediately thought of his friend and Chief of Scouts Chris Colt.

"My friend Chris Colt?" he asked simply.

"He lives," she replied with a big smile.

"All the *wasicun* are now speaking about the Battle of the Greasy Grass, but they call it the Battle of the Little Big Horn," she said. "But Sitting Bull wanted you to know the true story from the red men who were there, because Long Hair wanted to be the great White Father in Washington, and Sitting Bull knows the hearts of men. Some who want him to be chief will say Long Hair was a great warrior, and others will say he was a bad man with a badger in his heart. What I tell you comes from the mouth of Sitting Bull. He has packed up the lodges and the people head toward Canada, because the bluecoats will now be very angry."

Joshua was still in a bit of shock but not really surprised.

Lila said, "Sitting Bull said that Long Hair made a very big mistake. When the long knives would attack our lodges before, the chiefs would take the men and flee because our warriors are so few. We had to think about the war, not one battle. This time though, our people were like the bees in a hive. When they attacked the big village, the *wasicun* kept getting stung and could hide nowhere from the angry bees, our people. First, your friend Colt had become friends with Crazy Horse. He tried to come to the big village before the battle to speak with Crazy Horse and stop the battle. Crazy Horse had him tied and bound and held in the camp during the attack, because Colt would not give his word that he would not warn Custer."

Joshua started chuckling and shook his head while he poured them both more coffee. Lila took a break and went to the stream and washed her face. He stared at her bent over the stream, and grinned at himself. He was a man, and white or red, she was indeed one of the most beautiful women he had ever known. He wondered why he could not be more like other men and satisfy his natural impulses instead of trying to do what was right. She walked back and sat down, smiling softly, and sipped her coffee.

Lila went on. "Long Hair Custer was one of the first people shot in the battle."

"He was?" Strongheart said.

"Yes," she replied. "Our people did not know Long Hair was there. Sitting Bull learned that Long Hair's wife had a dream, a bad dream, and she saw a Lakota warrior holding Long Hair's bloody scalp high in the air. He had to promise his wife to cut off all his hair. So he was riding one of his big red horses."

Strongheart remembered seeing the two magnificent chestnut Thoroughbreds and interjected, "Vic and Dandy."

"They just knew this man was a chief, and he wore buckskins like Long Hair, but they did not know it was him until the battle ended," she went on. "He led one force down

Medicine Tail Coulee, right here"—she pointed on the
map—"and tried to attack the big village. Sitting Bull's
nephew, Yellow Bull, and two other old men were behind
some dirt along the Greasy Grass."

Strongheart interjected, "I met Yellow Bull when I was
there for the sun dance."

"He was the one who shot Long Hair, as he ran across the
river," she said. "He was hit in the chest, and they stopped
the attack. Two men jumped down and helped him back on
his horse. He was with his brother's group of men. They ran
up the hill on the ridge with many Lakota and Cheyenne all
around them shooting many bullets and arrows. *Wasicun* were
dying very fast. Only one horse lived. Custer was almost dead,
and up on the hill where they made their stand, he pulled out
his pistol and shot himself here." Lila pointed at her temple.

"Custer had three, uh, tribes, bands, uh, I do not know
the word." she said.

Joshua smiled, saying, "You probably mean companies
or battalions."

"Yes, I think," she went on. "One had a chief named Reno
and the other had a chief named Benteen. They were down
the Greasy Grass to the south of Long Hair on the big ridge
that ran along the river. You know the black scout?"

Strongheart said, "Yes, I do. Isaiah Dorman. He was with
Benteen or Reno as I recall, scouting."

"Yes," Lila replied. "He was dying and Sitting Bill
stopped people from killing him. They were friends. Sitting
Bull gave him a drink from his water bag and held him and
talked to him until he died. Another *wasicun* scout, Lonesome Charley Reynolds, gave away everything he owned to
friends before they left for the big camp. He knew Custer
was going to get his men killed. When it started, two more
of Sitting Bull's nephews were out getting stray horses,

Deeds and Brown Back, and they met up with another boy named Drags-the-Rope. Some Long Knives saw Deeds and one of them shot him in the chest. Brown Back and Drags-the-Rope hid in the bushes and made their way back to the big circle and started the alarm that the *wasicun* were coming. That is how it started."

"Wow!" Joshua said.

She went on, "After Deeds was killed, Sitting Bull had scouts following the Pony Soldiers. He thinks Custer found this out and decided to attack the village. We knew he was going to attack it at night until he found out our warriors followed him."

In actuality, one small band of Cheyenne was headed toward the encampment and although there were less than forty warriors in the band, they followed the column. Scouts who later found their tracks alerted Custer, and he did indeed decide to make the daylight attack. Benteen's battalion was in reinforcement and Reno's battalion were not given the opportunity to get into position. Both battalions ended up under attack themselves, cut off from Custer's column. She explained these attacks to Joshua.

Joshua went to his saddlebags and pulled out some bacon and some hardtack biscuits he already had. He put the pan on the fire and shaved off some slices of bacon. Lila made more coffee.

They sat down to eat, and she gave him more details of the battle.

"Up here on this ridge overlooking Medicine Tail Coulee and a little bit north of it, in the tall grass, was where Long Hair and his brother Tom died. Chief Rain-in-the-Face kept his word, too. He once told Tom Custer someday he would cut his heart from his chest and eat it. He did that while many warriors watched and yelled, 'Hokahey!' The women and villagers would not scalp or cut up Custer's body because he killed himself. But one woman, Monasetah, found him, and he had made her a baby with him a long time ago. She hated him, but he made her make a baby with him, his baby. She took her sewing awl and poked it into each ear.

"She yelled, 'Can you hear me now? I hate you!'

"They would not strip his clothing because he died a coward."

To the Lakota it was a disgrace to kill yourself in battle to save yourself from torture.

She went on, "Long Hair's brother Tom was very brave fighting and many warriors wanted to count coup on him."

Tom Custer had indeed been awarded the Medal of Honor, twice, in the Civil War.

His citations read:

The President of the United States in the name of the Congress takes pleasure in presenting the Medal of Honor to CUSTER, THOMAS WARD, Rank and organization: Second Lieutenant, Company B, 6th Michigan Cavalry. Place and date: At Namozine Church, Va., 10 May 1863. Entered service at: Monroe, Mich. Birth: New Rumley, Ohio, 25 June 1845. Date of issue: 3 May 1865.

   Citation: Capture of flag on 10 May 1863.

His second citation read:

The President of the United States in the name of the Congress takes pleasure in presenting the Medal of Honor, Second Award, to CUSTER, THOMAS WARD, Rank and organization: Second Lieutenant, Company B, 6th Michigan Cavalry. Place and date: At Sailor

Creek, Va., 6 April 1865. Entered service at: Monroe, Mich. Birth: New Rumley, Ohio, 25 June 1845. Date of issue: 26 May 1865.

Citation: 2d Lt. Custer leaped his horse over the enemy's works and captured 2 stands of colors, having his horse shot from under him and receiving a severe wound.

Rain-in-the-Face had been Tom Custer's prisoner when he made his famous boast that he would someday kill Captain Custer and eat his heart. It did indeed happen according to many warriors there, but instead of being a defiling act, it was actually a great show of respect for Custer's brother Tom who fought very bravely and courageously. He commanded the company that Lieutenant Colonel George Custer was with when he died, and eating the man's heart made Rain-in-the-Face feel he was not only exacting revenge but acquiring some of this warrior's powerful medicine or power.

Lila continued, "The man who owned the horse who lived was also a very brave fighter, and he was the very last man with Long Hair who was killed. He rose up on one knee and kept shooting while many warriors cut him down."

Strongheart would later learn that it was Captain Myles Keogh, the owner of Comanche, the battle's lone survivor.

Lila explained in more detail about the battle, told him that his friend Chris Colt had gone off looking for the woman he loved, who had been kidnapped by a brute of a man named Will Sawyer. Joshua also did not know at the time but would later learn that the woman was Belle's first cousin. She also owned a restaurant but hers was in Bismarck. She also told Joshua that Benteen and Reno suffered losses, and Reno's command was even cut off from water and ended up drinking their own urine before the siege ended, but Sitting Bull and the other chiefs were more interested in moving the big encampment and leaving that country.

Strongheart and Lila finally went to sleep lying near each other close to the fire. He did not know, but she stared at him sleeping for over an hour, dreaming about what might have been. He dreamed about Belle, but in his dream she rode off smiling on a large white horse, and he was smiling, too. He had finally, through the help of his cousin, learned how to let go of Belle.

12

GOING EAST

They both awakened early and gave each other farewell hugs. He was headed back to Denver to catch a train east, and she was heading north.

Joshua started to leave but stopped and said, "Come with me, cousin."

She was nervous as he led her into Denver and headed straight for the trainyards. Within an hour, Lila and her pony and pack pony had their own freight car with hay and bedding straw. Strongheart explained the entire situation to the brakeman and told her to only leave the train when that man told her to. Riding the train would save her many days' travel north, and it turned out to be one of her most memorable experiences ever. She would leave the train far to the north in Montana territory and would be amazed at how much time was saved by the rail travel.

He, too, was full of anxiety, as he sat down in his passenger car, Eagle safely loaded in a stock car. The Pinkerton had been to Chicago but never all the way back east. What new adventures lay ahead of him? he wondered.

The drummer sat down next to Joshua Strongheart and the detective knew immediately he was going to be in a long conversation.

The man wore a derby hat and a brown pin-striped suit. He stuck out his hand with a friendly smile.

"Howdy, chief," he said cheerfully. "The name is Lawrence Vosen."

Strongheart said, "I am not a chief. Why would you call me that?"

The man stammered and said, "Well, uh, ahem, uh, I don't know. I was just trying to be friendly and did not know what to say, sir."

Strongheart smiled and stuck out his hand saying, "My name is Joshua Strongheart. I know you were trying to be friendly, but many white men call red men *chief* like that and do not realize it is an insult."

Selders said, "You certainly speak English very well for a red man. I meant nothing by it."

Joshua said, "I know. I am half white and my mother made sure I got an education. I did not mean to be impolite, sir. Are you in sales of some sort?"

"Yes, yes, I am," Vosen answered enthusiastically. "I represent several furniture concerns back in North Carolina. I travel out west to make deals with large stores that can ship our furniture west on the rails to places like Denver and other large cities. Then, from there, they are transported by freight wagons all over the frontier."

Joshua said, "That is interesting. How long have you been doing that?"

"Ever since the Civil War ended. I make my home in North Carolina and have a wife and three fine children there. How about you? Where do you work? You have a family?"

Strongheart lied, "I work as a consultant on Indian affairs

and am traveling back to Washington from Denver for a meeting. No, I have never been married."

"Are you all right, Mr. Strongheart?" the drummer asked, as he saw the Pinkerton agent suddenly staring out the window.

Joshua gave a start and said, "Oh yeah, sorry. I just saw those thousands of buffalo skeletons out there all along both sides of the railway. It saddens me greatly."

Little did Joshua know that his enemy had started the shooting of this massive herd days before, and this herd of carcasses would be the first of several such scenes of carnage Strongheart would be witnessing along the way. His heart broke a little bit with each skull, with each pile of bleached bones he saw.

He looked at the salesman and said, "You know the buffalo sustained my father's people and so many are being slaughtered. It will end up killing many Indians."

The drummer said, "No offense, but I would guess that many right now would not mind that, after the heroic fall of General Custer."

Joshua did not raise an eyebrow and just said, "I heard about that. It is a shame the red men and the white men cannot simply live in peace."

"Well," Vosen said, "I agree. Live and let live, I always say. I read all about Custer's Last Stand. What a hero. He stood there with so many savages, no offense, charging down on him, a pistol in each hand, and he was the last one of his men to be cut down."

"How do you know he was the last to fall?" Joshua asked innocently.

"Well, I read the account in the newspapers," the salesman replied. "They thoroughly research stories like that before they put them in print, you know."

Strongheart just smiled politely and nodded his head. He thought to himself *If he only knew.*

"The Indian Ring!" Vosen said suddenly.

"What?" Joshua anwered.

"The Indian Ring!" Vosen answered. "Ever hear of it? I would wager a stout bet that it was behind Custer's Last Stand."

Strongheart acted innocent, saying, "The Indian Ring?"

The drummer replied, "Yes, I travel back and forth between the West and the East all the time. I have seen some of their people. They get money from the government to buy blankets and nice things for the Indians on reservations, but instead, they buy cheap rotgut whiskey and trinkets and things, then pocket the money."

Joshua acted shocked and simply said, "Do tell."

They talked a little longer, then both men fell asleep in their seats, while the train kept puffing across the golden-green seas of prairie grass. It was after breakfast and both men sipped coffee as the train pulled through Saint Louis. On the eastern side, they did not stop at one station but slowly passed through. There were two flashes and the window exploded by Joshua's head. A piece of glass cut him along the cheekbone, and he had his Peacemaker out and peered out the window. Two men were atop a water tower and were now scrambling down. He saw two distinctive horses tied below, a snowflake Appaloosa and a strawberry roan with four white stockings.

It was then Strongheart noticed the twitching leg kicking his foot. Lawrence Vosen had been shot through the head, dying instantly. Both bullets had just missed Joshua. Two women screamed in the car, but Joshua was too busy scrambling back out the car toward the stock car where Eagle was traveling.

He quickly saddled Eagle, opened the door, and as the train slowly went through the outskirts of Saint Louis, Joshua saddled up, watched for the best spot, squeezed Eagle hard in the ribs, and leapt out onto the berm the train was passing. The mighty paint hit the ground running and Strongheart raced back toward the big city to the water tower, which was still in sight.

Strongheart tore along the tracks toward the water tower. Nearby he saw where the two men fled away from the railroad bed. Instead of cantering, Joshua eased Eagle into a mile-eating fast trot, realizing he was in for a long race to catch up.

Eagle trotted along the trail following his nose and did not require neck reining or leg aids to indicate what to do. He sensed that he was to overtake the two unusually colored horses, who he could clearly smell with his giant nostrils.

In an hour, Strongheart spotted the two horses, both lathered up, because the killers were pushing them too hard. Instead of using a mile-eating trot like Joshua had done with Eagle, they had galloped until they had to stop, let each horse catch his breath, then start again. Both horses were already in danger of binding up, with their muscles cramping and causing the horses to stop.

As he trotted along, the Pinkerton pulled his Winchester carbine from the scabbard and held it across the swells of his saddle. After several minutes, one of the shooters looked back and saw Joshua. He drew his .44 and fired back toward Strongheart only to be ripped out of the saddle by a rifle bullet and a second following the first almost immediately. He spilled from his saddle as if he had been poleaxed and tumbled along the ground lifeless.

The second, on the roan, dropped his head down and put the spurs to his horse. Joshua did the same and Eagle leapt out in a mile-eating stride. As he quickly got closer the Pinkerton could see the other horse was very lathered. The man was large but very frightened and did not even think about shooting until Eagle was a few steps away and closing fast. He twisted in the saddle, a Navy .36 Colt in his hand,

and Joshua just switched to his left side from the right rear, and the man tried to twist to shoot that way. It was too late, Strongheart was alongside and dove sideways onto the man and both bodies flew off to the right of the horses and crashed and rolled on the ground with hard thuds.

Joshua was staggering to his knees when a meat hook–sized fist crashed into his left temple, and he saw stars. He shook his head and faced the large man who had a broken bloody nose from the fall.

Strongheart grinned and said, "Is that the hardest punch you've got?"

His ego bruised, the behemoth roared and charged forward, which is exactly what the Pinkerton agent wanted. He grabbed the outstretched wrists, skipped back on one foot, and placed the other firmly in the brute's stomach. He skipped back a step, sat down, and straightened his right leg out, sending the killer flying upside down through the air, and landing on his back with a loud thud. Joshua could hear the wind leave the man in a rush.

Strongheart grabbed the gasping sniper by the hair, forcing him to his feet, and he punched him hard three times in a row, in the stomach. The man fell to the ground, face contorted in panic as he tried to catch his breath. Strongheart pulled the man's gun out and tossed it on the other side of Eagle, who had walked up.

Strongheart drew his Colt Peacemaker and sat down on a trailside log.

He said, "Stand up."

The man complied, holding his stomach.

Joshua went on, "Mister, that train is stopping at the next town and is taking on wood and water. I plan on catching it, so I have no time for games. Who hired you to try to shoot me?"

The large man snarled, "Go to hell, half-breeed!"

Boom! Flames shot off the barrel of Colt's .45 and the man grabbed his right ear screaming. Half of it was gone and it bled profusely.

"Wrong answer," Strongheart said. "Hurry with the right one. You're running out of ears and other body parts."

He started talking, "I was hired by Robert Hartwell."

"Where is he?" Strongheart said.

He saw an almost imperceptible flicker in the man's eyes, which put him on guard immediately. The eye flicker turned to a deer-in-the-torchlight look, and he knew trouble was coming. The man's hand came up with a large-bore .45-caliber derringer apparently hidden in his pocket. Strongheart's gun boomed and the man's head almost exploded. Joshua looked at the man lying flat on his back unmoving, eyes wide open staring up at the sky, but actually seeing nothing. He shook his head.

"Wonderful. Good shooting, Joshua," he said to himself sarcastically. "Kill the man before he can give you any information."

Strongheart went through the man's pockets and then mounted Eagle on the run. He knew the train would be watering and taking on fuel at the next stop, so he hoped he could catch up. Eagle was still as strong as could be. He reined him into a mile-eating fast trot and paralleled the tracks.

An hour passed, and Strongheart saw the next town ahead where the train was stopped. He pushed forward, finally allowing Eagle to slow to a walk. They had made it. He had to cool the horse down before putting him back on the train, so he walked him back and forth on the loading platform before putting him back on the train. Meanwhile, he spoke with the brakeman and told him what happened. In the car, he gave the horse a good long rubdown. He decided to ride in the car with him awhile to make sure he was fine physically, and once again Eagle amazed him with his stamina.

As the train started up, Strongheart started feeling the strain on his muscles from the chases, fight, and adrenaline-pumping experience he had once again survived. Lying back on the golden straw, he closed his eyes and he drifted off to sleep. He dreamed about his youth in Montana.

Joshua's stepfather, Dan Trooper, was demanding but had to be to bring this young boy into manhood befitting the high expectations his mother had for him. She saw to it that Joshua had his nose in books in school, and she made him study Shakespeare and other great writers. She told him that as much as he was learning to shoot guns as well as bows and arrows, he also needed to learn how to communicate effectively if he wanted to get anywhere in life.

One time, Dan told young Joshua to take the old grade mare out and harvest a young bull or cow elk for the family for meat. The last time Joshua did that, he was told to shoot a deer, and did so but had been given only two bullets and took two to shoot the doe. He got a switching from his stepdad out behind the woodshed. Dan instilled in his young brain to only use one bullet to kill anything, to always shoot clean, so the animal would not suffer, and not to waste expensive bullets. He rode far out heading toward the darkest timber he could see, feeling that would be where he would surely find a large harem of elk bedded down.

The teenaged Strongheart entered the trees and skirted north through them, seeing some signs but nothing fresh. He heard shooting and yelling and made his way along the foothills toward the noise. Dismounting and creeping forward through the trees, he saw a small but fierce battle going on. Two large bearded mountain men who had apparently joined forces with about seven Crow warriors were fighting against a force of about twenty Blackfoot warriors who were all on foot. The mountain men and Crow all had horses, plus the mountain men had two pack mules as well. The goal of the Blackfoot war party was quite obvious to the young man.

This was less than six miles away from the town where his father was marshal and his young mother owned a popular general merchandise store. He felt that warning his pa was more important than taking an elk right now. He hopped on the mare, wove through the trees south, and when he was around the ridgeline out of sight, he pushed the small mare into a gallop toward the distant mountain valley town. When he arrived, he rode straight to the marshal's office and city jail and jumped off his lathered horse and ran into the building.

"Pa, Pa," he said excitedly, "I was out west scouting for elk and there were two trappers, joined up with seven Crows, and they were being attacked by about twenty Blackfeet."

Just then Joshua's beautiful mom walked in the door, smiling, and Dan snapped up out of his chair, and smiled broadly. She walked over and gave him a quick kiss.

"Finish talking to him, Joshua," she said.

"Yes, ma'am," he said. "So the Crows had ponies, and the trappers had riding stock and pack mules. The Blackfeet did not have any stock."

"Blackfoots," his mom interrupted with a smile.

Young Strongheart replied, "I thought the plural of *foot* is *feet*, Ma?"

As a teenager, he felt he had just counted coup on one of his elders and had a self-satisfied smirk.

She calmly replied, "That is true, son, but we are not discussing their feet. Their tribe is referred to as the Blackfoot, so the plural is Blackfoots. You would not say, *There were twenty Blackfeet warriors*. You would say, *There were twenty Blackfoot warriors*. Is that understandable, Joshua?"

Ego deflated, he grinned at himself and said, "Yes, ma'am."

Dan said, "Honey, can I come to the store in just a little bit and speak with you? Joshua and I were about to have a man-to-man talk."

She smiled and winked at the handsome, tall lawman and backed out of the door. Joshua, in the meantime, thought back to his whipping for using two bullets to bring down a deer. He wondered if he was in trouble again.

Dan surprised Joshua by pouring two cups of coffee, although the teen had never really drunk it before. He set one before Joshua and sat down himself, cup in hand, putting his worn boots up on the desk.

"Son," he said, "You were very observant figuring quickly that the Blackfoot were probably after horses, and you counted how many were in each group. I bet you could also describe a number of the men and the colors of many of the horses."

Proudly, Joshua said, "Yes, sir."

Dan said, "You are old enough, you should start giving thought to what kind of career you want. Your observation shows me you would probably be well-suited to be a lawman or a scout, either one."

Enthusiastically, Joshua said, "I've thought about both, Pa."

Dan said, "The important lesson here though is twofold. One, I am a town marshal, not sheriff of the territory. My concern is protecting the citizens of this town and enforcing the laws. My job is to concentrate on that and not go off a half dozen miles to attend to any other problem somebody is having, unless a sheriff or deputy needs help. Lesson two is that you had a task and that was to hunt and kill an elk for the family. I am glad you care about others, but those trappers are big boys who know what kind of country they are riding in and should be aware of dangers they might face. The Blackfoot and the Crows kill for a living, son. They are warriors. So are you, or at least a warrior in the making. Always finish the task you have been given. That is one of the measures of a man."

Strongheart said softy, "Yes, sir."

Suddenly Dan's face morphed into Belle's face, and she was smiling, and then she turned into a golden eagle and flew off toward the distant mountain range.

Strongheart sat up in the straw, blinking his eyes. He looked around the car and over at Eagle, who had been napping on his feet. Now, he lay down on a straw bed. Joshua stood and stretched, yawning.

He got into his saddlebags and got some oats for Eagle, some hardtack and antelope jerky for himself, and he ate like a wolf. After eating, Joshua gave the big pinto a good rubdown. Then he cleaned his saddle while he did a lot of thinking about the case.

Strongheart decided to stay with his horse for a while and not chance sitting by windows again. Hopefully, they may not even think he was back on the train. As the miles passed, he did a lot of thinking about his conversation with Lila. He had to truly let Belle go and stop blaming himself for her death. It did make him think a lifetime as his spouse would not be a good idea for most women he might fall in love with, but he would let his guard down more.

Strongheart was nearing Terre Haute, Indiana, when he heard the train slowing down and braking. It seemed awfully fast to him, and he wondered what the cause was. He immediately hoped and prayed there were no large herds of bison this far to the east awaiting further slaughter by blood-lusting rail passengers.

As the train stopped, Joshua slid the big side door open. He was shocked by what greeted him: a mob with badges.

The brakeman and fireman both came running up to the large posse. The prominent rider wore a sheriff's badge, and he handed a piece of paper to the brakeman who started reading it. The posse members all pointed rifles and pistols at Strongheart.

The sheriff said, "Joshua Strongheart?"

Strongheart replied, "Yes, what's going on, Sheriff?" He was puzzled.

"My name," the lawman said, "is Jewels Herculette and I am the sheriff. I have a warrant for your arrest for the murder of two men, Richard Landhart and Michael Reuben, just outside of Saint Louis."

Strongheart said, "That is ridiculous, Sheriff. Those men shot and killed a man seated next to me on the train, aiming for me. I got my horse, pursued them, and had a gunfight with them. I won. Simple as that."

The officer said, "You can explain all that to the judge. I have a warrant for your arrest for murder, period. Now, reach up and grab a chunk of cloud with both hands. Zeke, climb up in the car and grab his hogleg, rifle, knife, and any other weapons you see."

Strongheart complied but said, "Sheriff, I am a Pinkerton agent and on an important case!"

"Tell it to the circuit judge," the sheriff replied.

Joshua knew any further arguing would be fruitless. He would ask the sheriff to send an immediate telegram to Pinkerton headquarters in Chicago. Two men boarded the car and confiscated his weapons, then one saddled Eagle, while the other tied Strongheart's hands. The Pinkerton wondered why they did not use handcuffs, but he cooperated.

Twenty minutes later, with Joshua's hands firmly bound, he was mounted on Eagle and the posse rode away from the nearby town of Terra Haute. This also puzzled Joshua.

He said, "Sheriff, where we headed? Why we headed away from town?"

The posse member next to him said, "Shut up and ride."

Strongheart said, "Hey, Sheriff!"

The man next to him hit him on the back of the head with a rifle butt. The Pinkerton saw stars and shook his head to clear the blinking lights. The sheriff stopped, rode back to the man next to him, and lashed him across the face with his quirt.

He said angrily, "You were all told not to touch him."

He looked at Joshua and said, "You keep quiet. We will get to where we're going when we get there. Shorty, tie his hands to his saddle horn!"

A short, stocky man came over to Strongheart with some braided leather and lashed his wrists to his saddle horn. He remounted and the posse continued riding away from the city. Joshua was now totally suspicious of this sheriff and his posse. He had to start making escape plans, but how?

They rode for several hours and were riding through a wooded area when they arrived at a large farm complex. There were many outbuildings and several large barns. There was a very large farmhouse, a pond in front, and a large apple orchard behind the farmhouse surrounded by what appeared to be a large forest. Joshua Strongheart started cataloguing in his mind possible escape spots in case he did escape. He also had to make sure these men were not an actual sheriff and posse, as he could get fired from the Pinkerton Agency for not cooperating with a law enforcement investigation fully. He was certain, though, that his intuition was correct.

A very large man came out of the house dressed in coveralls like a farmer and pointed to the corrals behind the barn. The posse rode over there, following the sheriff. The farmer followed. Everybody dismounted and started stripping saddles, bridles, and other tack off of horses. Finally,

Josh was untied from the saddle horn and followed the sheriff and two posse members. Two more followed behind him. All but the farmer held their guns at the ready. The farmer led them to a large well. The sheriff looked over the edge and saw a deep dry well that went down about thirty feet or more. The sun was positioned so that he could see the bottom contained a few rocks and boards.

The sheriff stepped forward with his .45 stuck up under Joshua's chin, saying, "All right, half-breed, have a seat on the bucket and we'll lower ya down."

Joshua said, "What kind of sheriff are you?"

"Sheriff." The man laughed and replied, "I'm no sheriff, but my boss can sure get good printing done, huh?"

He chortled at his own joke.

Joshua was not laughing. He could see no escape, so he quickly looked around him and assessed the surroundings in case of future escape, which he now figured he would do.

"Who is your boss?" Strongheart asked.

"Get in the bucket now!" the man said.

Joshua knew there was no way out of this with all the guns pointed his way. He would have to go down in the dry well and then try escaping. He lifted his leg and placed it between the ropes and settled his buttocks on top of the wooden bucket.

Strongheart said, "I need my hands to hold the rope or I will fall off and then how are you going to explain a dead Pinkerton to your boss?"

The fake sheriff nodded and the coverall-clad farmer moved over to him and freed his hands. Joshua nodded, smiled, and grabbed the rope. They started lowering him down into the dry well. The rocks and dry boards he'd seen at the bottom earlier were heartening. That meant he would have tools and possible weapons. He also had his hideout emergency pocket knife, which he carried in a pocket inside his right boot. Nobody had checked him for such a small weapon. In fact, Joshua decided that once he did indeed escape this and prevail, he would buy a small derringer to keep as a hideout gun for any future problems.

He was soon down at the bottom of the well, and he remained in the bucket. The fake sheriff yelled down to him to get out of the bucket, and Strongheart refused. Joshua counted on the sheriff being under orders not to shoot him, probably so that Robert Hartwell could come and execute him personally and gruesomely. He wanted the rope and hoped his plan might work if he could frustrate the sheriff the way he figured he could.

The sheriff pulled out his pistol and pointed it down at Joshua, saying, "Strongheart, you get the hell outta that bucket! Now, or I'll shoot you."

Joshua had to take a risky but strong action. He yelled back up, "You have to be kidding, whoever you are! You sure aren't any sheriff! That bucket is the only way I am getting out of here, so I am staying on top of it until you hoist me back up!"

"The hell you say!" the angry man replied. "See how this sows yer bean crop!"

Joshua saw a flash in the man's hand, and he grinned. The large knife passed across the rope all the way up at the crank and sliced through it, letting the large rope fall down into the well. That was exactly what Strongheart wanted. Now he felt he could escape, and would be unbothered until the boss arrived, maybe a day later. His guess was that they had telegraphed Hartwell, and he wanted Joshua imprisoned until he could arrive and deal with him personally.

He only had minutes left of daylight to see what materials he had to work with in the dry well bottom. There were several boards, a large hard stick, a handful of fist-sized rocks, an old pair of dirty trousers, and several pieces of twine. Joshua immediately gathered wood he would use to built a teepee-type fire, and used his little pocket knife to shave off wood to use as kindling. He cut a small section of the twine to use with the kindling to start the fire. He would wait until after dark before lighting it. In the meantime, he would sleep. Most of his activity would be at night. He correctly figured that, with the rope cut, they would assume he could not possibly escape and would just occasionally look down into the deep hole to ensure he had not miraculously figured out some way to do so. Not seeing or hearing any activity, they would probably not check as often and get more careless, simply assuming that he was safe down there until Hartwell showed up the next day.

Joshua lay at the bottom of the well the rest of the day, feigning sleep sometimes and sometimes getting up. He would wait until somebody checked on him, looking over the edge of the well, then he figured he had a little time to work. He took the pole and started whittling the end with his knife. He was able to sharpen the blade on one of the rocks, and he continued this throughout the day. After dark, someone would come up with a torch and look down, so he kept up the same ruse throughout the night.

It was two hours before daybreak and Joshua had just seen a lookout check on him. Now, he was ready to make his daring move. He had been preparing all night. He had carved the end of the large stick into a spear. Now, he held his first board with the end whittled to an edge, grasped the rock wrapped in his shirt, and pounded the board into the wall of the well about five feet up. He set the rock on the board close to the wall and pulled himself up and stood on the plank now sticking from the wall. He lifted the spear, and wedged it up well above the board between the walls, and now pounded a second board into the wall of the dry well five feet up. He repeated the procedure and was now standing on a board ten feet above the bottom of the well. He had placed a third board on this second one, and he pounded that one into the wall, too.

He now stood fifteen feet up in the well and was ready to carry out the next part of his plan, but suddenly he heard spurs jangling and heading his way. Joshua thought quickly.

Bugger McDonald liked Robert Hartwell simply because both men were the same size—tiny—and Hartwell wielded tremendous power.

Bugger looked down into the hole with the lantern in his hand, simply trying to be cautious. He had heard the dull thudding sound of Joshua pounding the boards into the wall, and Bugger wanted to impress his bosses by doing his job thoroughly. He knew something was wrong before his lantern could shed its full light down into the deep hole. However, a spear came up out the shadows directly below him and hit him under his chin and went up through his throat and penetrated directly into his brain. He died instantly. His body slumped lifeless over the edge of the well, and the lantern slipped from his fingers. Reacting quickly, Joshua stuck his hand out and the bottom of the lantern struck it, halting its fall, and he withdrew it and immediately inserted his fingers into the handle, grabbing it before it could descend any farther.

Strongheart whispered, "Whew!"

Now, he had a new challenge. He had to get Bugger's body out of sight quickly. He wiped the point of the spear and wedged it across the well again, so he could grab it if needed. Next, he took the important well rope that was coiled diagonally around his muscular chest. He formed a double overhand knot. On the second toss, he got it around the neck of the dead Bugger McDonald. Carefully, Strongheart tightened the lasso, then using one hand pulled on the rope and lifted the dead weight of Bugger's body up over the edge of the well and finally, with a jerk, sent it falling past him down to the bottom of the dry well. It hit the floor with a thud. It actually took him longer wiggling and shaking the rope to get the lasso loop off of the dead corpse than it did to lasso him. He finally got the rope free.

Joshua coiled up the rope again, and attached it to the spearhead with a loose knot in a leather thong from his clothing. He reached up with the spear and was able to just get the coil of rope over the top of the crank for the well. He held the end of the rope and the weight of the coil pulled the loose knot free and the rope fell down into the well, where Josh easily grabbed it. Quickly, the Pinkerton agent formed another loop and immediately stuck his left toe through it, like a stirrup. He stuck the end of the spear into his boot and attached it to his belt with another thong from his fringe, so it remained alongside his body, and he did not have to worry about it swinging from side to side or banging it into something.

He pulled himself up quickly to the edge of well, peered over and saw two guards sleeping by a campfire made out in front of the main farmhouse. They seemed to be sleeping soundly, and he dropped into the shadow of the well on the far side of it opposite from the two guards. Undoing the spear, he freed it from his boot and started crawling on his belly toward the barn and corrals where his horse had been placed. Trying to stick to the shadows, it took him nearly a half hour to make it the short distance to the barn. There, he found a very alert guard looking all around with a Henry carbine in his hand. It was getting close to dawn now, but Strongheart took his time sneaking up on the man. He removed his boots and crawled around the barn, then got to his feet and went forward barefoot. Joshua was ten feet away when the man turned, bringing the rifle up. Strongheart had wanted to get close enough to stab, but had to throw the spear, with adrenaline coursing through his body. The spear actually went through the guard's body right in the abdomen, slicing the celiac artery in the process, and the man sensed he would be dead in seconds. He instantly thought he had to fire a warning shot, but he could not pull the trigger. His fingers would not work. Then, as if in slow motion, he saw the carbine tumble from his hands onto the ground. The last thing he saw was Joshua Strongheart pulling out his .44 revolver and grabbing the Henry repeater. Everything went blank.

Strongheart quickly searched the man's pockets looking for clues but found nothing but tobacco and some paper money, which he left. He was so thankful that his mother took him to his father's village circle so often as a child so he could learn the skills of the Lakota warriors. He now had the man's Henry and pistol, so he went into the barn searching for his saddle, tack, and saddlebags. Strongheart found a well-appointed tack room and there was his gear and, surprisingly, his guns and knife.

He quietly saddled Eagle and led him from the barn, then disappeared into the orchard, grabbing some apples as he moved along. Deep into the trees, Joshua saddled up and moved away heading into deeper woods. Strongheart identified several higher wooded hills, so he headed for them so he could look out and get a vantage point. As always, he had paid attention to what direction they had traveled in to get to the farm he was escaping from.

13

THE CHASE

Joshua soon found himself atop the highest ridge around, which would not even compare with a small rise in his part of the country. Nonetheless, he got a view of the countryside around, and he took in drainages, thick woods, trails and roads, including the one they rode in on. Strongheart planned his escape routes in his mind, thinking of each possible attack. He saw movement down below and got his telescope out of his saddlebags. There was a posse following him and there was a tracker in the lead.

"Shawnee," Strongheart said to himself. "Let's see how good you can track."

Strongheart took off down the other side of the ridge, then doubled back, reached the top of the ridge, and doubled back again down the gentle ridgeline, making three sets of tracks going both up and down the ridge. He went into a stream running along the bottom of the gulch to the east and slowly walked through the stream until he came to a rocky bank, left the stream, and carefully rode up the opposite ridge a short distance. There, he dismounted, left Eagle grazing on the wild grasses, and he went back to the stream, and covered up all signs of him leaving the waterway. He thought about even drying the grass where they came out and went up the bank, but he figured that the sun would dry the grass by the time the tracker led the posse there.

The Pinkerton returned to Eagle, and took the leather hoof covers from his saddlebags and slipped them over each hoof, tightening them at the top of each. He then slowly walked to the top of the ridge and removed the leather horse moccasins. It was important to Joshua to remain on high ground, so he could see when Robert Hartwell was coming on their backtrail.

He soon found a thick stand of hardwoods on the south side of the ridge overlooking the trail the posse brought him in on. It was not as high as the previous ridge and there was plenty of grass for Eagle to graze on. Strongheart made camp.

Hokolesqua, which was a Shawnee name for "cornstalk," was simply called Johnny in this part of the country. He was the only tracker around and was frequently hired by hunters and lawmen searching for fugitives. He had a great reputation locally, but he had never tracked anybody like Strongheart before. He was still working out the jumble of tracks going up and down the end of the ridgeline across the valley and had not even gotten to the creek yet.

Knowing he still had hours of time separating them, Joshua made camp and built a small low smoke fire out of very dry wood, knowing the heavy cover from the oaks and maples about him would dissipate the smoke as it filtered through the tree canopy. He took a risk and decided to take a nap, sorely needing sleep.

Joshua's eyes opened, and he looked around. It was nearing dark. Quickly, he saddled Eagle, leaving his camp in place, and rode back to the other side of the smaller ridge he was on. Reaching a good vantage point with cover, he retrieved his telescope. Far down the valley, he spotted patches of color here and there as the posse moved along the creek. He finally spotted Johnny as he walked along the small waterway, searching for clues. Strongheart rested easy, knowing he had been very effective so far covering his trail. He decided he would nap for a few hours, every once in a while awakening and checking for both posse and Robert Hartwell.

Eagle whinnied lightly and Joshua's eyes came open. His hand was already on his Colt Peacemaker, and he doused the small fire and then urinated on it. He then covered the fire completely with soft dirt. Strongheart ran through the trees and saw that a second posse was coming up one end of the ridgeline, and the first with Johnny tracking was coming up the backside. The two would soon meet on both sides of his makeshift camp. Strongheart made it back, saddled Eagle, and scraped out the fire pit, quickly rebuilding it. He lit the fire and fanned the flames. He then stacked some pine boughs he had used as a bed so from a distance in the dark they might look like a sleeping man's figure. With the flames licking up higher, he tossed nine bullets into the fire and crept away into the darkness. Retrieving Eagle, the two quietly slipped down the steep side of the ridge between the two posses.

Down below, Strongheart slipped into the saddle and grinned as he heard his rounds now cooking off in the fire. As he hoped, both posses opened fire on the camp and each other. The large farmer with the coveralls was hit in the heart and killed instantly with the very first shot. Several men on both sides lay on the ground moaning with wounds.

Joshua Strongheart was now in the creek bottom down below the northernmost ridge and would exit the stream on the main road. Once on the main road, his tracks would mix in with all the other tracks. He would move farther down the road, find another vantage point to see the road, yet still be far enough away that he could catch up on some much-needed sleep. If Robert Hartwell ever appeared, Strongheart would snipe him out of the saddle. He was a very destructive force, especially for the American Indian nations, and most especially the Plains tribes. It was a matter of national security and Joshua saw Hartwell as a traitor and enemy combatant. He needed to be killed on sight.

He rode down the road over a dozen miles and was now at the end of the long valley where he could see from the high ridge before. If Hartwell came, he would have to come that way, as the railroad was that direction.

Strongheart hid his sign well as he left the road and went into the trees and made a safe camp in a thicket with lots of sign of game, but no humans. He built a smokeless fire and a comfortable bed of pine boughs, left Eagle to graze nearby, and went to sleep. If riders came, Eagle would whinny or snort when he smelled or heard them in the distance, and Joshua would check it out. In the meantime, he had to get caught up on sleep.

The Pinkerton agent slept the sleep of the dead for hours. When he awakened, it was dark out, and he built up the fire a little, made breakfast and coffee. He checked on Eagle, who grazed peacefully in the trees nearby. Joshua felt much better after food and a few cups of coffee. He needed some more meat though, so he got his Lakota bow and arrows from their hiding place in his bedroll. Stringing the bow, Joshua slipped on his moccasins, and left the camp, not intending to go far.

As the first streaks of daylight began to slice their way through the green forest canopy, Strongheart drew the bow, and launched an arrow into the left ribcage of a young white-tail buck. He was less than one hundred yards from his camp. He rolled the buck on its side and quickly field-dressed it, then cut the two scent musk hocks out of the inside of the hindleg kneecaps. He carefully cleaned his knife blade, knowing the strange gland scent could taint the rest of the meat. He carried the deer back to his camp and started cutting meat. He put a couple backstraps on the fire and ate until he was stuffed. He knew the protein, the meat, would help him be more alert and stronger, and Strongheart did not know when he might have his next meal.

After preparing some of the meat and placing it in his saddlebags, he packed up his camp and started covering all signs of its existence. He then headed back toward the road to get a closer vantage point. Right after dismounting, Joshua spotted a group headed toward him in the distance. The group had men all dressed in suits, and then he spotted him. It had to be Robert Hartwell. In the midst of the group was a tiny man, even obviously so without Strongheart's telescope. He was riding a large black horse, larger than the others in the group. Joshua ran to his saddle and grabbed his Winchester carbine. He found a stump where he could rest the barrel, and he ran to his saddlebags and grabbed his spare shirt, brought it back and used it as a pad for the rifle. The group was riding slowly, carefully. He would simply bushwhack Hartwell from a distance, shooting him out of the saddle.

Strongheart laid the rifle across the shirt on the stump and aimed at a spot in the road. He was conflicted, because everything in him wanted to challenge the man to a gunfight and shoot it out with him no matter how many shootists accompanied him. Then he thought back to his shootout in Florence, Colorado, and how close to death he was, how many bullets were in him.

He decided back then in the hospital to be much smarter in the future and not let his emotions influence his decisions.

He knew that Robert Hartwell was an enemy of the United States, and enemy of the American Indian nations, an enemy who manipulated the system for personal gain and cheated Americans out of their taxes and the red man out of lands and promised compensation that was part of various peace treaties. One of the biggest problems affected Joshua's people. Gold had been discovered in the Black Hills of South Dakota territory, very sacred lands to the Lakota. Hartwell kept his crew very busy. He paid them very well, which bought much loyalty, and he was building a very financially successful power base nationwide.

Joshua knew he had to stop him for the sake of the country and his father's people, so fair play was out the window. He would easily take the henchman out with the sniper shot he planned. Robert Hartwell would soon be in the killing zone of the ambush.

No sooner had the Pinkerton agent thought this than a group of four riders came running down the road from his left and rode straight up to Hartwell, who halted. Joshua knew the conversation going on. They had just told him about Strongheart's escape and that there were two posses out trying to find and catch him, maybe more than two posses out now. He could not hear the words, but he saw that Hartwell was angry. Then, the ruthless killer nodded at two of his henchmen, and they drew, shooting the man out of the saddle who had just warned him. Hartwell spoke to the assembled gang, and they turned and galloped away. Joshua almost came close to cursing he was so frustrated. The other three dismounted and loaded the dead man on his horse and headed back toward Joshua's prison compound.

He saddled up and took off after Robert Hartwell and his crew. Joshua would plan as he rode, keeping out of sight behind them, but something happened he did not count on.

One of the three riders who rode back with the dead body of the fourth had to return and catch up with Robert Hartwell to give him a message. He was galloping hard behind Strongheart, and within a few miles he came running around a bend and spotted Joshua Strongheart far ahead following Hartwell's trail. The Pinkerton did not see him, even though he frequently checked his backtrail. The man immediately slid to a stop, turned his horse, and put the spurs to him. He did not have to be hit over the head to know what was going on. He would return and tell the rest of the group that he had spotted Strongheart following Hartwell and his gang. They would want to pursue Joshua from the rear.

Hartwell had ridden hard for several miles when he stopped and appointed two men, who were good rifle shots, to lie in wait along the road to ambush Strongheart if he might be coming along behind them, tracking them, or just coincidentally going down that road, his only way back to the railroad. Feeling more secure knowing the two men were covering their rear, Hartwell had his men slow to a walk, which he would alternate with slow trotting, As bad as he was as a man, he did take good care of his big Thoroughbred. That, however, was quite common among outlaws, because they were frequently pursued by posses, legal ones. Outlaws quite often had the best horses around and usually treated them well.

Both men were named Shorty. One was Shorty Medina and the other was named Shorty Atha. Shorty Atha was nicknamed that humorously because he actually was tall and lanky, at about six foot four. The other was five foot two and very stocky. Medina took cover right next to the road where he could not possibly miss. There were some thick bushes around the base of a large oak tree. He crawled under them on his belly with part of the oak hiding most of his body.

Shorty Atha, in the meantime, climbed up and lay down on a flat-topped short grassy hillock about thirty feet beyond Medina's position. They waited patiently for fifteen minutes, and suddenly a chill crept up Shorty Medina's spine. He felt like someone was staring at him and he rolled over, and sat up looking up the short ridge behind them that skirted the roadway. He gulped as he stared at the grinning face of Joshua Strongheart, who was up the hill and aiming an arrow directly at him. He saw the Pinkerton wink at him, then release the arrow, which whooshed through the air and buried itself in his chest right through the heart. His head slumped forward on his chest, and his lifeless eyes stared at the ground.

Joshua nocked another arrow, and his moccasins made no sounds as he padded along the low ridge to his right, until he was behind Shorty Atha. He gave a whistle and Atha whirled, pistol drawn and in his right hand, but the arrow penetrated his forehead immediately passing out the back of his skull. He died before his hand dropped the gun.

Joshua ran forward and checked both men for .45-caliber bullets, which would fit his gun. Medina's body had them and Joshua took the dead man's pistol as well, tucking it into the back of his waistband.

Strongheart knew that Hartwell had not survived this long by being stupid, so he would probably set up an ambush on his backtrail. He had simply kept under cover on the high ground, and saw the two bushwhackers when he slowly came to the part of the ridgeline and stopped to scour the area with his telescope, as was his custom. He had indeed learned his lesson about just wading into an entire gang of bad men gun ablazing. However, the tall half-breed had no idea he now had ten men in front of him and would soon have twenty more behind him, all wanting to tear him to shreds.

He knew one thing and was very single-minded about it.

Strongheart had to fight or think his way past all the gun hands and kill Robert Hartwell, for the sake of his country. To that end, and not wading into a gun fight, he decided very firmly if he had to lose his life to accomplish that goal, so be it. He definitely would.

Joshua decided to risk it and go back into the road and speed along for a while at a mile-eating fast trot. He rode for miles and the tracks of the gang were still there. He saw where they had stopped twice, apparently to give their horses a breather. Then he saw where they took a side road south.

Thinking they might again set up an ambush or might be stopping to set up a camp, he went off the road and worked his way through the trees paralleling the road. His hunch was a wise one, as they did indeed set up a camp in a clearing bordering the side road, or trail, actually. He circled around to some wooded high ground south of them and saw he could keep an eye on their camp, the road, and make his own campsite on the opposite side of the small ridge he was on.

Four hours passed, and it was well after dark when five riders, as well as Johnny the tracker, rode into the camp carrying a couple large torches. Joshua watched as they spoke with Robert Hartwell.

"Darn it all!" Joshua said, as he saw Hartwell call his men together and then make their fire smaller, and sent several as lookouts on their backtrail.

By Hartwell's immediate reaction, Strongheart knew immediately that he had been spotted by someone, and they knew he was trailing them. The henchman would not be putting guards up on his backtrail if that were not the case.

Joshua said, "Shakespeare said, 'Our doubts are traitors and make us lose the good we oft might win by fearing to attempt.' Forget the amount of men you must face, Joshua, just use your brain before you use your guns."

He glassed around with his telescope, so he could understand the land before him once again. He would enter the enemy camp this night and give them some food for thought. Instead of waiting to see what Hartwell would do, he decided to take the fight to the enemy. He wondered if he could sneak in and do harm to Hartwell himself, but Strongheart thought better of it, knowing that the professional shootists that the killer boss surrounded himself with would not fall asleep on watch, like others would be likely to. He figured, though, that he could indeed do damage to their sense of well-being and maybe cause some sleepless nights, as well as potentially eliminate a few of the enemy.

Using his telescope again, Strongheart surveyed the area around Hartwell's camp and figured approaches and hiding places. He changed into his moccasins, darkened his face with charcoal from his small fire, and retrieved his bow and quiver full of arrows from his bedroll. Leaving Eagle, he went downhill through the trees.

In an hour, he was outside the killer's camp in the dark shadows of the surrounding forest. His plan was simple. He would avoid the part of the camp where Hartwell and his bodyguards slept as he scouted the perimeter. He had already noted where the outer guards were. He had plans for them, too.

Twenty minutes later, he was on his belly crawling through the undergrowth toward the southern part of the perimeter around the camp fire. He saw several guards near Hartwell carefully watching mainly the northerly part of the campsite area. The obvious guard here was propped against a log by the fire, in deep slumber. Joshua low-crawled to the first man and saw he had removed his double-draw holster. Strongheart buckled it and slipped it over his neck and under one arm, grabbed the man's Henry carbine, and crawled into the darkness. He stowed the weapons there and crawled back into the circle just outside of the flickering light of the camp-fire. He took this man's holster and gun, buffalo gun, and Henry carbine, as well as a very fancy beaded sheath holding a large bone-handled and engraved Bowie knife.

Then, he thought about the dramatic effect he could really bring with a very bold move. He returned to the man, thought again how this was war and what he did could prevent an even greater catastrophe in the United States. The welfare of the Indian nations and the country was at stake. He pulled out the Bowie knife and felt the blade, which was as sharp as his own knife. Joshua froze as a man sat up suddenly, then just as quickly lay back down and was snoring in less than a minute. Strongheart hated to kill this way, but again thought about the greater good, and he placed his hand firmly over the outlaw's mouth and nose and sliced his throat. He held the kicking man until he no longer moved. Then, he raised the knife and brought it straight down into the saddle that the man had been using for a pillow. He crawled to the next man, stole his guns, and crawled away into the darkness.

At his cache of weapons, Strongheart got on his feet, slinging various holsters around his shoulders. He carried everything off toward his camp. He was upset with himself for slitting a man's throat while the man slept, but he knew it was something he needed to do to gain an edge. Joshua knew when the man's body was discovered, it would really unnerve many of the members of Hartwell's gang. He put .45 rounds in with his own cache of bullets, and figured out how many of the weapons he could use. He knew he would be in some running gun battles, so he would bundle rifles together behind his saddlebags and bedroll and use them when necessary, discarding the long guns if need be.

Now Joshua was ready to return to take on a bigger chal-lenge. Johnny the Shawnee tracker was one of the sentries that Hartwell had sent out to watch their backtrail. He was hunkered down between several small leafy trees overlooking the main trail back to the farm where Joshua had been held. He had a good clear field of vision on the road, but unfortunately could not see much behind him because the foliage was so thick. It also blocked out a lot of moonlight.

The Shawnee tracker was disciplined, as he had been taught as a child, and sat very still. Joshua had to sit above him in the trees and watch with his telescope for twenty minutes before Johnny moved slightly, slowly to look behind and beside him. However, his movement occurred exactly when the Pinkerton was holding the spyglass in his direction. Telescopes and binoculars help one see much better at night, as they capture available moonlight, starlight, and any other light to help one see objects more clearly in what seems like virtual darkness.

With a fellow red warrior, Joshua had to use much more stealth this time. He moved slowly down the ridge, bow in hand. He would have to take Johnny from more of a distance, but it was very important to the detective to kill Hartwell's tracker, as it would have a tremendous psychological impact on the gang. He was still bothered about slitting the man's throat, and decided he at least had to have this Shawnee looking at him when he killed him. He would, however, definitely kill him.

Joshua moved down until he was close enough to easily shoot him with an arrow. The whole way down the ridge, Strongheart stared to the right and left of the Shawnee, as many warriors have a highly developed sixth sense, a sense of knowing. He knew if he stared at the Shawnee, even his back, the man would sense it. Quite often, this starts with a shiver running down the spine or similar phenomenon. This happens with animals who are often prey, such as deer, so

Strongheart when stalking deer or elk for meat would never look directly at the animal, but usually a few feet behind it.

At one point, Joshua froze as Johnny looked around to his sides and directly behind him, but failed to see the motionless Pinkerton in the shadows. Strongheart was in place now, and stood facing the unwitting tracker's back. He would not launch an arrow into it though, but at least let him see what was coming. He nocked an arrow and slipped his index, middle, and ring finger on the bowstring ready to draw, while his left hand gripped the bow. The nock of the arrow was firmly against the bowstring and nestled between the first two fingers.

Joshua drew the arrow, held at his anchor point at the back of his right cheek, and softly said, "Shawnee."

He saw Johnny's shoulders jump up with a start, and then the tracker whirled, trying to draw a pistol. Strongheart released the arrow, and it passed cleanly through Johnny's left lung, nicking the heart. He looked down and clutched at the hole, and reached back toward the exit hole in his back. Blood streamed from both wounds, and he quickly felt the life draining out of him. He slid down the trunk of the tree with his back against its rough bark, but Johnny never felt that. He looked at Strongheart and gave him a little smile and slight nod. His eyes closed, and his breathing stopped.

Joshua had to move quickly to get back to his campsite before dawn. He had to get a little sleep, some nourishment, and then move on to his next challenge. Within minutes of returning, he was fast asleep and not concerned about being discovered. His hideout was far enough away that he would not be discovered except by some fluke.

Joshua's mother sat on the edge of his bed and smiled at him when he opened his eyes.

"Where am I, Ma? What happened?" he said.

Smiling softly, she said, "You are in bed, Joshua. You have had a very bad experience, but the doctor said you will be fine with rest. Do you remember what happened?"

The fourteen-year-old boy looked down at his body under the goose-down quilt. He was naked, and he could see four straight lines going down his right rib cage on an angle and crossing over onto his belly under his navel.

He thought for a minute and remembered he and Dan had been out hunting for an elk or mule deer for the family coffers. They had split up and decided to work both wooded sides of a large draw. The ridges were steep, and they walked along the draw keeping fairly abreast of each other's location by using bird whistles occasionally.

Dan was following a set of tracks of what appeared to be a large buck, which he knew probably was bedded down somewhere above the head of the draw. This was something old bucks frequently did, so they had a broad sweeping view of anything approaching up the draw and it carried strong breezes. They also could get over either ridge in case of trouble. He also knew that big bucks did this instinctively and could not actually reason such things out.

Joshua was following a narrow game trail through the trees and went around a bend silently and slowly and froze. There before him, not twenty feet away, was a large tom mountain lion on top of a fresh deer carcass. The doe's neck was broken and twisted in an odd way. The big cat had just about finished eating the entrails. Strongheart knew that was the first part of a deer that cougars ate after making a kill. The lion looked at Joshua, laid his ears back, and bared his fangs, hissing. A low growl began in the big cat's chest, his ears were back, and then Joshua saw the big tail start swishing back and forth. He knew from his hunts with Dan and hunts with Lakota in the villages that swishing the tail back and forth like that was what mountain lions did right before making a charge. They normally shied away from humans, but he had come upon this one eating a fresh kill, which the cat would protect. Joshua slowly raised his rifle and aimed at the lion's forehead. It was too close to aim at his chest and take a chance on wounding him. A cougar like that could cover over twenty feet in one leap. The animal's muscles tensed, and Joshua took a deep breath and let it out halfway. The cat sprang, took two big strides and leapt at his face. The shot rang out and the lion hit the ground after crashing into Joshua, his left front paw scratching him where the marks were now. They bled some but were bad scratches and not deep cuts like his father Claw Marks had from the grizzly. The cat crashing into him was two hundred pounds of dead weight and, landing on top of him, knocked the wind out of him, plus his head snapped back and slapped into a log. The sky spun around in circles as he panicked and fought to regain his breath. Then everything went black. Dan found him with the dead mountain lion on top of him.

He awakened in his room at home with his mother babying him, and it was one of his warmest memories. Like most males of any age, Joshua loved getting babied by his mother when hurting. On top of that, he had stood in the face of danger and done what was needed, while maintaining a cool head. We develop poise and confidence in life from little successes, and this was a big success that was important in Joshua's personal development.

His mother bathed his head with cool water, and he closed his eyes. It was so soothing. He opened them again and looked into the deep, bright blue eyes of Annabelle Ebert. His head was in her lap, and she was rubbing his face with a cool wet piece of petticoat. Annabelle Ebert: This was the woman he loved and planned to marry. Suddenly, the door burst open and seven-foot-tall Lakota maniacal killer We Wiyake, Blood Feather, stood there with Strongheart's Bowie knife in his hand, ready to plunge it into Belle's back. The sun was bright behind the killer in the doorway, almost blinding.

Joshua wanted to scream no as he sat bolt upright and opened his eyes, his chest heaving.

He looked around and realized he was lying next to his campfire. Shards of fiery bright sunshine streaked through a break in the wooded canopy above as the late morning sun bathed Joshua in an all-out attack on his eyesight.

He had just relived his most common dream and blinked his eyes against the bright morning sunlight, rubbing his eyes. Strongheart immediately looked over at Eagle grazing nearby. The horse's ears were his large danger signals. If the horse's head was up, ears focusing a certain direction, nostrils flaring in and out, Joshua knew danger was approaching. They were not though and the horse grazed contentedly.

Strongheart grabbed his telescope and ran through the trees to his vantage point where he could see Hartwell's camp. He immediately began grinning as he saw the activity below. The rest of his men had joined the camp and were bringing in Johnny's body, and Joshua saw Hartwell throw his hands up to his face and then sweep them downward in frustration. The Pinkerton chuckled out loud. He saw some of the gang members gathering around the other dead bodies he was responsible for, and noticed their heads were down and some were shaking them. He knew he first had to defeat this superior enemy in their heads, and then he could more easily defeat them on the ground.

Strongheart was playing the deadliest game of chess he had ever played, and so far he was winning. His next challenge was even more daring, and the loser of the game would be facing certain death, not just defeat. He pulled a large pencil and paper from his saddlebag and sat down to carefully write in large plain letters. Joshua rolled up the finished paper and stuck it down inside his shirt.

He again grabbed his bow and cougar-skin quiver full of cedar arrows. Joshua camouflaged his face using a piece of charcoal and headed on foot back toward Hartwell's camp. Wearing his moccasins, he would approach from the thick woods on the far side of the camp.

He carefully scouted around, moving through the thick vegetation and watching the men who rode for Hartwell until he found his target. Buffalo Lombardi was a monster of a man, one of the largest men Joshua had ever encountered. He had spent almost two decades as a mountain man all over the West, but several murders had sent him back east for the past two years. He yearned to get back out west, but figured he would bide his time and make some great money working for Robert Hartwell. Although he had never even spoken to the tiny bad man, Hartwell helped keep him in the Midwest.

Hartwell knew full well about Buffalo and the stories surrounding the giant. Buffalo grew up in the eastern part of Kansas near Topeka. He was full of wonder as a boy and loved the outdoors and spent many days honing his stalking skills with red and gray squirrels. He learned early on to carry pebbles in his pocket. When he made a squirrel scamper up a tree, it would always go on the far side of the tree trunk. So, Buffalo would toss several pebbles beyond the tree at once. The noise would alarm the squirrel and it would run around to his side of the tree, where he would pick it off.

Even as a boy, he was known as Buffalo, and the lad hunted squirrels all the time. When he was fourteen, he was taller and much stronger than any of the men in his town. He dreamed about moving out west and becoming a mountain man. He finally did go at seventeen and grew up quickly, but he got in fights with two different miners in mountain mining camps and killed both with his bare hands. Buffalo spotted a wanted poster on himself and that sent him back east until things could cool down.

Now Buffalo spotted some movement in the thick forest directly behind him. Unlike some of the killers in the gang, he relished the opportunity to go after whatever or whoever was moving. If it was Strongheart, that would be even better. Buffalo had never lost a fight in his life using his bare hands. Even against knifes. In the close proximity of the dark woods, a gun may not even be practical.

Joshua Strongheart wore a grin on his face. His goal was not to use his guns or knife, but to beat this behemoth with his hands and feet and, more importantly, his mind. As the man looked for him, Joshua waited patiently in his hiding place and thought back to his youth.

The one thing Joshua remembered most about the only father that he'd ever known was how good the man could fight even though he was much smaller than some of the giant buffalo hunters and mountain men he'd had to arrest. Dan had taken a section of log weighing more than two hundred pounds, shaved the bark off of it, and the two thick branches that extended out for two feet, which he had also shaved and sanded, rounding the ends, so they would resemble thick arms. Joshua would watch the man for hours on end tossing the log backward, sideways, and various combinations of those directions working on numerous grappling moves.

Joshua thought back to a very familiar scene that really influenced him as a youth, seeing his stepdad in action. The incident, which initially made him fear for Dan, had impressed the young dark-skinned cowboy. Some of these big men that came into town to blow off steam looked like they were related to the buffalo they hunted they were so large, and some were very nasty and mean.

Three behemoth mountain men were drinking heavily in the saloon and soon were slapping customers around. One of the customers came to fetch Dan, and Joshua happened to be with him. He tagged along behind.

Thinking back again, Joshua had watched Buffalo Lombardi from a distance with his spyglass, and he was even larger than any of these three giants.

Each of the men had murdered before but was never caught. Dan walked fast with long, easy strides. He, with Joshua following, walked briskly to the family's mercantile store. Joshua was very curious. Dan walked up to Abby, Joshua's mom. and she forced a kiss. Joshua grinned knowing this man hated to show affection, but his ma would never let Dan get away with that with her. He walked over to a shelf with clothing and grabbed a pair of socks and then walked to the hardware supplies along the far wall and grabbed a large wooden ax handle. Next, he went to a large jar of marbles and started pouring handfuls into one of the long boot socks.

Joshua was still perplexed.

"Got these marbles, Abby, pair of socks, and this ax handle. Put them on our account. Gotta get back to work. See ya."

Curious, she gave a half wave as he strode out of the store.

Tying a knot into the end of the marble-filled sock while he walked, he stuffed it into the right pocket of the long tan duster he was wearing. Next, he slid the handle of the ax up his right sleeve, but it stuck out. He pulled it out, put it under his left arm, inside the long coat, squeezing it along his body with his left elbow and forearm. Without hesitation, he stepped up onto the wooden boardwalk and into the saloon.

He spotted the three giants in front of the bar where one had lifted a woman of pleasure up in the air, taking his own pleasure at the very abject fear clearly showing on her painted face. That man looked at the others and laughed, a deep, booming guffaw seemingly echoing from a deep cavern.

"Lookee, boys," he mused. "A teeny little lawman come to arrest us!"

He laughed at his own joke and was joined by the others. Dan never broke stride and walked straight up to him. Off-balance, the brute dropped the red-haired tart on the rough-hewn bar with a thud, and tried to gather his thoughts. He did not have time. The sock filled with marbles came out of the right pocket of Dan's duster, swung around one time, and struck him with a louder thud on the left side of his jaw, breaking it, and dropped him to the floor unconscious. Now, Dan had one giant behind him and one in front of him, and they immediately closed in, but Dan had already untied the sock and with his left hand let the marbles fall to the floor behind him. That brute saw them too late and stepped on them, going down unceremoniously on his back with a thundering crash. In the meantime, Dan's right hand grabbed the ax handle and raised it high, taking hold with both hands now facing the third giant in front of him. The brute's eyes opened wide as he saw the massive piece of wood come down toward his head, and his eyes crossed, looking up before rolling back as he fell on his back unconscious.

The victim of the marbles had now regained his footing and was about to grab Dan from behind, when Dan shoved the ax handle straight backward into the man's solar plexus and heard the wind leave him with a rush. Dan spun around and swung it upward like a butt stroke with a rifle, and it caught the three-hundred-pounder under his chin, and his head snapped back with the force, as he, too, went down out cold.

Dan grabbed the woman and helped her down off the bar, saying, "Lucy, isn't it about time you consider a different profession?"

She was so amazed and still frightened, she could not even speak. She just fluttered.

Dan said to the frightened, but now very relieved, bartender, "Fred, get some men and a buckboard, and get these three down to the jail before they come to."

Fred said, "Yes, sir, Dan, and thank you very much."

Joshua was bursting with pride over the coolheaded way Dan had handled that crisis.

As if he were reading Joshua's mind, Dan put his hand on the young man's shoulder, spun him around, and said in a low voice, "When you are outnumbered, keep them off-balance, and do the unexpected. Come on to the office with me."

They walked out the door, Joshua half running to keep up with the stern lawman's long stride.

Joshua said, "Pa, how come you didn't just pull your gun and arrest them?"

Dan said, "They kept their knives sheathed and guns holstered. Remember what I told you. If you draw a gun, use it. Don't pull it just because you're afraid."

Joshua said, "I ain't ever seen you afraid."

"You just did, son," Dan said, giving a slight grin, which hardly anybody ever saw from him, "You see the size of those three grizzlies?"

Strongheart grinned as he once again recalled that story and the lesson learned.

"Keep them off-balance," Strongheart whispered.

Besides the men he had already killed, the most effective way to psychologically terrorize the Hartwell gang was to pick out their biggest, toughest brute and kill him with his bare hands, or at least make it seem so in their minds.

Buffalo made his way with a bit of stealth and speed for his enormous size. He came through a stand of scrub oaks, and immediately found himself in a thicket of pines with branches all the way down to the ground. He kept coming closer and closer, and was now within an arm's length of the large oak tree that Strongheart was hiding behind. The giant man knew something was wrong, and he just stood there breathing heavily and looking around.

In an odd twist of irony, without realizing it, Strongheart used one of Buffalo's own tactics. He grabbed several rocks and, careful not to expose his arm or make noise, he tossed them down the hill behind Buffalo, just like the big man had done hunting squirrels as a boy. Hearing the rocks hit, Buffalo moved quickly to hide behind the big oak tree.

Joshua had hidden about fifty marble-sized rocks in the empty sock. He started swinging the sock from way back, and it came around catching Buffalo squarely on the jaw, judging by the sound. The big man's knees buckled and he heard his jaw break, before he temporarily went unconscious for a few seconds. The fact that he came to shortly after was a testament to his enormous size and capacity to take such a hard hit.

He shook the cobwebs out of his head and clawed for his gun, but Joshua's second swing caught him on the gun arm as he was drawing. He screeched with pain, dropping the gun that look like a derringer in his massive hand. He doubled his fists and swung at Strongheart, who grabbed the first with both hands, pulled, and swung the man toward the downhill side. Because of his own momentum, he went flying down the hill and crashed into a maple tree with a large trunk. The air left him in a rush, and Joshua punched him twice on the end of his jaw, sending a front tooth flying from his bloody mouth. Now Buffalo's head was really spinning, and Joshua knew he had to end this before they got close enough to the camp to be seen or heard. As the behemoth rushed forward, hate and rage in his eyes, Joshua swung the loaded sock again and the bulk of it crashed into the side of Buffalo's face, immediately swelling the eye shut and shattering the cheekbone. It also hit the man across the temple, and in Buffalo's head everything went black. He felt his body hit the ground, but then there was nothing.

Looking at the face of the corpse, Strongheart saw that it was badly beaten up. He also saw exactly what he wanted. Anybody looking at the bruises and marks could believe they were made by a fist, instead of a sap made of a sock filled with small rocks.

He used the lasso he brought with him to fashion a harness for the big man's body and for his own shoulders, and he started dragging Buffalo back toward the camp. He got close to the camp and saw a few men moving around engaged in various activities.

Joshua had to come up with a plan now to lure the men away. He spotted three small deer on the far side of the clearing where the camp had been built. The clearing was long and narrow, maybe sixty to seventy yards wide in most places. The three does had come out of the trees on the far side, and were grazing on grass. Joshua waited patiently until all three were close together. He raised his bow and drew an arrow. Normally while hunting he would never take a shot this far away, but he felt one of the does would have to sacrifice its life to save his own. He took careful aim and released the arrow. It sailed over the backs of all three and embedded itself in a tree trunk. His goal was to shoot a deer and attract attention, but now all three bolted, their big white tails waving from side to side like nature's metronome as they bounded away from the arrow and toward the camp, then veered to their left and headed up the valley. This had an even better effect than expected, as the men in the camp thought that Strongheart must have been over there and spooked the deer. The five men witnessing this, ran toward the trees, guns in hand. Joshua quickly dragged the big body back to his sleeping spot, then placed the sign he'd carefully lettered on top of the body. He quickly melted into the trees and made his way back to a safe spot to watch them from with his telescope.

One of Hartwell's minions summoned him, and surrounded by his personal entourage, he moved cautiously toward the assembled men now moving into the trees at the edge of the clearing. He and his bodyguards stayed back and watched from the camp for an hour, until the men emerged from the woods. The last one found Strongheart's arrow stuck in the tree trunk, and when he told the others, they finally realized that he had been on their side of the clearing all along. They headed back toward the camp and briefed Robert Hartwell. Now, all eyes focused on the trees on Joshua's side of the little valley.

Hartwell was very bothered seeing big old Buffalo Lombardi napping in the middle of the day with this hunt for Strongheart going on, It was just out of character for the big man, who always wanted to be in the midst of any action.

"Buffalo!" he hollered. "Get the hell up!"

Buffalo did not move, and Hartwell nodded toward him. The closest man ran to Buffalo's area, where he lay head on his saddle. He stared at the giant's form. The man turned, looking as if he had seen a ghost and signaled Hartwell and the others to come over. They all briskly walked to the body and gathered around the body and stared at Buffalo's lifeless corpse and the letter on his chest.

It read: "So far, you have seen what I can do with a knife, my bow, and my hands. I am better with my guns. Leave Hartwell today or tonight when he is not looking, and I will spare your life. Stay with him or wait until tomorrow and die. Strongheart."

Joshua could tell by the body language, even at that distance, that his message had had its desired effect. There was not a man in the group who did not immediately think hard about the warning.

One of the men said, "Look at the marks on Buffalo's face. They were made by fists. I never thought I'd see anybody who could take him in a fight, or even hit him in a fight."

One of Hartwell's immediate bodyguards, with over twenty gunfights to his credit, boldly stated, "Mr. Hartwell, you shore pay good, but that ole boy's medicine is too strong fer me. I ain't still alive by being stupid. I'm pulling out."

He headed toward his horse and his riding partner thought about joining him when Hartwell drew his pistol and fired, hitting the man squarely in the back. He went down writhing in pain, and the little boss man walked over and calmly put two more bullets in the back of his head.

Hartwell turned to the men, his face red with fury, saying, "He was wrong. He was very stupid. Anybody else want to be stupid? Anybody who runs out on me, dies. I want double guard tonight and any man trying to ride out of the camp will be shot on sight."

Several men glanced at Buffalo's battered body and thought they would rather have this man trying to kill them than the man who beat Buffalo Lombardi to death with his bare hands.

Strongheart watched the men during the rest of the day and a couple looked like they were trying to subtly get their things together to be ready to leave. Darkness came and Joshua moved in much closer, where he could see men moving around using his telescope. Over the next several hours, it looked to him like more than ten men crept away from the camp circle through the night, two of them together. He also saw two guards who sat on a log together creep away while on watch duty. In the distance, he saw several of them leading horses away toward the road. The two on guard together looked like they were two of Hartwell's inner circle. Joshua grinned in the darkness. The odds were getting better but were still very much against him. He did not really know how much.

The two who left together were indeed two of Hartwell's most trusted gunslingers, and he had told them privately to steal away as if leaving but to circle back and scour the land south of the camp, as that was the direction the arrow had been shot from. He reasoned that Strongheart was outside the camp somewhere in that general direction.

Joshua had been outsmarted.

14

REFUGE

Joseph "German" Dietrich and Slim Jim Selders were two of Robert Hartwell's toughest gun hands and most trusted henchmen. They were now circling behind Joshua's position, just hoping they would find something, anything that would give them a clue to his whereabouts. Shortly after reading Strongheart's ultimatum, Hartwell made the plan with them, understanding human nature and knowing that some of his men would desert him.

The two came up on a small ridge and dismounted among the trees. There was a small valley next to that ridge with another heavily wooded rise just to their north. The two, as planned with Hartwell, would glass every wooded rise carefully. They lay down in the trees, and watched the ridge Strongheart was on for an hour, when they spotted some white. Watching more carefully and moving positions, they saw it was Eagle grazing among the trees.

They discussed whether to put the sneak on him, or ride around and warn Hartwell. They chose the latter. These two were the two best gunmen he had in his employ, and between them had many kills. They knew Strongheart's skills and knew they had to be very careful. However, like most gunmen, they always felt they were faster and better than any living legends.

German Dietrich came from Germany when he was a boy. He killed his first man in New York City while he was still a young lad. There had been no shootout involved. He saw the man had money, so he stabbed him in his sleep and stole his money belt. He still had a little bit of an accent that especially came out before gunfights. By the age of eighteen, he was already working as a gun for hire.

Slim Jim Selders, like Dietrich, lived in Denver and Washington both, serving at the whim of Robert Hartwell. He truly enjoyed killing and was a rapist as well. He had to be more careful about that, because there were so few quality women in the West, there was an unspoken rule about not touching women. There were many outlaws who actually shot or even hanged men riding with them who molested women or girls.

The two men looked carefully at the rise north of them where Strongheart slept. They decided they would go up the small hill, which led to rocky ground that rose above the nearby river. The farm where Joshua was held was far to the northwest of Terre Haute. This was to the southeast of the farm.

The two killers both carried Henry repeaters and had their double dig holsters carrying .44s. German also had a .36-caliber Colt Navy as a belly gun. They spread out about thirty feet apart and slowly, very slowly started making their way up the hill, keeping to the thick woods.

Joshua Strongheart was exhausted. He had been doing a lot of fast traveling through thick trees, doing adrenaline-pumping experiences, and was going on very little sleep. He slept deeply now, soundly.

The two moved slower than they ever had when trying to be stealthy, because they both understood their adversary's superior skills. They had seen his handiwork the past two days, and heard all the stories about his gunfights, and the survival of the grizzly mauling he endured. They were very careful and ended up seeing the sleeping man and the small fire he had going. At one point Slim Jim even spotted Strongheart rolling over under his blanket. This was going much better than they thought it would.

Both men had their pistols ready, and both had their rifles cocked and held them with both hands at the ready. The hammers were back on their repeaters. Slowly, methodically, carefully, they approached the sleeping Pinkerton.

When they were still out of sight of Joshua, the ever alert Eagle gave a slight whinny. His nostrils several times the size of a bloodhound's, his eyes much larger than a deer's, his ears able to twist and turn and focus on even the slightest sounds, which they were now making, Eagle saw his master's eyes come open although Strongheart did not move his body. He looked at Eagle's ears and could tell he was focusing on two different people or animals approaching from downhill. Joshua turned under his blankets to look like a normal man sleeping, but actually it was so he could see the two directions the ears aimed at. Keeping his eyes squinted he saw the men approaching, and he had his own Peacemaker out under the blanket and one of the belly guns he had picked up in his left hand. He would let them get even closer. Strongheart recognized the dress of both men and knew them to be two of Hartwell's immediate bodyguards. Hence, they would be outstanding gunfighters. Because of that he also knew they would have their guns cocked and ready to simply squeeze the trigger. Strongheart knew only one way to handle that situation and that was to get and maintain superior firepower.

He aimed his guns at each man, shooting from the hips, the way he had practiced for countless hours with each hand. He would let the pair get closer and closer and then squeeze both triggers simultaneously and pray he was on target. His plan was then to start moving and rolling while continuing to shoot rapidly, keeping them off-balance and unable to make effective shots. The one drawback was that both had been in many gun battles and were very tough killers. He would watch their body language to make sure they did not shoot him first. So far they had their rifles up, ready to fire, but did not have them up to their shoulders, aiming, yet.

He saw both stop and German nod at Slim Jim, and both shootists raised their rifles. The blanket over Strongheart exploded and smoke literally came out of the two holes. One bullet slammed into German's right shoulder, spinning him halfway around, and making him drop the rifle. His left hand immediately clawed for his left hand gun. At the same time, blood appeared in Slim Jim's, and he dropped his rifle, a gurgling sound coming from his bloody mouth.

Strongheart immediately knew that German was the immediate threat. He rolled with a bullet kicking up dirt right next to his head, blinding him in the left eye. He kept his right eye open and fanned his Peacemaker, tucking the belly gun into his belt. His bullets hit German in the thigh, left hip, and slammed into the killer's chest.

German tried to speak in the German language, but only blood came out of his mouth. Joshua aimed and the next bullet hit the man directly in the face, killing him instantly. He swung the gun to Slim Jim, who now had his wits about him but was in a panic, drowning in his own blood, which was frothing out his mouth and throat. Joshua drew the belly gun again, and emptied it into the torso of Slim Jim who went down in a heap, his eyes opened wide in total panic.

Strongheart walked over to the dying man and kicked his gun away a few feet.

Slim Jim tried to say, "Kill me, please?"

However, his mouth would not work and his vocal chords were gone. He just looked at his conqueror and his eyes remained open although he could see and hear no more.

Joshua quickly reloaded and walked over to Eagle, petting him and loving him.

"You save my life again, old buddy," he said softly, then added, "We better get out of here."

He was correct with that assumption, because Hartwell was rallying his men to charge after the gunfire and hope they would finally stop Strongheart. Joshua grabbed his telescope, ran to one of his vantage points, and saw Hartwell's men saddling and grabbing their weapons. He ran back to his campsite, extinguished his fire, urinated on it and kicked dirt all over it. He then quickly packed up his bedroll and saddlebags, saddled Eagle, and headed southeast, angling toward the road back to the railroad many, many miles distant.

The pair were on the road within fifteen minutes. Hartwell had his men all around the rise of ground by now, and they were moving in. When they came upon the two bloody bodies, even some of the crime boss's bodyguards were unnerved seeing both German and Slim Jim shot up so badly. Robert Hartwell was furious and could not understand why he could not outfox this man. He had always outfoxed everybody before.

"All right men, gather 'round!" he commanded.

The entire gang, or what was left of it, gathered around him.

He yelled, "These two boys are gone, and we will send men to fetch them and bury them proper, but Strongheart is uncanny.

We have to get after him, and we are going to put all our eggs in one basket. He has to be heading back toward the railroad, so we have to lather some horses and catch up to him."

Robert Hartwell could have cared less how loyal these two men were. He had no intention whatsoever to waste men on burying them, so he simply lied to his men. This was something that came naturally to him, and he gave it no thought.

The gang was soon back in the saddle, heading after the fleeing Joshua Strongheart, who was pacing Eagle with his customary mile-eating fast trot. Joshua had gone fifteen miles when he noticed an almost imperceptible limp in Eagle's front leg.

"Easy, Eagle," Strongheart said and slowed the big horse to a stop.

He dismounted and looked at each foot. Eagle had partially thrown his shoe on his right front hoof and had a stone lodged in the frog of his hoof. Joshua immediately pulled a hoof pick from his saddlebag and worked the rock out, tossing it off to the roadside. He walked forward and turned to watch Eagle. He could still see a little bit of a limp, which most cowboys would not even notice. The pinto had just saved his life again and Strongheart was not going to injure his foot even more by pushing too hard. He had shoes in his saddlebag, but he had to file the hoof, put salve on the frog, and nail on a new shoe, before he would push his equine friend any further.

Walking in front, he led the horse down the road until he found a depression where he could take him off to his left and into some thick trees. There, he could properly take care of the horse out of sight. If the gang of outlaws came by, hopefully they would bypass him. Joshua led the horse several hundred yards before finding a small meadow with a brook running through it. He removed Eagle's bridle and let him drink water and graze, while he jogged back to where they'd left the road. He grabbed a large maple branch, hacked the limb off with his big Bowie-like knife and went to the end of his tracks in the road. He then erased tracks in the road, going forward one hundred paces. He made a big deal of making big sweeping marks side to side with the branch.

Then he carefully returned to where he'd dismounted and led the horse into deeper greenery. He removed his boots and slung them over his neck with a leather thong from his fringe and carried them off the road and tossed them into some grass alongside Eagle's tracks. Joshua, now in his socks, returned to the road and using road dirt he scooped up, he carefully, methodically spread dirt over each boot print and hoofprint going off the road. It was slow painstaking work, but he had to completely cover his trail and that of his horse, so he could take time to fix Eagle's foot properly.

Doing the task of covering his trail would allow Hartwell and his gang to catch up or get closer. When he brushed the road for one hundred paces, and brushed it so demonstratively, his hope was to fool Hartwell into thinking that he was actually trying to brush out his tracks on the road for a while. Most outlaws figured that they were much smarter than people like Strongheart, so he hoped what he did was not too obvious and Hartwell might actually think he had outwitted the Pinkerton. Joshua hated doing this task, as he had to be so meticulous or he and Eagle would be found out, but he learned as a boy not to do any job unless he planned to do it right.

He obliterated all the tracks on the road, without any telltale signs of covering them. He then moved into the grass and trees where he'd led the pinto away from the road. Here, he had to dig chunks of sod in some spots to cover their tracks. He also had to bend blades of grass back until they sprang back into their original positions.

In the meantime, Robert Hartwell was almost upon him, and Joshua guessed they had to be getting close but he could not approach his task halfway, or he and Eagle would be found out. Fifteen minutes later, the detective was able to now ignore his tracks, as their path could not be detected by anybody coming down the road. No sooner had he stopped, when he heard a large group of horses trotting up the road. He ran as far as he could to judge how close the horses were, then dropped into the thick foliage.

Strongheart had wisely brought his telescope with him and pulled it out to observe the gang. He could tell Hartwell was pointing at his brush sweeps and was laughing at the amateurish attempt to cover his trail. The half-breed chuckled to himself, as he could almost imagine Hartwell's haughty words about him and his reputation. He slithered through the foliage until he could stand without being seen at all and made his way to Eagle.

The handsome detective quickly went to his saddlebags and pulled out his nippers, file, and one of the four steel shoes he carried for Eagle. He also had a small oilskin of salve made of pine tar and several other ingredients he'd gotten from his father's village to use on horse's hooves. The pine tar was mainly to seal the salve in but the main ingredient was called by the Lakota *śuŋkhú śtipiye*. Its scientific name was *Hymenopappus tenuifolius* but it was commonly called the chalk-hill woolly white plant. It was a plant that stood about three feet tall and the name was kind of a misnomer because the plant had small yellow flowers.

Joshua thought for a minute and made a decision. He lifted Eagle's right front foot and pulled the shoe using his steel nippers. He then filed the heads off the nails sticking out of the hoof and pulled the shaft out with the nippers. He dabbed some of the salve into the frog of the foot and then removed the shoe on the left front hoof. Instead of filing the hooves, he would let the ground do it naturally. He pulled the left shoe, so the legs would feel equal to the horse and the hooves would be filed by the ground to the same approximate size. He would take the horse to a safer place far away from the route to the railroad and nurse his hoof.

He mounted up and leaned his body forward barely squeezing his calves together and said, "Walk."

Eagle started at a walk in the same direction they had come to this hiding place, putting the roadway behind them with each step. Joshua rode the big horse for several miles into deep woods and made camp along a shallow stream in a thick stand of evergreen trees. He would find some very dry hardwood sticks and make an almost smokeless fire, allowing the numerous pine needles and thick branches to diffuse the smoke before it exited the emerald canopy. He could now take his time cleaning and nursing the injured hoof. He could also hammer his horseshoe nails into place without worrying about the noise carrying to his enemy's ears.

Joshua was very attuned to the movements of the big horse, and he was very heartened to not sense a limp in the animal's gait. Apparently, removing the shoes and dressing the wound had brought a lot of relief. Joshua cleaned the hoof very thoroughly and treated it with salve. He then got the shoe back out and, facing the horse's rear, he pulled Eagle's foreleg up between his two knees and held the leg up with the inside of his thighs. He lightly filed the hoof until it looked totally flat. He placed the shoe on it, and it fit like it had been filed using a level. He then pulled the nails out and put three between his lips and one on his hand. Then using the butt of his gun like a hammer he started tapping the nail into the shoe. When the point came out of the hoof one-quarter inch up, Joshua held the point in place with the

handle of the steel nippers, and kept hammering. This bent
the point back toward the shoe. When the horseshoe nail
was all the way in, he bent the point all the way back to the
hoof. Then, he snipped it off with the nippers. He did this
with the three other nails. Then, he repeated the procedure
on the other front hoof.

Strongheart was feeling the effect of his effort in the small
of his back, but knew the soreness would go away. He made
some food and let Eagle graze and rest for a while. He would
eat, take a nap, and get back in the saddle. As soon as Joshua's head hit the saddle, he was fast asleep.

The click of the rifle hammer brought him wide awake,
but he did not move anything but his eyelids.

"Blanket nigger," the voice said, "do not move an inch.
Slowly now, very slowly move that blanket off ya using the
toes of yer boots. If I see either arm movin' under the blanket, yer gonna git opened up with this here smoke wagon."

Joshua was wide awake now and trying to figure out
where the shooter was. He voice came from above. Strongheart had wisely kept his Peacemaker and holster under the
blanket, but it would do him no good right now. He moved
the blanket off of him.

The voice said, "Awright, mister, real, real slow with yer
arms way up above yer head, roll away from that gun belt.
Roll toward me mebbe three times."

Joshua could tell this man was not stupid, so he kept his
hands away from the gun and knife. His belly guns were in
the saddlebags and out of reach, too. He rolled over three
times slowly and then stood. He finally saw his assailant.
The man was twenty feet up in a large white oak tree, wearing coveralls, old boots, and a brown homespun shirt under
the coveralls. The shirt was almost as dark as the man's
skin. In his hands was a Winchester carbine.

Joshua had made his camp right where there was a large whitetail deer scrape, and this man had been in the camouflaged tree stand waiting for the large ten-point buck that checked this scrape frequently.

Bucks, during the rut, or breeding season, in early fall, have a large territory that they patrol. Around the perimeter they make scrapes using their front hooves, and they paw the ground out. A good hunter can estimate the size of a buck by the size of the scrape. Joshua had seen the scrape and ignored it, as bucks can make them anywhere they wish. After pawing out a large area, the male deer then stands on its hindlegs under a low-hanging branch and rubs its forehead scent on it, sometimes chewing it a little for good measure. He then stands in the center of the scrape with all four hooves together and urinates, with the urine running down the inside of its hindlegs, washing across two powerful musk organs on the inside of its hind knees. This scent marks the territory, so does in estrus will come by, smell it, and urinate so he can smell it and follow her scent trail to her. It also warns smaller bucks to stay out of this territory. They are like signposts for whitetail deer bucks and does, almost like no trespassing signs for most. Successful whitetail hunters know that a buck, especially a large one, will patrol its territory smelling each scrape looking for mates and challengers as well. They also know they need only remain in a tree stand or fork of a tree, up off the ground, where their scent will not carry as well, and where deer seldom look, simply be still and wait.

This man shot deer for meat whenever he wanted to feed his family, but he enjoyed occasionally taking a large buck for its antlers. It was simply a skill he'd acquired years earlier and took pride in being good at.

Joshua stood slowly, his hands raised. It immediately

became clear to him that this man was not connected with Robert Hartwell in any way.

Strongheart said, "I mean you no harm, sir. My name is Joshua Strongheart, and I work for the Pinkerton Detective Agency."

The man said, "I've heard of you."

Joshua said, "Can I put my hands down?"

"Nope," the man replied, "Walk over to yuh gun belt."

Strongheart complied.

The man said, "Use yer toe and turn it over, so I can see yer knife."

Joshua did and the man smiled.

He said, "Now, turn it over again, so I kin see yer holster."

Joshua did, and the man saw the miniature sheriff's star on his holster and grinned.

He lowered his rifle and said, "You kin grab your hogleg and rig, Mr. Strongheart."

The man started climbing down from the tree stand, and Joshua pulled on his boots and walked over, retrieving and buckling on his gun belt. He walked up to the man and shook hands with him.

The man said, "Ya got coffee? My name is Sammy Davis."

Strongheart grabbed his coffeepot and the makings and set it on the small fire, building it up a little.

They were soon sitting by the fire drinking coffee while Joshua briefed him on what was going on. The middle-aged black man had an easy smile, and a build that showed many years of using his muscles. His hands were rough, too, and Strongheart could tell they had handled many tools over the years. There was a hint of gray creeping into his curly black hair.

Joshua said, "Hey, Sammy, you are not what I would call snow white. Why did you call me a blanket nigger?"

Sammy chuckled and said, "Wal, I seen you was either an Injun or half-breed, and I wanted to git your attention right off. I was nervous. Looking at you riding up, I could see you was a man who had ridden the river a time or two."

Strongheart said, "You sure got my attention. You were in that tree stand the whole time?"

Sammy replied, "Darned shore was."

Joshua shook his head, grinning.

Sammy said, "I know what yer thinking. Why do I talk this way instead of like a Southern former slave? I was a slave and escaped by way of the Underground Railroad and made it to this part of the country. Then, I headed west and stayed fer a long time. Picked up this accent, too, I s'pose."

"Why did you come back to this area if you were living in the West?" Joshua asked.

Sammy replied, "I done a lot of stuff, but didn't feel like I was accomplishin' a thing. I wanted to come back here and help out with the Underground Railroad."

"The Underground Railroad?" Strongheart said, "I thought that ended years ago, even before the Civil War?"

"Thet's what everybody thinks, but it still exists," Sammy said, "Not like it was before, but we help a few here and there. I'm called a conductor."

Fascinated, Joshua said, "What does that mean?"

"Well, just 'cuz slavery is outlawed don't mean that a lot of landowners in the South abide by thet. The KKK still runs amok, and they is quite a few little towns and communities thet keep stuff hushed up," Sammy answered. "There is still a real quiet Underground Railroad, mainly in Ohio, but some around here and in Pennsylvania, too. We get stories 'bout slaves or sharecroppers thet are about like slaves in the South. I go there, bring 'em up here, and we give 'em clothes, help 'em find jobs, or move 'em further east to find jobs, mainly in Ohio. We got some ole boys with money who donate a lot to help out. I can trust you with all this, 'cuz you know what folks like mine go through with bein' a half-breed."

Strongheart poured them both cups of coffee, and Sammy went on, "We're gonna have to sneak you outta here usin' the Underground Railroad."

"Why?" Joshua asked.

The former slave replied, "'Cuz, all the bad men around these parts was hired up by thet character on the big black horse, and I jest heerd he has some headin' this way on the railroad. He ain't gonna want you makin' it ta Washington from what you told me."

"How?" Strongheart asked, "How did you learn that?"

Sammy took a long sip of coffee and grinned broadly, "I told you, I'm with the Underground Railroad. We have us a network across the North and parts of the South. We know what's goin' on and git the news out to each other fast."

Strongheart took a thoughtful sip on his coffee and asked, "Then, can you find out for me about the condition of Lucky DeChamps with the Pinkerton Detective Agency? He was shot up bad and in a hospital in Denver."

Sammy said, "Shore. We can find out about him. Where's he work outta?"

"Headquarters in Chicago," Strongheart replied.

"Well, we need ta git you in a good hidin' place," Sammy said, "You git back to takin' yer nap, and I'll stand watch. I may take me a looksee in a little bit, too."

Strongheart said, "Are you sure, Sammy?"

Sammy chuckled.

He said, "Son, I been around heah a good bit, and I know all the woods in the area like the back of this old, wrinkled, scarred-up, brown hand."

Joshua nodded in appreciation and lay back down. He

closed his eyes and thought about Lucky and the first time they'd met. Oddly enough, many miles to the northwest in Chicago, Lucky was also thinking about it.

One of Pinkerton's supervisors was Francois Luc DeChamps, who was born in Paris, but came to the U.S. as a young boy and changed his name to Frank DeChamps, but all in his family and American friends started calling him Lucky, for his middle name, when he was a slightly larger than a bean sprout. He considered Joshua Strongheart a tremendous asset for the Pinkertons.

Lucky was dining with a date in a very popular upscale restaurant in downtown Chicago, a city already known for great eateries. Lucky noticed his date eyeballing a man who walked in and who was escorted to his table by the maître d'. Tall, broad-shouldered, and very handsome, he was obviously half-Indian and half-white and Lucky could not help but notice the way all the women looked at him.

At the table next to him was a very large, boisterous, obviously drunken police lieutenant. It was obvious that was his profession because he made it clear in a loud voice that that was what he did. The man was a mean drunk and wanted to intimidate all who were within earshot. Worse yet, he intimidated and embarrassed his wife seated at his table. The man was complaining about anything and everything. Cursing the wine steward and his waiter both, this finally brought over the maître d', who tried to politely ask the man to leave.

The large man stood and shoved the maître d', who fell over a chair, and several people in the room murmured. The waiter helped the man up.

The bully bellowed, "Do you know who I am? I am Lieutenant Daniel Alexander of the Chicago Police Department! If you think you can bamboozle me, you . . ."

His slurring was stopped when Joshua Strongheart stood up. Alexander gave him a mean look and said, "What do you want, you blanket nigger? What are you even doing in this place?"

Joshua kept smiling and said, "Sir, didn't you say you were Lieutenant Daniel Alexander?"

"Yea, so what?" the man snarled.

Joshua extended his hand saying, "I have heard all about you and your heroism, sir. I just wanted to shake your hand."

The drunk was taken aback, and he extended his hand, but when they shook Lucky noticed the big man grimace in pain. That was when Lucky saw that Strongheart, while shaking, stuck a pencil between the policeman's ring finger and middle finger and then squeezed his hand while pretending to shake. He then grabbed the man's elbow and, appearing to be friendly, strong-armed him toward the door, all the way talking nicely to him. The wife sat in her chair and buried her face in her hands and cried.

Lucky excused himself and walked over to the window, where he watched as, outside, Strongheart stuck his foot out and tripped the big man and slammed his head into a gas lamppost. He slumped to the ground unconscious. Joshua then summoned two police officers over and spoke to them, and they began to laugh and shake their heads. They both shook hands with Joshua and grabbed the officer by his upper arms. Lucky sat down with his date.

Strongheart came back in and was asked by Lucky to join him and his date. He told Joshua about seeing the pencil and appreciated Joshua's quick thinking and classy handling of the matter. To make a long story short, he found out that the half-breed was job hunting and Lucky hired him on the spot for the Pinkerton Agency.

Joshua opened his eyes when he smelled meat cooking

with lot of spices on it. Sammy was over a frying pan cooking potatoes and corn and had backstraps from a young doe already broiling over the fire on a green stick spit.

Joshua said, "I heard you leave and heard you come back, but knew you had me covered."

Sammy grinned. "You shore slept good, Strongheart. You been conked out fer a good two hours," he said.

Joshua Strongheart said, "That venison sure smells good. I guess you checked the area out?"

Sammy handed him a slice of backstrap, potatoes, and corn and Joshua dug in. It was some of the best cooking he had tasted in a long time. The two spoke over a great meal and more coffee, then broke camp, covering all evidence of their presence. Joshua looked over at Eagle. His ears were up, his nostrils flaring, and he gave a low whinny, a signal to his master.

Sammy and Joshua both stood.

Sammy said, "Grab yer gear and climb up into mah tree stand."

Joshua looked over at Eagle and gave him a shooing motion.

He said, "Eagle, go!"

Eagle seemed to understand and trotted off. Both men clambered up the branches to the camouflaged tree stand, carrying Joshua's saddle and gear. They held still. Two of Hartwell's henchmen came into view minutes later. They had carbines across their saddle swells and their heads were moving side to side. Both men had the look of two little boys tiptoeing through a cemetery at midnight.

The reason that tree stands have always worked for hunting deer is because prey seldom look up in the trees. Most animals and humans will look all around them but never remember to look up above for danger. The two gunmen below were about to learn an expensive lesson. They came directly below the tree stand after fifteen minutes of scouring the ground looking at Eagle's tracks. One of them finally spotted Joshua's boot tracks running to the base of the tree.

Joshua whispered to Sammy, "Stay back out of sight."

Both men followed the tracks right to the tree and looked up the trunk, and straight into the broadly grinning face of Joshua Strongheart, holding two cocked weapons pointed at the two would-be killers.

Strongheart said, "Howdy, boys. I've been waiting for you. I have been wanting to send Robert Hartwell a message. You can deliver it for me."

It was well after dark when the horses of the two gun hands rode into the circle of light of Hartwell's camp, which had lookouts all around the tight perimeter. Both men were gagged with their scarves, both were wearing only their long johns, both were missing their boots, clothing, hats, and guns, and both were tied backward in their saddles. Hartwell looked at both men, and they each had the deer-staring-at-torchlight look on their sweaty faces.

Sammy had trotted next to Eagle for a mile, and they had come to his mule grazing near a creek. He was now mounted up and riding alongside Strongheart. They rode along slowly through the darkness.

Strongheart said, "Earlier, I told you to stay back, because I do not want Hartwell knowing you are helping me."

"Believe me, Strongheart," Sammy replied. "I understand."

"Mule man, huh?" Joshua replied.

"Nope," Sammy said. "I have a nice big chestnut Thoroughbred I travel on, but I always use a mule when I'm hunting deer, buffaler, or bears. They pack a lot better."

Strongheart said, "We're heading east. Where are we going?"

"Ohio," Sammy said with a grin.

Joshua said, "You don't have any gear or anything."

He saw Sammy grinning in the moonlight.

He said, "We're not going tonight. I'm taking you to a safe house tonight."

They rode for hours mainly through woods, and Strongheart found himself impressed with this unusual man. He moved easily through the darkness and showed he was clearly a man of the wilderness.

After he escaped and fled the horrible plantation he was raised on back in North Carolina, Sammy made it west to Charlotte, where he met a member of the Underground Railroad. Eventually he was smuggled to Cleveland, Ohio, where he was given housing, a little money, and a job in a steel factory near where the Cuyahoga River met Lake Erie, which was like the ocean to Sammy. Later, he made it out west, where he worked as a cowboy on several cattle drives. Then he tried his hand as a mountain man trapping beaver mainly in the Wind River Range. Following that, he journeyed to California, where he prospected for gold in several places. The whole time, he thought back to how much he had been helped by the Underground Railroad, and it kept drawing him back.

They rode for hours and came upon a very large house with a number of barns and outbuildings. There were many flowers around the house and a vegetable garden. In the moonlight, Joshua could tell this big property was well taken care of. Right below the house was a bubbling creek, a dam, and a large pond, the surface rippling in the moonlight. In the middle of the pond was a large island covered with trees, and cattails were clearly visible around the edges.

Lanterns were lit in the big house when they rode up. The front door opened and a man came out holding a lantern. Joshua and Sammy dismounted and Sammy took his reins and led both the horse and mule to the man.

He said, "Buck, this is Mr. Strongheart. Please take his horse to the safe place, put up hay and feed for him. Let Mr. Strongheart get his saddlebags and rifle."

Joshua nodded at Buck and said, "The name is Joshua."

The short, stocky black man smiled and waited for Strongheart to take his rifle, bedroll, and saddlebags. He led the two equines away toward the barn complex.

Strongheart said, "Is this your place?"

Just then, the door opened and a ravishing brunette woman walked out the door, also carrying a lantern, and wearing a very expensive long gown, which could not hide the curves. She glided down the steps, and it was obvious there was an immediate attraction between her and Strongheart. He had not had feelings like this since Belle died. She stuck out her hand, and he shook it, noticing the softness and the firm handshake.

"Brenna Alexander," she said. "Welcome to my home, sir."

He smiled, doffed his hat, and said, "Joshua Strongheart, ma'am."

She said, "Pleased to meet you, Mr. Strongheart. Hi, Sammy."

Sammy removed his hat, smiled, and replied, "Hello, Brenna. Sorry to come so late, but it's a Railroad problem. We need to hide him and his horse for a while."

"Joshua, please, ma'am," Strongheart said,.

She replied, "Okay, Joshua, and please call me Brenna."

He nodded. She led the way up the porch steps and into the mansion.

She said over her shoulder, "We can discuss it over breakfast, but for now let's get him hidden and rested."

She led the way through the massive great room and into the library. Sammy walked over and reached up inside the fireplace and pulled a hidden lever. One of the bookcases popped open, and he swung it out like a door. They entered and went down a stone stairway ending in a long, dark, cold passageway. She led the way for what Joshua figured had to be at least four hundred feet, and they came to another stairway. They ascended, she opened a door, and they landed in a small room in a comfortable cabin. Joshua was amazed and impressed.

She lit another lantern and a wood-burning stove with kindling already in it. There was a coffeepot on the stove. She took it over to the sink and pumped water into it from a pump handle in the sink.

Smiling, she said, "This will be your home for a while, Joshua. It even has its own well, and this cannot be seen from anywhere. Only chimney smoke when there is no wind or breeze."

Joshua smiled and shook his head, saying, "I'm dumbfounded. Where is this located?"

She said, "Did you see the island in the moonlight?"

"Yes, I did," he said, "You mean we are on that island?"

Brenna grinned, "That passageway is under the floor of the pond. My father had it excavated when he created the pond and built all this. This cabin has shuttered windows and there are trees and vegetation blocking the view of the cabin. You will be free to relax here. Many runaway slaves were hidden out here and nobody ever discovered the passageway or the cabin. I purposely have no boats on the shore. You'll be safe here until we move you, Joshua.

"That stove heats the place nicely, but there is a fireplace over there as you can see, if it gets too cold. There are two bedrooms and you can pick and choose your room. We will talk in the morning. You both need sleep now. Sammy, do you want to sleep in the other room or the main house?"

He said, "I'll bunk here, Brenna. Obliged. I'll see you in the morning and explain everything."

Strongheart fell asleep when his head hit the pillow and awakened the next morning totally refreshed. He really did feel safe here. It was a natural feeling, not something artificial. He also could not wait to see Brenna in the morning light. He found the outhouse and then explored the tiny island, emerging on a small path to the pond apparently made by occasional deer who would swim to the island and back.

Since he was on the side opposite from the house and outbuildings, he slipped off all his clothes and dove into the cold water. He swam for a few minutes, and rubbed his body down with his hands. Emerging from the water, he shook himself off like a dog and squeegeed his body with the edge of his hands. He stood there by the pond shivering but exhilarated and let the warming morning sun dry him a little. He pulled his clothes back on, promising himself to wash them after breakfast. There were flowers all over the little island, and he picked some, making a bouquet for Brenna, hoping she was single. He had not seen a ring the night before. Sammy was already gone, presumably to the big house.

He went in shaved, brushed, dressed, and found a lantern and made his way under the pond back to the big house. He walked in and found Sammy, Brenna, Buck, and another woman, presumably a maid, all sitting at the large dining table in the dining room. There was a big spread of food on the table with eggs, pancakes, ham, fruits.

Brenna got up and walked over to him, saying, "Good morning, Joshua. I trust you slept well."

He smiled and handed her the flowers. She blushed and smelled them.

"Just thought you might like these, ma'am," he said.

She replied, "Thank you so much. I love all of these types of flowers. Let me put them in a vase, and I'll be right back."

Joshua shook with Sammy and sat down to breakfast.

Sammy said, "Morning, pardnuh. I tole Brenna all about ya and what yer up against."

Brenna returned with the flowers in a nice vase and placed them on the table. She smiled at Joshua and marveled at how good-looking and strong he was.

"Joshua, thank you so much for the flowers. That was very thoughtful and kind," she said. "Please enjoy the breakfast, and if you don't mind, we will talk about your situation while we eat."

The group ate and talked, and then Strongheart walked outside with Brenna. She showed him her flower garden and vegetable garden as well.

He said, "You live here alone?"

She smiled demurely, saying, "No, the help lives here with me."

He said, "I am sorry. I am being forward but should have simply asked you if you are married or not."

She grinned, "No, Joshua, I have not married yet. Are you?"

"No," he replied. "I was engaged and very much in love, but she was murdered some time back. It took me a while to come to terms with her death, but I have."

She responded, "I am so sorry. Did they catch the assailant?"

Tight-lipped and looking off at the trees, he said, "No, I did."

She said, "And . . . what happened?"

"He saw the error of his ways."

"You killed him?" she asked.

"Yes," Strongheart answered.

He waited for her response. He was not used to Easterners and wondered if he would get a lecture about not seeking revenge.

She smiled and said, "Good for you. I would hope that someday a man would love me enough to want to avenge my death if I came to a violent end. I would love to know some man would hunt down and punish my killer."

"I personally believe a man in love should," Joshua responded. "If he is capable of doing so."

"You are indeed an unusual man, Joshua," she said. "Most men are afraid to even utter the word *love*, yet you are not afraid to speak freely of it."

Joshua replied, "William Shakespeare said, 'Who could refrain that had a heart to love and in that heart courage to make love known?' To me, Brenna, if you're going to be a man, you often have to prove yourself. You have to conquer fear and do what is right. To me, that includes being courageous enough to speak thoughts that most keep hidden in their hearts."

Brenna felt her heart beating in her ears and thumping in her chest. She was flustered.

"My, Joshua, you even quote Shakespeare," she said, red-faced. "You seem quite the poet yourself, but you seem so, so . . . Well what I mean . . . On the other hand, you strike me as a man who could indeed kill any murderer that you choose to hunt down. What a combination!"

Strongheart said, "I am simply a man trying to do what is right. Tell me, Brenna, how did you come to live here?"

She said, "My father made a tremendous amount of money, a fortune, actually, shipping goods on the Great Lakes. He left it to me, the only child. My mother died when I was very small, and he left me to go home about ten years ago. He also worked very hard on the Underground Railroad before, and after, the Civil War."

Strongheart said, "I am very sorry for your loss. It sounds like you and your father were very close."

She said, "Yes, we were. My father spoke out very fervently and passionately against slavery and racial discrimination. He also told me if God blesses you with a lot, you must give to others, or God may take away your blessings. That was why he got so involved in the Underground Railroad, and I am of the same mindset."

"I always thought the Underground Railroad was a great thing," Strongheart said. "But until yesterday I had no idea that it still existed."

Brenna answered, "It must exist. There are so many fools in this world. Some are very narrow-minded. I grew up almost believing that annual death threats are a way of life for a person."

They walked along and Strongheart seemed to be thinking long and hard on something. They stopped, and she sat on a stump surrounded by beautiful greens and a few wild flowers.

Joshua said, "You reminded me of something that occurred in my childhood. I was a young boy, and we had a very tough schoolmarm, plus my mother made me study and read all the time. I tried to be nice to everybody in school and out."

He grinned, adding, "If I didn't treat everybody nice, my pa would have tanned my hide."

The Pinkerton went on, "I was at school, and we got to

go outside and eat lunch on warm sunny days. There was
this little girl named Rebecca, with red hair and lots of freckles, and I sure was sweet on her. So were most of the boys in
the school. I picked some daisies one day and handed them
to her, while she sat on a bench with three other girls. She
got a mean, nasty look on her face, and slapped the bouquet
out of my hand. I was shocked and hurt, I guess. Then, she
said, 'I don't want no flowers from no red-skinned blanket
nigger. My pa said yer a smelly half-breed.'"

Brenna shook her head.

Joshua continued, "That was the first time I ever heard words
like that I had never seen such hatred. I mean this cute little girl
seemed to turn into a demon with her demeanor. It sure made
me smell the coffee for the first time. When I got home, I was
doing chores and slamming things down and just letting off
steam. My father was town marshal and was at home recuperat-
ing because he had been shot in the lower leg during a gunfight.
I didn't know it, but he was watching me out the window the
whole time and knew I was upset. I had just finished stacking
fire wood, and he came out the door using a cane. He walked
up to me and said to join him.

"We sat down on the bank of the creek near my house,
and he asked what was wrong, and I told him."

Brenna said, "What did he say? And, I must ask. You
clearly are half white and half red and said your father was
town marshal, so was your mother an Indian?"

He grinned, "No, sorry. She was white and a very successful merchant starting at the age of fifteen, when she had
me. My father was a Lakota Indian. You folks call them the
Sioux. His name was Claw Marks, and he was a member of
the Strongheart Society, a group of the very best warriors.
That is how I got my last name. He never married my ma,
because he knew what you were talking about: Many people

are narrow-minded and ignorant. He told her he knew that I would be a boy when I was born, and asked her to give me my last name, and he left me this knife and sheath, and he told her to take me to Lakota villages, his village, and let me learn the ways of his people, as well as of the white world. The man I called my pa was a lawman named Dan Trooper, who left me this pistol and fancy holster."

She saw the miniature lawman's star on the side and also admired the intricate beadwork and fringe.

Strongheart went on, "He was actually my stepfather, but he was like a real father to me. Very strict."

She said, "Fascinating. Very fascinating life, Joshua."

"Getting back to what my pa said," Joshua continued. "He asked what happened, and I told him. Then, he said, 'Son, I am not a Bible-thumper but one verse I learned and liked when you were a toddler because of comments I had to deal with about you was Romans chapter 12, verse 21: "Do not be overcome by evil, but overcome evil with good." I always say that the very best revenge in the world is success.' I tell you, Brenna, those words have never left me."

He then said, "Brenna, I really need to check on Eagle, my horse. I need to feed him, and—"

Brenna laughed and interrupted, "Come with me. I think you will be surprised."

They walked to the large barn and entered. Joshua had never seen such a well-appointed stable. There was a large pump handle at the end of the building and piping that ran downhill on an angle from that, with spouts at each individual stall over the stone watering troughs for each horse. It had an upstairs hayloft and the stalls were impeccably clean with fresh bedding straw and Strongheart saw that each stall had what looked like rich green hay in the corner feeders. The horses, all handsome, were very well groomed. At the very far end, a large wooden door was closed and locked shut with a pair of lawman's handcuffs. There was a sign on the door, which read, KEEP SHUT, FRESH FEED.

They got to the door, and Brenna, yelled, "Buck!"

He emerged from the far end stall and ran down to her and unlocked the cuffs, sliding the door back. Strongheart followed her and saw there was no feed at all. There were two larger stalls, presumably for stallions, with tall rock walls for the runs instead of fencing like all the other stalls. This apparently was to keep studs calmed and not see other horses and get excited. There stood Eagle eating hay in one stall, and he gave out a low whinny when he saw Joshua.

Strongheart went into the stall and fussed over him a little, while Brenna watched on, smiling. Eagle had been cleaned, groomed, combed out, and someone had worked on his hooves, which looked great. He had a run, privacy, and nobody coming into that barn would know he was there unless they heard him whinny.

"Oh my gosh," Joshua said. "Brenna, this is too much. You are too kind. How can I thank you?"

She said, "Do not get killed or caught and finish your job."

He smiled.

They left the barn and Strongheart was very amazed at the wonderful care Eagle was being given and how well hidden he was. He was also amazed at the beauty and grace of this woman beside him. He felt stirrings that he had not felt since Belle was murdered.

At first, Joshua resisted the feelings, but he remembered the talk his cousin Beautiful Woman had given him. He was a survivor, and he knew that as much as he loved Belle, he would dishonor her memory by curling up in a fetal position like a dandy and just giving up on life. That was not him. He was a warrior, a man, and he was indeed a romantic. He could not help himself, probably because he was the love child of an adventurous fifteen-year-old girl making her way west, having had both parents killed on the way yet forging ahead, and a handsome Lakota warrior who saved her life from a grizzly, almost dying himself in the process. How could Joshua not have become a survivor and a romantic?

He also knew that this refuge was wonderful, but he had to get to Washington, D.C., and try to end the horrible antics of the Indian Ring, and he had to eliminate Robert Hartwell and his henchmen. However, he had to make sure they did not eliminate him first, and he did not know that a local had seen Sammy Davis with him and where they were riding to.

15

TOP OF THE DIRT PILE

William W. Belknap was born in 1829 in Newburgh, New York. Having graduated from Princeton, he got his law degree at Georgetown University. He passed the bar exam in 1851, and then practiced in Iowa, before running for and winning a seat in the state legislature.

During the Civil War, William Belknap fought in the Fifteenth Iowa Infantry and saw action at both Shiloh and Vicksburg. By the end of the war, he had been promoted to brigadier general and become close with General William Tecumseh Sherman.

After the Civil War, Belknap became the head tax collector for Iowa until 1869, when President Ulysses S. Grant appointed him secretary of war. Almost immediately, in what became known as the Trader Post Scandal, Belknap started taking kickback payments every three months from a crooked Fort Sill tradership contract between Caleb P. Marsh and sutler John S. Evans.

At the very beginning of the Civil War, Union soldiers began purchasing supplies from private vendors known as

sutlers. These sutlers set up trading posts inside U.S. Army
forts and were at that time chosen by regimental officers to
do business. That policy changed completely in 1870, when
Belknap lobbied and got Congress to pass a law in July to
grant him the sole authority in the War Department to
license and choose each and every sutler at Western military
forts. Both U.S. Army soldiers, civilian workers, such as
scouts, and Indians, shopped and bought most of their supplies at these trading posts. Controlled by Secretary Belknap,
the trading posts became very lucrative monopolies, and he
attracted people like Robert Hartwell, who was an empire
builder in his own right. As secretary of war, Belknap not
only appointed handpicked sutlers, but made sure that soldiers stationed at forts could only buy supplies from the
trading posts. Soldiers in the West, who were forced to buy
supplies at higher than market prices, were left destitute.

Behind this scam was William Belknap's second wife,
Carita, who initially got her husband to appoint a Caleb P.
Marsh to the trading post at Fort Sill located in the Indian
territory. John S. Evans, however, had already been appointed
to that position previously, so to settle the question of owner-
ship regarding the trading post, Belknap had an illicit part-
nership contract drawn up and then authorized by him. The
contract allowed Evans to keep the trading post at Fort Sill,
provided that he pay $12,000 out of his annual profits to
Marsh. Evans would keep the remaining profit. Then Belknap
had Marsh pay half of his money from the contract or $6,000
per year to Carita so it could not be traced to him. She only
lived to receive one payment, dying from tuberculosis during
childbirth. So Belknap then had Marsh continue to pay
Belknap Carita's share directly, with the secretary claiming
he would save it for their child, but the infant child died one
year later, so Belknap pocketed the money and had Marsh

keep paying him directly. Then in less than a year, Secretary
William Belknap remarried, but this time it was Carita's
sister, Amanda, and she gladly accepted Carita's portion of
the quarterly payments from Marsh so they could not be tied
directly to Belknap as easily.

This was the birth of the Indian Ring.

National attention was drawn to the plight of the American Indians two years earlier in 1874 when world-famous
paleontologist Othniel Marsh revealed that the Lakota had
"frayed blankets, rotten beef, and concrete-hard flour." Secretary of Interior Columbus Delano, responsible for Indian
Bureau policy, resigned the next year. Following that, the
New York Herald, a Democratic newspaper, reported the
rumors that Secretary Belknap was receiving kickback
money from various trading post sutlers.

Prior to this, Allan Pinkerton had personally conducted
some very quiet investigations along with some of his
Washington-based agents into the Indian Ring, on behalf of
private requests from various politicians. On February 29,
1876, during the Great Sioux War and a presidential election
year, Democratic U.S. Representative Hiester Clymer headed
an investigation into the corruption under Belknap in the
War Department. The Democratic Party had recently
obtained a majority in the House of Representatives and had
immediately begun a series of queries into corruption charges
throughout the Grant Administration. Clymer's committee
barely began investigating when they learned about Belknap
and both his wives receiving the quarterly bribes from the
Fort Sill trading post contract. However, Washington, D.C.,
has always been loaded with deal-makers, cronies, and politi-
cos and Congressman Clymer was among them. Even though
he was investigating him, he advised Belknap to resign his
office to keep him from going to prison. Belknap hired an

attorney, Montgomery Blair. Secretary Belknap defended himself by admitting that the payments took place. However, he proclaimed his innocence, stating that the financial arrangements were instigated by his two wives, both sisters, used to high society living standards and opulence. Clymer, however, had Caleb Marsh, who exposed the Fort Sill ring under Congressional testimony. And to save his own hide, Marsh testified under oath that he had directly made payments to Secretary Belknap and that Secretary Belknap even gave Marsh receipts for these payments.

It was at this time, foreseeing Belknap's end, that Robert Hartwell started using more strong-arm tactics to keep the monies flowing in, through him, from all the trading posts that were part of the scam. There were also a number of political leaders and investors around D.C. who wanted the Indian Ring to keep operating and wipe out the tribes, so various ventures such as gold prospecting in the Black Hills could be carried out without attacks. A number of investors had put money into the trading post scams and were reaping benefits quarterly.

William Belknap, along with his attorney, testified before the Clymer Committee on February 29, 1876. Belknap then withdrew from giving any further testimony. Now, his attorney Blair approached members of Congress and proposed that they drop any and all charges against Belknap if his client would simply resign. The Clymer committee refused the offer. When a cabinet member named Bristow went to the White House and sought out President Grant, who was eating breakfast and getting prepared for a studio portrait session with Henry Ulke, Bristow told President Grant all about Belknap's trading post scams. He suggested that the president speak with U.S. Representative Bass for more information about the Indian Ring. Grant scheduled an afternoon meeting with

Congressman Bass. Grant started to finally leave for Ulke's studio for his portrait sitting, when he was interrupted by Secretary Belknap and Interior Secretary Zachariah Chandler in the White House's Red Room. Bawling like a two-hundred-and-some pound baby, Belknap literally threw himself on the floor in dramatic fashion in front of the president. He confessed the kickback scam to Grant but blamed everything on his two wives. Belknap begged the president to please accept his resignation. U. S. Grant, knew both sisters' reputation as elitists who always seemed to want the best of everything. Actually moved by William Belknap's plea and dramatic scene, the president wrote the resignation for Belknap himself, and then accepted it at 10:20 A.M.

Even though Belknap resigned, the angry and indignant House of Representatives voted to impeach the now former secretary of war. Members of the House argued about whether they had any right to impeach Belknap, since he was now a private citizen. A couple of outraged Democratic congressmen really criticized Grant for accepting Belknap's resignation. The House finally, after arguing all day, passed five articles of impeachment, to be presented to the Senate for trial.

In May 1876, after a lengthy, often political, debate, the Senate voted that Belknap be put on trial by the Senate. Although there was a great deal of strong evidence that Belknap willingly and knowingly accepted quarterly bribes from sutler Marsh, Belknap was actually acquitted when the Senate vote failed to achieve the required two-thirds majority for conviction. This was because most of the senators present were against conviction, feeling that the Senate had no right to convict a private citizen.

George Armstrong Custer was now dead and being lionized in the news back east. The Battle of the Little Big Horn, which Joshua had recently learned about, was already being called Custer's Last Stand. He was an egomaniac who graduated at the very bottom of his class at the U.S. Military Academy of West Point and received more demerits than any previous cadet. He did well leading men, as he was very ambitious and wanted medals, and his long-range goal was the presidency. The reddish-blond George Custer, known to friends as Autie, but to his wife as Cinnamon, wanted one, too. He did however gain national fame as the "boy general," as he was promoted to brevet brigadier general, a temporary rank, at twenty-three years of age during the war. After the war, he fell to the rank of captain and was later promoted to major then lieutenant colonel, but was used to the accolades and respect of being a general officer.

Earlier in the year, Reprentative Clymer had met with Lieutenant Colonel Custer, who was a Democrat with his eyes on the presidency and who was also quietly feeding stories about Belknap and Grant to the news media. Clymer continuing his investigation into Belknap's War Department, having called upon Custer at Fort Lincoln, Nebraska. Autie then testified in the nation's capital on both March 29 and April 4. Custer was rumored to have anonymously aided the *New York Herald* in its investigation into Indian trading posts in a March 31 exposé, entitled "Belknap's Anaconda." Custer boldly swore to Clymer's committee that sutlers gave a percentage of their profits to Secretary William Belknap. He was genuinely upset about it, as he become suspicious in 1875 that his men at Fort Lincoln were paying ridiculously high prices for supplies, and then found out the sutler at the fort was only being paid $2,000 out of the trader-ship's $15,000 in profits. Custer believed that the $13,000 difference went to partners in the trader post deals, or to Belknap himself. With much of his testimony based on hearsay and always also eager to feather his own political nest, Custer testified that he had heard that President Grant's brother, Orville Grant, was an investor involved in the trading post rings, having invested in three posts with the president's blessing.

President Grant was furious that Custer did this. Custer also testified that Colonel William B. Hazen had been sent to a remote post, Fort Buford, as punishment for Hazen having exposed Belknap's trading post scam in 1872. That testimony really angered General Philip Sheridan, who wrote to the War Department and contradicted Custer's claims, including his remarks about Hazen's so-called isolation. Prior to that, Sheridan had been a staunch supporter of Custer's until the boy general's testimony before the Clymer committee. Although Custer's testimony, as mentioned, was based on almost all rumors and innuendo, his national reputation as a military commander really impressed the Clymer committee, so they gave more weight to his gossip. Belknap, despite his resignation and damaged reputation still had many strong connections in Washington, D.C., and he used his influence to try to discredit George Armstrong Custer's testimony.

So, now in actuality William W. Belknap was a has-been and no longer relevant. Hartwell was the head of the now-invisible but still functioning Indian Ring. Oddly enough, Joshua Strongheart was now being helped by the now-invisible but still functioning Underground Railroad.

Joshua Strongheart faced and defeated the infamous and frightening We Wiyake, Blood Feather. He had defeated many powerful foes, but he had never been up against such a powerful and extensive machine that could reach all the way across the country. Worse yet, this man was not seven feet tall like Blood Feather. He was slight and short and weak, physically, but he was gigantic in his ruthlessness. He also had an inordinate amount of power and his money was in a steadily increasing unending supply. Even worse, all of his money and power had been accumulated at the expense of the true Americans, not immigrants, Strongheart's father's people, the American Indian. He despised the red man and could care less if every man, woman, and child perished. Unfortunately, there were also many greedy investors in the Indian Ring who wanted Hartwell to succeed and make them money. There were also those in power who wanted the red man to become a nonfactor, so they and their cronies could prospect and mine the sacred Black Hills for gold, as well as violate other American Indian rights.

This was indeed Strongheart's biggest challenge, and it was starting to present an even greater threat.

16

HIDE AND SEEK

Joshua and Brenna were walking back toward the many farm buildings, when they heard hoofbeats approaching. Strongheart took her by the hand, and they ran into the greenery along the wooded farm road. They ran through the woods back toward the farmhouse, but stayed out of sight of the driveway road. The hooves got closer and closer, and they both hid behind trees as the group rode by. Many more had joined Hartwell's gang, and at least a couple dozen gun toughs rode down the farm lane. Brenna recognized the man in the lead, who was a local farmhand saddle tramp who lived about twenty miles to the west but was frequently in trouble all over the area.

Strongheart recognized several of the riders and their horses, and said, "Hartwell's gang, and they have added some more gun hands."

Brenna added, "The ugly skinny man in the lead with the pockmarked face is a local tough. I bet he saw you and Sammy headed this way and led them here for some cheap money."

Joshua said, "Makes sense. We need to get into the house, and I need to hide on the island."

Brenna said, "We are about to get to a path that runs right to the back, and we can hopefully go in one of the back doors without being seen, or we can get to the fruit cellar and take that tunnel into the basement."

"Your father thought ahead," Joshua said.

She smiled, saying, "I had that tunnel dug attaching the fruit cellar and the house, actually, in case of a tornado. We get them once in a great while."

The hoofbeats were thundering as they came within sight of the big home. Through the trees, they saw one man pointing out locations to the rest, and he was consulting with the ugly one who led them there. Brenna nodded toward the fruit cellar door and Joshua felt they should dash for it right then before men started spreading out looking around the property. With Joshua holding Brenna's hand, they dashed across the backyard, which slanted downhill toward the large pond. They made it without incident. Inside, they lit a lantern, and she led him into the basement of the mansion, then up the stairway. They paused at the door, and she looked at the windows to ensure nobody was looking in them yet.

"It is safe," she whispered.

They scurried through the doorway into the kitchen, and she led them to the hidden door that would lead him to safety. Strongheart stopped there and took her in his hands. She melted looking up into his dark brown eyes. They reminded her of something recent and powerful. Then it dawned on her. Just months earlier, she had traveled east to go shopping in Cincinnati, Ohio, and visited the new zoo there. The Zoological Society of Cincinnati was founded in 1873 and opened for visitors two years later. The Cincinnati Zoo & Botanical Garden, the second oldest zoo in the United States, had an early collection of animals that consisted of less than a dozen apes, two silvertip grizzly bears, three whitetail deer, six raccoons, two elk, a buffalo, a hyena, a tiger, an alligator, a circus elephant, and over four hundred birds. The zoo was sixty-five acres in size in the middle of the town. It hit her that she was totally fascinated looking into the eyes of the tiger. She saw so much power behind the eyes, and so much mystery in them. Joshua's eyes were affecting her the same way, except his eyes also made her feel tingly.

Strongheart said, "Brenna, come to the island and hide with me. You shouldn't talk to those men. They are looking for me. That man apparently saw Sammy and me coming here and will know I have been here."

She said, "Joshua, please. My entire family and I have had to deal with several raids by members of the KKK looking for slaves. Many in the area knew we were part of the Underground Railroad and this was the first place they checked when there were reports of runaway slaves in the area. I have been threatened and even manhandled once. I will handle them. You must hide, please. I will be okay."

Joshua winked at her and stepped back into the secret passageway. He closed the hidden door until it was just a crack, and she walked to the front door. Buck was running up the front steps of the porch as she walked out the door. Numerous horses pulled up in a semicircle in front of her.

A man in a black suit and twin tied-down pearl-handled Peacemakers looked at the pockmarked man and said, "Take Shaughnessy, and check the barns for his horse. Lady, we have already been told you took in a fugitive, Joshua Strongheart. Give him up and save yourself. Owens, ride back and fetch Mr. Hartwell. Tell him it is safe to ride up."

A man took off at gallop while the other two headed toward the barn.

Brenda smiled saying, "Whatever do you mean, sir? All I have seen are a bunch of ruffians who refuse to act like gentlemen in the presence of a lady. Now you all can leave my property!"

Sammy Davis walked out the door and came down the step partway to stand next to her. He was holding his rifle.

Nobody spoke for several minutes, everyone just kept staring at each other. Suddenly, Robert Hartwell, looking very tiny on his big black Thoroughbred galloped up, accompanied by his top five gunmen.

He looked at Brenna and then Sammy, then back at her, saying, "Lady, one time and one time only: Where is Joshua Strongheart?"

She replied, "I don't know who you are but you all get off my property right now."

Hartwell nodded and all five gunmen drew and fired at Sammy, hitting him multiple times, and killed him instantly. Brenna screamed and Joshua came flying out of the passageway and ran to the front window, immediately seeing what happened. He drew his pistol and aimed at Hartwell, but did not squeeze the trigger, worried that a hail of bullets would rain down on Brenna. He ran to the front door and burst out boldly aiming his Peacemaker at Hartwell.

"Freeze, everybody, or Hartwell dies!" Strongheart commanded.

He could see that many men wanted to go for their guns, but a few others really had scared looks on their faces. His earlier terror tactics had apparently worked on some. He also noted that all the blood had drained out of Hartwell's face.

Still aiming at the center of Robert Hartwell's chest, he said, "Brenna, inside. Buck, you get inside, too."

As soon as both were safely inside the house, he backed up, seeing that several gang members really wanted to draw.

One finally did, and Joshua stepped back, shooting. His bullet was a little off, slamming into Hartwell's shoulder, and it spun him off the horse. A hail of bullets hit the front of the house and the doorway and one clipped Joshua's right triceps, as he backed into the house. He fanned his pistol as he backed up and shot two more. One fell out of the saddle half-dead and the other tried to spur his horse away in panic, but the blood quickly spilling out of him made him fall off the horse, dead before they went out of sight.

Inside the house, he grabbed Brenna and dropped her to the floor, his arm protectively around her. His arm hurt, but it could be used.

She said, "Joshua, you've been shot."

Ignoring her, he said, "We need to get into the passage-way and over to the island."

Now it was her turn to ignore him saying, "Buck, go through the basement and out the side door, go through the orchard to the back of the stable. Saddle his horse and put his saddlebags and bedroll on it. Put his bridle in a saddlebag and turn his horse loose in the trees. Also, quickly saddle my big chestnut and do the same thing. Turn them out together. Then, you hightail it out of here through the woods."

Buck said, "I ain't leavin' you, Miss Brenna."

"Nonsense," she said, "I am with Mr. Strongheart. He won't let me get hurt. You get out of here. They will start in the front of the stable. You hurry and don't argue, Buck. Get out of here, and go home to your wife and kids. Stay out of sight."

"Yes'm," he said.

Joshua interrupted, "He doesn't need to risk that. I'll go the stable."

She quickly replied, "Joshua, he needs to get out of here anyway. Buck will be fine if he leaves now. Go, Buck, and thank you."

Buck nodded and crawled on his belly toward the basement door. He went through it. Strongheart was very glad she'd thought of getting Eagle out of there.

Two men attended to Hartwell's shoulder, quickly bandaging the entrance and exit wounds, and getting the bleeding stopped.

He looked at two of the men and said, "Take one of the locals and get me a doctor."

They nodded, and one grabbed another gang member, and the three sped off.

Hartwell hollered, "We finally got Strongheart where we want him. Surround the house and torch it. We'll shoot him when he is running out. Watch for shooting from the windows."

Inside, Strongheart wrapped his arm protectively around Brenna and got her to the passageway door. She tore a strip off her petticoat and started wrapping it around his massive arm while she spoke.

"My father had a Gatling gun he kept just in case something like this happened."

Strongheart said, "Where is it?"

She pointed at a door across the room, saying, "In his study! It's on wheels, Joshua."

Strongheart said, "Great! Run to the house on the island and stay there. I'll join you."

She stopped and looked up at him, tears starting to well up in her eyes. He pulled her into his arms and kissed her deeply.

Bullets still flying through windows, he looked into her eyes and said, "I'm so sorry I brought this misery down upon you, Brenna."

"Nonsense," she said, "I was born into it."

Strongheart said, "You know Hartwell will burn this house down?"

She nodded and said, "I am not about possessions. Things can be replaced."

She grabbed a lantern and matches and turned into the passageway. He looked at her back and could tell she was sobbing. He ran to the study and found the automatic weapon.

The Gatling gun was a machine gun that consisted of ten barrels revolving around a central axis, and was able to fire .30-caliber bullets at a very rapid rate. An earlier .58-caliber version of it was first used by General Benjamin F. Butler of the Union Army first at the Battle of Petersburg, Virginia, in 1864.

The inventor, Dr. Richard J. Gatling, a physician, had hoped that the overwhelming power of his new invention would discourage large-scale battles and maybe end wars. He actually sold the guns to the Union during the war, but secretly belonged to the Order of American Knights, a clandestine group of Confederate sympathizers who also committed acts of sabotage.

The army adopted the version of the Gatling gun Joshua now had in his hands in 1866. It was mounted and had two wheels and could fire four hundred rounds per minute. There were several loaded magazines with it.

The Pinkerton ignored the pain in his right arm and wheeled the deadly gun to the front door. He moved it off to the side a little and opened the door, hiding behind the heavy oak of the doorframe. He peeked out and saw Hartwell had been carried out of sight, but most gang members were now dismounted and were yelling to each other about the door being opened. He soon had the result he wanted as many assembled together near the front. The half-breed quickly wheeled the gun in front of the door and started turning the crank, causing immediate carnage in Hartwell's ranks, as they fell bloody all over the ground.

One of Hartwell's bodyguards, Kirby Hoover, moved forward along the trees to find out what was happening because of the thunderous shooting. He saw bloody men sprawled all over the front area of the house. While there, Kirby saw four who took off into the trees west of the house at a dead run, apparently quitting the gang as quickly as they had joined it with promises of rich bounties.

Hoover returned to his boss and knelt down saying, "Mr. Hartwell, we need to get you out of here and to a doctor. That hombre has a Gatling gun in the house, and he just killed over half the posse in just a couple minutes' time."

Hartwell said, "Very well. Tell them to continue the siege but to be careful. Then set fire to the house and barns."

The bodyguards got Hartwell up and into the saddle.

He said, "Kirby, you stay here and run this thing. I want Strongheart burned to a crisp if he doesn't come out. No witnesses."

"You got it, boss," Kirby said, as he took off toward the house.

One brave soul made it up close to the eastern porch on the side of the house and tossed a torch up onto the veranda. It started catching the outer wall of the house, and the flames quickly started shooting up. All the rest were hiding behind trees, rocks, troughs, or anything available. The Gatling gun had made believers out of most of them.

Strongheart, in the meantime, out of bullets for his machine gun, dismantled it from its mount so he could carry the big gun through the hidden door and place it inside the passageway. He just wanted to keep Hartwell's men from getting their hands on it. He carried the gun into the passageway, ran back to the front windows, and fired a couple shots out into the midst of the besiegers. Joshua wanted to keep their heads down longer. It worked.

He went into the cabin on the island and Brenna ran into his arms. She started sobbing and then caught herself and stepped back.

She said, "Take off your shirt and sit down here at the table."

She already had medicine, bandaging, a pan with soap and water, and a small bottle of whiskey. He complied, and she started dressing his wound.

"Thank you, Brenna," he said, not knowing what else to say.

They could now hear the crackling and explosions from the mansion burning and tears started dropping down her cheeks. He took her hands and set down the rest of the bandage and pulled her against him, letting her head rest on his big chest. She started bawling her eyes out, while Strongheart softly stroked her hair. She cried for five minutes, then collected herself and stepped back with a sniffle here and sniffle there. She set her jaw defiantly.

"Joshua, thank you, but it is gone now, and I can do nothing about it," she said, sniffling. "I would be glad to lose it all just to have Sammy alive right now. Will we be killed, too?"

"No, we won't." Strongheart said. "I promise you."

"What will happen?" she replied.

He said, "We need to pack what we can for tonight. We will leave after dark and find our horses. We should take naps, eat, and get ready in a while."

"Okay, you know how to handle things like this better than me," she responded, fighting tears now.

They both lay down in the two rooms to take naps, but after a few minutes she called Joshua. He walked to her doorway. She was crying again.

Sticking out her arms, she said, "Joshua, please hold me awhile?"

He smiled softly and walked over to her bed and lay down. He gently placed her head on his massive pectoral muscle, and she started sobbing again. They awakened a few hours later and the sun was still in the sky but getting ready to disappear under its covers for the night. Joshua gave her a kiss and walked to his roll and saddlebags.

She got up, joining him, and said, "What do we do?"

She watched with curiosity as he spread out his large slicker. Then he carefully folded his stuff on top of it. Then he walked out of the cabin, returning a few minutes later with his shirt removed. He had tied the neck together with a piece of fringe and used it as a bag. It was filled with small sticks and pine cones. He poured them all over his equipment on the slicker. Then he rolled up his shirt and put it in the pile. Brenna marveled at his rippling muscles and the numerous scars all over his upper torso. They told a story of danger and excitement, and this man excited her more than any she had ever met. In fact, she knew she was already in love with him.

"What are you doing?" she asked.

"Well," he replied, "making a raft, a waterproof one."

She cocked her head to the side wondering what he meant.

He explained, as if reading her thoughts, "I am sure I saw a couple tarps in the other room, oilskin, I believe. I will tie these up tight, so that water cannot get in. With pine needles, pine cones, and sticks they will float. I'll make one for you and one for me. We will float across the pond just quietly kicking with our feet, so we do not make noise. Then we will run a ways through the trees and then stop and get dressed."

"Get dressed?" she said.

Joshua smiled, saying, "Brenna, this is a life-or-death situation, so I hope you are not going to be too modest.

Whatever we wear will get wet, and we will be riding hard, for hours, wearing it wet. I will be naked, and if you are smart, you will be, too."

She replied, "Oh my. Will you look?"

He smiled, "Probably."

She grinned, her face tomato red.

"I will do whatever you say, Joshua. Like you, I am a survivor," she said.

They ate and then shortly after, made their way through the trees to the end of the island, seeing easily in the dense small forest because of the flames still licking the sky from the burning mansion, barns, and outbuildings. They could hear happy voices, and Strongheart knew that the fools figured he and she had perished.

At the end of the point, sitting between some pines, they both started undressing, packing their clothes in the two rafts, which Strongheart tightly sealed by rolling the seams together and then tightly bound them with his lariat and some piggin strings.

Now, seeing each other's nude bodies clearly in the glow from the flaming sky nearby, they both marveled at the other. They did so in silence, though, because, as Joshua had said, this was survival, pure and simple. They made it across the pond, only visible to Hartwell's group for maybe ten feet and nobody was looking anyway and might mistake them at a distance for geese or a couple of beavers.

Entering the dark trees on the far shore, Joshua reached back, taking her hand and, both carrying their rafts, he led them through the darkness. Joshua could see much better than she because he closed his left eye whenever they were in sight of the bright flames from the heinous act of arson. As a warrior, he knew that closing one eye when exposed to light and then opening it after getting back into the dark, makes the eye quickly adjust to the darkness. This happens within seconds, in fact. As they wound through the dark trees, they heard the voices and sounds behind them disappear.

Joshua stopped, hearing a familiar whinny and strained to look between the trees. In a small clearing ahead was Eagle and her chestnut standing side by side.

Joshua, smile unseen in the blackness, whispered, "Our horses are ahead, maybe forty feet."

As they made the clearing, they both saw the horses clearly in the silvery light from the full moon. Behind them in the cracks of the emerald curtain, the sky was cloaked in bright red and yellow. They got up to the horses and dropped their rafts, and a figure stood up between the horses.

Buck gulped, as he looked upon Brenna in her nudity, and Joshua, too. He turned his head.

Brenna was embarrassed, as she said, "We had to swim across the pond and keep our clothing dry, Buck. Buck, why did you stay here? I told you to make it home to your family. They need you."

Buck nodded, smiling, with his head turned, hearing them both toweling off and getting dressed.

He said, "Yes'm, but my family dey know how to take care of demselves. Dey have had to hide befo'. Dey will do it if'n anybody comes ta mah house."

"Are you sure?" she said.

"Yes'm," he replied.

"But why did you risk your life and stay here?"

He looked now, as she and Joshua were dressed except for boots.

"Because ma'am, you risked yo' life befo' fo' me," Buck said, "I wanna make sho dat ya both got yo' horses."

"Thanks, Buck," Strongheart said and extended his hand. "Thanks a lot."

Buck had heard many stories about Strongheart all the way there in the Midwest and to have him shake hands with him and thank him was like getting a roll of bills. Then he looked down at her hand extended forward and in it was a tight roll of bills. She put it in his hand.

She said, "I will be insulted if you try to give it back. I grabbed some money and put it in my pocket before, when I saw those ruffians riding up. Just in case. I will have to go away now, Buck. However, I will come back someday and find you and your lovely wife. You have been a wonderful help to me over the years and a loyal friend. God bless you."

He hung his head down trying to hide his own tears. She grabbed him in a big hug, and he turned and disappeared into the trees just like that. She dabbed at her eyes.

By this time, Joshua had the gear stored on his horse, which was already saddled and bridled. She took the reins to her horse and gasped. There were saddlebags on her horse, too. She reached inside, and saw that Buck had grabbed food, apparently sneaking to the fruit cellar, and put a store of it in there. He also grabbed some of her clothing off the line out back, and shoved it in there as well, and some matches. He had also rolled up her rain slicker and bedroll, including a bag and oilskin and had them rolled tightly behind her saddle cantle.

Again, she got tears, and said, "He risked his life to get me some food and clothing, Joshua. What a wonderful man."

He said, "Sure is loyal. Salt of the earth. Brenna, we need to put some miles between us and them. Do you know where you want to go?"

She said, "Yes. Chicago."

He did not wait for her to say any more, but said, "Then we will head west."

He was headed east, but this woman had risked her life

and lost everything to protect him. Sammy Davis had given up his life, too, and Strongheart became even more determined to make Robert Hartwell pay. The Pinkerton looked up at the sky, located the Big and Little Dipper, then the North Star, and headed west.

They rode for hours, and Joshua knew he had to give her and the horses a rest. Hartwell knew he was headed to Washington.

He found a nice quiet grove along a wide stream and made camp. He built a small fire, and they quickly curled up, using their saddles for pillows, and both slept until the sun awakened them.

Brenna was still tired and sore, but said, "I will be ready in a minute."

Joshua said, "No, ma'am. The horses need rest, and we can eat a good breakfast, some coffee, and take it easier. Those fools think they burned us to a crisp, and will never look to the west. Hartwell knows I am heading to Washington."

Shortly after, during breakfast, she said, "Why are you heading to Washington?"

He said, "To expose Robert Hartwell and his followers in the Indian Ring to Congress."

She said, "Joshua, I want to ask you a serious question. You are definitely a man of sorts, and a man of the wilderness. Do you think a bald eagle could fly down and kill something in a place like New York City?"

"Definitely," he said with a grin, not knowing what she was after.

"Do you think a bald eagle would enjoy being in or around a place like New York City?"

"No, not at all," he answered, "Eagles treasure their freedom. Too many people, houses, and buildings in a place like that. I suppose an eagle would feel very confined."

She said, "Since we talked about this case, I've done a great deal of thinking. According to what you told me, many people back east and out west know about the Indian Ring, and Secretary Belknap was caught and forced to retire."

"Yes," Joshua said.

She went on, "And many investors in Washington and similar places put money into the trading posts and other parts of the Indian Ring."

"That's true, too," he replied, "So, what are you getting at?"

She went on, "You, to me, are like that eagle. Yes, you could go to Washington and kill Hartwell and many of his people, but you would be confining yourself to a part of the world that is not your territory. You can do it, but is it right? Why not leave the politics to the political buzzards in Washington who are expert at it, and you do what you're expert at? Hartwell obviously wants you dead, so why not make him come to your territory to try to kill you, especially since you are up against so many other killers. By chasing him to Washington, it seems that you are playing into his hands instead of the other way around."

Joshua took a sip of coffee and grinned.

"What is so funny, Mr. Strongheart?"

He chuckled, saying, "I am trying to figure out if you are simply wise, or actually brilliant, or I am just plain stupid? This has happened twice within a few weeks that two women, my cousin and you, have made me stop and think clearly."

She chuckled, too. Then she set her coffee down and came over to him and put her arms around his neck. They kissed softly, then passionately.

"You know," she said, "I have always had to be so strong, so guarded. I feel totally safe when I'm with you. When I cried on your chest, I had never done that before with any man. This is very forward, but I have fallen in love with you, Joshua."

Strongheart kissed her again, then sat back and refreshed his coffee and hers.

He said, "Brenna, you are very, very beautiful and free-spirited. Like a female eagle of sorts yourself but you could function well in Washington, New York, or Chicago. However, you said it. I am a man of the West, and I am a man of two worlds. You would not be happy there."

"I would be happy with you anywhere, Joshua," she said her eyes welling up again, as she knew deep down he was correct.

Strongheart said, "Those who move west have a stirring in their soul. They hear about harsh blizzards, and many more grizzly bears and wolves than you would find where you live. They hear about Indian raids, stage holdups, hardships, many more rattlers than you find where you live, and gun fights. Yet, they are drawn there like by a magnet. Brenna, you have never had those feelings, have you?"

She said, "No, I haven't. I just wish."

He said, "I know."

He grabbed the frying pan and knelt down by the stream. He reached down into the water and grabbed a handful of sand and half filled the pan with water. He dropped the sand in and started swirling it around. In short order, the pan was clean. Then, Brenna tossed him a bar of soap from her saddlebag, and he scrubbed it with that, and rinsed it. Strongheart stood and shook the pan and then put it away in his saddlebags.

They both knew the conversation was over.

He walked over to her, and held her upper arms, saying, "Are you going to be okay? I am so sorry you lost your home and all your belongings because of me."

She put her hand on his and said, "Not because of you! It was because of Hartwell. I'll be fine, really. I am very wealthy, Joshua, and everything I lost were simply things. I have relatives I will stay with in Chicago until I figure out what to do next. Maybe after you destroy Hartwell and his gang, I'll return, but I am thinking maybe I should move to Washington myself and try to influence lawmakers on race relations."

"The Pinkerton Agency headquarters are in Chicago," Strongheart replied. "Maybe when I come there, we can have dinner."

"I would love that."

17

BACK HOME

Within a few days, Strongheart rapped on the door of the palatial mansion on Wacker Drive. Brenna stood next to him, eyes glistening. One of the massive double oak doors opened, and a man with a face similar to Brenna's looked at Joshua then at her. His face broadened into a beaming smile, and he swept her up in his arms.

"Sis!" he yelled. "Honey, Brenna is here! Come in, come in!"

Strongheart remained for dinner at the insistence of Brenna's older brother, but then he left for the hospital.

An hour later, Lucky looked up from the newspaper he was reading to see Joshua Strongheart walk into his private hospital room. Lucky smiled and the two shook hands.

Joshua said, "Well, it looks like you pulled through. I'm glad. I would hate to have to break in a new boss."

The two chuckled.

Lucky said, "The last reports we had, you were in Indiana or Ohio somewhere, were arrested for murder, and taken away by a posse. That was days ago."

Strongheart smiled, "Yes, I ended up in Indiana, and I

think southwestern Ohio, too. I'll file a detailed report later, but I have been through a bit."

"How did you end up back here in Chicago?"

Strongheart responded, "After you got shot, I was determined to chase Hartwell to Washington, D.C., and take care of him and his men there, if need be. Someone I was with, who I brought here to Chicago, convinced me I should go home and have Hartwell come after me, on my ground, on my terms."

Lucky smiled, "Was she beautiful?"

Strongheart said, "Very."

Lucky smiled, "I'm glad you have gotten back to living."

"Life goes on," Joshua said. "In fact, Shakespeare said, 'The golden age is before us, not behind us.'"

He went on, "Lucky, I need a few agents to help me. I am heading back to southern Colorado and will make sure that Robert Hartwell knows it. He will come. He is obsessed with killing me now. He cannot help himself."

Lucky said, "He does not want you destroying his money well. You will have your agents. Just end the Indian Ring."

Strongheart said, "That's simple. It will end with the end of Robert Hartwell. The problem is the nature of man. It may not be called the Indian Ring, but there will always be such policies as long as one group has dominion over another."

Lucky said, "Very true. I am glad to see at least you are not full of holes again."

Joshua laughed, touching his bandaged upper arm, which was not visible because of his shirt's now-repaired sleeve, saying, "Only one hole this time, but not so bad."

Lucky smiled and just shook his head.

Two days later, Strongheart got off the train in Denver and made arrangements to take one to Pueblo and then connect to another going to Cañon City. He knew that by now Robert Hartwell would wonder if they had really gotten lucky and killed him, or if he was still alive. He knew that by now, Hartwell would have sent some of his gunmen out, maybe in twos or threes to major population centers to see if Joshua would show up. He would ensure that he was seen, and he was positive that Hartwell would definitely have people in Denver, his home base and the hub of Strongheart's travels.

Instead of riding in a passenger car, he stayed in the comfortable and safe confines of the boxcar Eagle was traveling in. They rode away from the train station looking for any of Hartwell's well-dressed shootists. He did not see any around the depot, so he figured since it was lunchtime, they may have gone to a saloon to have a sandwich. He rode to the saloon where Hartwell could always be found.

Strongheart entered the saloon, and immediately spotted Kirby Hoover and Ed Ragan, another gun tough of Hartwell's. Both wore tailored gray suits and both wore tied-down guns with double holsters. They spotted him, and he saw Kirby tap Ed and whisper something. They were back in the far corner of the saloon. At an unspoken signal, both men stood, pulling back the tails of their suit coats. Men seeing what was happening jumped up from tables and back up to both side walls of the saloon.

Joshua said, "It does not have to be this way. You can slowly unbuckle your gun belts, and we can march to the police department."

Kirby snarled, saying, "You go to hell, Strongheart."

Joshua smiled and replied, "Naw, you two will be there in a minute. I am planning on heaven."

He had walked into the saloon not expecting action so fast. He also knew that the men around Hartwell were the toughest and the best gun slicks around. To outshoot them he would need an edge, and the only one he could think of was beating them to the draw. Instead of waiting for either to make a move, he drew first.

"Draw!" he commanded, as he whipped out his Peacemaker and fired, his first bullet slamming into Kirby's belly, folding him like a new suitcase.

He stepped to the right, fanning his gun. The next two bullets slammed into Ed's chest, and then his left cheek. He spun and slammed face-first into the wall, and his limp body crumpled and fell to the floor, like a burlap bag full of rags that had just been dropped. Strongheart quickly ran over to Kirby and kicked his fallen pistol away. The man started crying like a baby and screamed.

"You gut shot me, Strongheart! Git me a doctor, please!" he yelled.

Joshua shook his head seeing this big gun tough bawling like an infant child. He thought about the fact that so often these supposed tough guys were nothing more than scared little boys with grown-up bodies and six-shooters.

Strongheart hollered out, "I am a Pinkerton agent! Somebody fetch the police and a doctor!"

He looked at the saloonkeeper and remembered his times with the man before. Two Denver police officers rushed in, guns drawn, and Joshua quickly identified himself and briefed them.

Kirby lay on the floor moaning, with tears still running down his face. Joshua knelt down next to him and said quietly, "A doctor's coming, but you are gut shot, and you are dying. Do you want to do one thing decent in your life, for a change, and talk to me about Hartwell?

Hoover was scared, and his chest was making a sucking noise.

He said, "Mr, Hartwell's in Washington, D.C. He thought

you were burned up, but wanted to make sure. He told Ed and me either one of us could outdraw and outshoot you."

"Will the bartender here send him a telegram about me being here?" Joshua asked.

Kirby smiled, "Hell yeah. Mr. Hartwell owns this saloon. Ya didn't know that?"

Joshua started to answer but saw that Kirby Hoover's eyes were unmoving, as was his chest. He died just like that.

He went to the police department and filled out a report, then sent a telegram to Chicago reporting the incident. He also reported that Hartwell owned that saloon.

The next day, he boarded a train for Cañon City via Pueblo. He arrived in Cañon City that afternoon. Strongheart was glad to be back to southern Colorado. He loved the climate, especially the very mild winters, and the many days of sunshine. More than three hundred thirty days per year, in fact, and less than a foot of snow in the winter usually, often only an inch or so at a time. And even that was almost always gone by the following day.

The following morning, Joshua rode Eagle to the west end of town, passed the big state prison, Old Max, and went to one of his favorite places by the river near the mouth of Grape Creek where it poured into the Arkansas River. Situated very close to the east entrance of the Royal Gorge, which was known as the Grand Canyon of the Arkansas, the Hot Springs Hotel was one of Joshua Strongheart's favorite spots. It was constructed in 1873 by Dr. J. L. Prentiss of Cañon City. The hotel consisted of thirty-eight rooms. It also had a very large lobby and a large dining room that also doubled as a ballroom, which cost $38,000 to build in 1873. There was also a popular swinging bridge over the river and a railroad depot as well. When Joshua had gotten shot up in a gunfight with an outlaw gang in nearby Florence several years earlier and when he was recuperating from an attack by a large grizzly bear, he spent many days at the Hot Springs Hotel just soaking in the hot mineral water.

He decided he had a little time before the vultures would start appearing, and his arm was very sore from the bullet graze. Strongheart almost fell asleep in the hot water.

"Wal, youngster, I reckon I might jest as well soak these old bones, too," said a voice that brought a smile to Joshua's face.

He turned to see his old white-bearded friend Zachariah Banta from Cotopaxi, about thirty miles west along the rumbling, tumbling whitewater Arkansas River.

"Zach, what a coincidence," Strongheart said looking at the leathery-skinned seventyish or eightyish storekeeper. "How are you doing?"

Zach said, "Wal, I guess a whole lot better 'n' you. I ain't been in no shooting scrap back east, saving no purty gals."

Joshua just shook his head. It seemed like every place that he went in the West he would find people who knew Zach from his current or one of his many past ventures. He always knew what had happened with Strongheart long before anybody else knew.

The township of Cotopaxi was located at the juncture of the railroad and river road between Cañon City and Poncha Springs a couple days' ride to the west. Because of the jutting rocks around the little community, it was named after the Cotopaxi Volcano in Ecuador, which was one of the highest active volcanoes in the world. Henry Thomas, a prospector, was the man responsible for naming Cotopaxi, which he had seen in Latin America. Strongheart had a lot of history already with Cotopaxi and with Zach Banta, a man always with a twinkle in his eye and something clever to say.

Chances were, Strongheart would soon be leading or

maybe stalking Robert Hartwell and his gang in that area. He could see, from the Hot Springs Hotel, the little gulch opening for Grape Creek, and he may just lead them up that gulch for starters. Strongheart was very thankful to Brenna as this was indeed his area now, and he knew it all very well. Joshua spent an hour in the mineral springs and had a good talk with Zach, telling him about his most recent adventure.

Two hours later found him on the river road to visit his young friend Scottie Middleton. Joshua thought back to his very first encounter with Scottie.

18

THE HANDSHAKE

Scottie Middleton was a towheaded youngster with freckles and an infectious smile. He had a serious set to his jaw when he looked at the imposing three-story brick Fremont County sheriff's office and jail on Macon Street one block over from Main Street. It was 1875, and Cañon City, Colorado, home of the territorial prison, was a small bustling town enjoying the best climate in the Colorado territory, which would become a state in less than a year.

It had been less than a year since Strongheart had lost his fiancée and true love, Annabelle Ebert.

Scottie hitched up his homespun trousers, wiped the drainage from his nose, and walked into the big, imposing building. In the front, he first stopped and looked again at the tall black-and-white half-Arabian, half-Saddlebred gelding, Eagle, which was ridden and owned by the famous half-Sioux, half-white Pinkerton agent Joshua Strongheart. When he got inside, he saw a large sheriff's deputy with a large muttonchop mustache.

"Well, saints preserve us!" said the deputy. "It is a lep-rechaun we have here. Or is it just a strappin' young lad?"

"I'm a boy," said Scottie, his jaw set despite feeling intimidated in the strange surroundings. "I want to see Mr. Strongheart, sir," Scottie said.

"Well, he is here visiting Sheriff Bengley," the deputy replied. "Let me tell him you are here. And what be yer name, lad?"

"Scottie Middleton, sir."

"You stay right here and have a chew on this wee bit a lico-rice I had back here, an' I'll go fetch him," the deputy replied.

He handed a small licorice whip to the boy, who took it with wide eyes saying, "Thank you, sir."

A few minutes later, the deputy had the little boy follow him and escorted him into the sheriff's office. The sheriff sat behind his desk grinning, and the boy looked with awe at Joshua Strongheart. He took it all in with his jaw hanging at knee level. Strongheart stood and winked at Scottie. This man was such a giant in Scottie's mind and now he was looking at him in person.

His long, shiny black hair was hanging down his back in a single ponytail, and it was covered by a black cowboy hat with a wide, very flat brim and rounded crown. A very wide, fancy, colorful beaded hat band went around the base of the crown.

He wore a bone hair pipe choker necklace around his sinewy neck and three large grizzly bear claws helped sepa-rate some of the rows of bone hair pipes. Just months earlier, a massive grizzly had mauled Strongheart, who'd eventually killed it with his knife and pistol, and he still bore many scars from the attack. They fit in just fine with the many bullet scars covering his body. His soft, antelope-skin shirt did little to hide his bulging muscles, and the small rows of fringe, which slanted in from the broad shoulders in a V shape above the large pectoral muscles and stopped at mid-chest, actually served to accentuate the muscular build and narrow waist that looked like a flesh-covered washboard.

Levi Strauss had two years earlier patented and started making a brand-new type of trousers made of blue denim, which folks were calling Levi's. They had brass rivets and Joshua had bought a couple pairs from a merchandiser, who bought them himself for $13.50 a dozen. They were tight, and they too did little to hide the bulging muscles of his long legs.

Around his hips, Joshua wore his prized possessions: one a gift from his late stepfather and the other a gift from his late father. On the right hip of the engraved brown gun belt was the fancy holster, with his stepfather's Colt .45 Peace-maker in it. It had miniature marshal's badges, like his step-father's own, attached to both of the mother-of-pearl grips and fancy engraving along the barrel. It was a brand-new single-action model made especially for the army in 1873, and this one was a special order by his stepfather's friend and Strongheart's new friend Chris Colt, who was a nephew of inventor Colonel Samuel Colt.

On his left hip was the long beaded, porcupine-quilled, and fringed leather knife sheath holding the large Bowie-like knife with the elk antler handle and brass inlays. It was left to him by his father.

He wore long cowboy boots with large-roweled spurs with two little bell-shaped pieces of steel that hung down on the outside from each of the hubs and clinked on the spur rowels as they spun or while he walked. These were called jinglebobs.

Joshua stuck out his hand saying, "Sir, I heard you were looking for me. My name is Joshua Strongheart, and what is your name, sir?"

A little of the trepidation disappeared while the kid's shoulders went back a little, and he shook hands with his hero. He tried to lower his voice and said, "Howdy, sir. My name is Scottie Middleton."

Joshua stuck out his hand and shook, saying, "I like that. You have a good, firm handshake and you look a man in the eye. Now, what can I do for you, young man?"

"Well, Mr. Strongheart," the tyke said, "I want to hire you."

Strongheart looked over at the sheriff and grinned.

He replied, "You want to hire me? What makes you want to do that?"

Scottie said, "Yer a Pinkerton agent, ain't ya?"

Strongheart said, "I am that Scottie. So, what is this all about?"

"Well, sir," Scottie said bravely but still nervously, "my pa said that you are the best there is even though you are a blanket nigger."

Joshua interrupted, grinning. "Son, first let's start things off right. Do you think calling me a blanket nigger is the kind of language we should use for somebody that does not look like us?"

Scottie hung his head and Strongheart felt bad. He knew this must be tough for him already,

He said, "Go ahead, Scottie."

"Well," Scottie said, "my ma died last year of consumption. Then some bad men come last month and killed my pa."

"I am so sorry, Scottie," Joshua said. "Do you have folks to live with?"

Scottie said, "Yes, sir. My sister and I live with my aunt Kathy and my uncle Dave, but he is a drunk and don't amount to much. She is nice to me."

Strongheart said, "So what did you mean you wanted to hire me?"

The little boy reached into his trousers and pulled out a small leather bag, He opened it and marbles rolled out on the desk. He reached in and pulled out some change and held it out.

He said, "Mr. Strongheart, I saved me up some money and have four dollars here. I want to hire you to find the men who stole my pony Johnny Boy and get him back for me. Ma and Pa gave me Johnny Boy last Christmas, and it is all I have from them. That gang a men burnt our house down when they kilt Pa."

Strongheart winked at the sheriff.

He said, "Well, Scottie, you brought too much money. I only charge one dollar to recover ponies." He took one dollar in change from Scottie's hand.

Scottie beamed.

He said, "My pa told me to always sign a paper when you make a deal. But I heard you was gonna marry that sweet Missus Ebert, the widow woman with the café and she got kilt. But I heard, before, some bad men stole her ring and you give your word you would get it back. Then I heard you went out and tracked each of them down and kilt them and got her ring back. I just want to know if you will give me your word to get me Johnny Boy back."

Strongheart got choked up thinking about Belle Ebert who had been murdered earlier in the year by the seven-foot-tall Lakota mass murderer named We Wiyake, Blood Feather. The monster paid dearly for that, his greatest mistake ever.

Scottie's words snapped him out of it as he heard the little boy get choked up, too, while saying, "I can't have my ma and pa back, but getting Johnny Boy back would be kinda like getti' part a them back, Mr. Strongheart."

Joshua stuck out his hand and said, "If he is alive, I give you my word I will get him back for you."

The little boy proudly shoved his hand into Strongheart's, and they shook.

He said, "Scottie, I will need you to tell me everything that you can remember about those men. Sheriff, I remember hearing about this case and believe you had a posse after them for a while. I need to know all the details."

The following day, shortly before daybreak, Joshua Strongheart rode his big majestic half-Arabian, half-Saddlebred black-and-white pinto, Eagle, out of Cañon City headed in pursuit of the killer horse thieves. First though, he stopped at Scottie Middelton's house, where he lived with his aunt and uncle, on River Street. He had to cross the Fourth Street Bridge over the fast-moving Arkansas River. The Arkansas River due west of Cañon City, where it churned its way through a rocky canyon for miles, dropped thousands of feet and produced some of the largest and wildest whitewater rapids in the world. After it poured out of the Grand Canyon of the Arkansas, which was starting to be called the Royal Gorge, the whitewater rapids disappeared pretty much, but the water still rushed with more power than most rivers in the West.

Seeing Scottie's place he rode up to the front of the modest home, dismounted, and Scottie rushed out of the house, grinning broadly. A middle-aged woman with a kind but haggard face walked out, and Strongheart doffed his hat to her. She was followed by a staggering brute of a man who obviously had been drinking.

As Strongheart walked up to the group, he said, "You have a fine young man here in this nephew of yours. My name is Joshua Strongheart." He tipped his hat brim again. This brought a big smile to her tired but pretty face.

Strongheart walked straight up to the uncle and said, "And you must be Dave."

The man started to say something, but his words were

shut off when Joshua suddenly reached out and grabbed him, spinning him around. He then grabbed the back of the man's unkempt hair, then grabbed the waistline of his homespun trousers in his other hand, jerked up, and gave it a twist. Now holding Dave up on his tiptoes, he started marching him toward the river in a rapid manner. Reaching the river's edge, Strongheart pitched the drunk into the cold glacial-fed water. The man went under and came up ten yards downstream gasping and flailing at the water, while his family watched from the house in horror. Strongheart jogged along the river's edge and waded into the water at a shallower spot.

He grabbed the drunken uncle and pulled him to the water's edge, dragging him up on the bank. The man lay there gasping and sputtering.

He finally sat up and said, "What d'ja do that fer?"

As the man flinched, Joshua reached down, grabbed him by the collar and dragged him, screaming, back into the water. He held him by the lapels and shoved his head under the fast-flowing current and held it there. After several more times, Strongheart pulled him out of the water and once again up onto the bank, where the man moaned and groaned and sputtered for several minutes.

"I did all that," Strongheart said, "just to make sure I had your full attention. Are you paying very close attention?"

"Yes, sir!" the uncle said with great enthusiasm.

Strongheart said, "Good. That is a fine young man, and he recently lost his ma and pa. He needs a strong man in his life to teach him how to grow into a man. Just like me, mister, you cannot hold your liquor. Therefore, just like me, you are making an iron-clad decision today, right now, to stop drinking. If you don't, every time I am in town and find out you drank, you will go back into the river but a little longer each time. Do we understand each other?"

Now the uncle's masculinity had been challenged, so he flexed his whiskey muscles and straightened his back a little, hand hovering near his pistol, saying, "Yeah, wal, what if ya was to try to throw me in the river, and I yanked my hogleg and put some holes in ya first?"

Joshua stepped forward, his own hand near his gun, saying angrily, "Go ahead, grab that smoke pole, and start the dance! Please do. Skin it! Draw down on me, and see if I don't punch your dance ticket for you!"

Joshua moved in as the man's eyes opened as wide as a canyon, and he obviously was in a panic, looking for a place to hide. Strongheart's hand shot out, grabbed the uncle, by the lapels, and by pulling and taking two steps backward, he flung the uncle through the air one-handed. The man hit the river once more with a splash and came up sputtering and coughing again.

Strongheart walked back up to the front of the house and took the reins from a broadly grinning Scottie and mounted up. He doffed his hat to Scottie's aunt and got a slight self-satisfied smirk and almost hidden grin and nod of gratitude from her. He galloped away from the house, and rode toward the depot. He would telegraph Lucky, his boss in Chicago, to keep him apprised of what he was doing, then book a train to Pueblo and from there north to Denver.

A few reports stated that a gang had been in Denver and had moved into the mountains northwest of there. He suspected it was the gang responsible for killing Scottie's pa. The pony, Johnny Boy, which was not albino but pure white, had been used as a pack animal. He got a train fairly quickly to Pueblo but had a two-hour wait there before he could load Eagle on a car and get a seat himself.

It was nighttime before Joshua had gotten Eagle fed,

bedded down in a livery stable, got dinner, and a hotel room. He was going to be busy the next day, he knew.

The next day at daybreak, Strongheart went to the Pinkerton Agency office in Denver and started researching all the reports he could find about the gang. He found two of the alerts indicated the gang had been in a place in Denver called the Cowboy Saloon and were nothing but trouble. He would start there.

He rode toward downtown crossing a bridge over Cherry Creek and pulled up in front of the Cowboy Saloon, which was in a two-story redbrick building with rooms above it. He tied Eagle to a hitching rack and went inside. He was almost knocked over by painted ladies, and there was a man with gartered sleeves in the corner playing tunes on a piano. It was raucous, and he saw a number of drinkers giving him dirty looks, probably simply because he was an outsider.

Six cowpunchers confronted him: Two were white, two were black, one was Jicarilla Apache, and one was Mexican. They came up around him at the bar giving him the evil eye.

The bartender said, "What do you want?"

Joshua said, "I need some information about a gang that was in here causing trouble."

The bartender grinned, saying, "Mister, information does not go across this bar if money is not being spent."

Strongheart smiled. "Fair enough. There is a new drink just been around a few years I have taken a liking to. It is called iced tea. You serve that?"

The bartender pulled a jug of sun tea from behind the counter and chipped some ice off a block, filling a mug with tea.

He handed it to Joshua saying, "I have taken a hankering to it myself."

Joshua said, "Then let me buy you a glass, too. Here, this should take care of both of us."

He tossed ten bucks on the bar. The bartender made himself a glass of iced tea, too, and they touched glasses in salute.

The bartender said, "The gang is called the Teamsters, 'cause every dang one a them drove a freight wagon in this area. We got over a hundred people moving into Denver every single day, and these boys found out instead of earning honest keep it was a lot easier to steal possessions from innocent families. Their leader is a big man, even bigger than you. His name is Crabs Hamrick. Red hair and big, big frame. He grabs ahold a something, it moves."

Strongheart said, "That sounds like them. Do they have a white pony they are using as a pack animal?"

The bartender said, "That's them all right. Suspected in two killings of new settlers lately. They busted this place up and beat up one of our girls upstairs one night just out of meanness. I heard they have a hideout on the Cache La Poudre up beyond Fort Collins maybe ten, twenty miles. You know where I'm talking about?"

Strongheart said, "I have heard from others about it. Have not been up that river myself."

The bartender looked at the six men who were closing in a lot on Strongheart, obviously trying to make him feel uncomfortable.

He gave Joshua a questioning look and Joshua quietly said, "That back door, what is behind it?"

"Just empty fields, then trees along Cherry Creek, why?"

Strongheart said, "If I want to get those bad boys, first I will need to take care of these."

He turned around and faced the six cowhands, who had clearly been doing some drinking. They each braced themselves for trouble and two let their hands hover near their six-guns.

Joshua said, "Boys, you seem very friendly, so let me buy each of you a glass of iced tea. It tastes great on a hot day, especially if you add sugar."

One of the white punchers seemed to be the leader, and they were all young.

He said, "We don't need your stupid dandy-boy drink, mister."

He started to say more, but Strongheart's upraised hand stopped him. "Wait, gentlemen." He took a long swallow of iced tea and said, "Hate to see you pass this up. As soon as I walked in I saw what was going to happen. You don't know me, so you guys want to come up and sniff around, pee on trees, and growl a little, and see if I act like a coyote or a rabbit. Come with me, please."

Curious, but still trying to look tough, they followed him to the back door. He opened it and faced the doorway.

Strongheart said, "Just watch."

He set the glass with just the little bit remaining of his iced tea on the back of his hand palm down. He balanced it there, and several other patrons gathered around, curious. It was a blur when his hand whipped down and suddenly his Colt Peacemaker exploded and pieces of glass, ice, and tea flew everywhere in the back. He had drawn his pistol that fast, cocked it, and fired, shattering the glass before it had even dropped five inches. Joshua then smiled, spun the Colt backward into the holster.

The leader said, "Wow! I have never seen shooting like that anywhere! Sorry to bother ya, mister. We was just going to fun ya a little."

Strongheart said, "I was just leaving anyway."

He stopped by the bartender and asked what the glass cost.

The bartender said, "You're Strongheart, ain't you?"

Joshua said, "Afraid so. How much for the glass?"

The man said, "No worry on the glass. When you walked in here I figgered you was Strongheart from all I have heard. I am pleased to meet you, sir. Ed LeDoux."

He stuck out his hand. They shook and Joshua tipped his hat.

"Thanks, Ed. Guess I better get to Fort Collins."

He went out the door and the six cowpunchers walked to the door and windows and watched him ride away.

The bartender called them over and said, "You owl hoots better start watching who you try to tangle with. That was the Pinkerton agent Joshua Strongheart."

The tallest cowboy, who was black and had a thick Southern accent, said, "Y'all hear that? Ah tole y'all he looked like trouble when he come in. I tole ya not to bother him. Y'all coulda got me kilt dead. Gimme a whiskey, Ed."

Strongheart had to take another train north where he could unload at Fort Collins, which was about sixty miles north of Denver.

Scottie's uncle moped around the house for the next day, and several times he started to head to his favorite saloon on the corner of Fourth Street and Main Street. Each time, he thought about his dunking and the look on Strongheart's face when he braced him and that stopped him. He remembered most being flung through the air, one-handed, as though he were a rag doll.

The second day, he got up shortly after daybreak and his wife noticed he was shaky.

He smiled for the first time in years and said, "I'm going into town and see if I can get a job at the territorial prison or driving a stagecoach."

She had not been so excited and happy in years and made him a heaping breakfast.

Scottie took all this in and thought about what a hero Joshua Strongheart was and vowed he would grow up to be just like him. In fact, Scottie at first decided he would become a Pinkerton agent someday, but then decided he would be a town marshal or a county sheriff.

Two days later, Joshua was riding in the Cache La Poudre river canyon along the river trail. The mountains on both sides were heavily wooded with tall timber and were on very steep, very high ridges. High up in several places he saw little white spots moving in the alpine areas and knew these were Rocky Mountain goats. Twice, he passed bighorn sheep herds watering at the river, and he came upon a pack of wolves feeding on a cow moose carcass near the river. In fact, moose tracks were what made him turn left and head southwest away from the river along a raging whitewater creek with many large boulders and waterfalls in it. Strongheart knew it had to lead to some flat areas, maybe a lake, because that is what moose like. It had to have good moose habitat, or they would not have turned up this offshoot canyon. He figured that would also provide good opportunities for a hideout for a gang for extended periods, plenty of good graze for horses, water, firewood, and plenty of hiding places both rocky and wooded. He knew what his friend Chris Colt already knew: Common sense was the most important aspect of tracking anybody or any animal.

Eagle's ears were where most of Strongheart's focus remained. They were like radar beacons. If there was a sound off to the side, the ears twisted toward it, if someone approached from behind, they turned backward. If the big pinto scented someone to the front, his ears would go forward, listening for any perceptible sound.

Joshua's eyes swept the ground in front of him in wide arcs back and forth going out twenty yards ahead, then thirty, and forty. He was riding the stream trail on a hill that ran above the whitewater creek with straight drops down of about fifty feet. Joshua noticed the leaves on the trees were being blown from the left to the right and the longer weeds were bending to the right. At the same time he spotted what he had been looking for, a sloping down to the stream with a well-worn trail going to and from. This is where somebody had been getting water as well as watering horses.

At the same time, Eagle turned his head to the left and his eyes looked up the steep vegetation-covered ridge, his ears directed that way, and Joshua saw his nostrils were flaring in and out. He whinnied and far up the ridge an answering whinny came back.

Strongheart patted his neck saying, "Good boy, Eagle. Now we have to keep going because they will watch us to make sure we are not a threat. They heard their horse a lot easier than we did."

He kept riding up the trail acting like a hunter or trapper and not like he was looking for signs of the gang. Up on the ridge, one of the Teamsters watched through his binoculars and saw the man far below nonchalantly riding down the trail. He kept watching until Strongheart was out of sight and rejoined his friends at their game of poker.

Joshua waited until he could no longer be seen, then turned left and started going up the slope, going back and forth in a switchback. He climbed Eagle up about two thousand feet, estimating the outlaws were maybe a thousand feet higher than the trail he had been on. Strongheart dismounted and let Eagle get rested up after the climb. Directly above him there were cliffs and down below he saw a kind of a broken terrace in the landscape. Apparently, the gang was camped on one of the terraces, which were each covered with lush green grass. Unlike the area around Cañon City where he lived, which was semi-arid, this was northern Colorado territory. There was much more rain and snow in this area, and consequently a lot more green vegetation. Right around Cañon City there was much vegetation, because the area near the mighty Arkansas River was very lush and green, with many apple orchards and grape crops. In fact, years later it would come out that Cañon City had a wider variety of types of trees than any city in the entire country. Joshua knew these outlaws could stay up there out of sight for months, like a cat hiding from the dog on top of the china hutch.

Strongheart knew he was up against big numbers and a couple years earlier, he took on a gang of wannabe gunslingers in a shootout in Florence, Colorado. He got them all but was shot to doll rags himself, and it had taken months to recover. He decided back then while he was healing, he would never just wade in like that again, but think things through better first.

He would first ride along the base of the cliffs and work his way around the many giant rock slides with horse-sized and even house-sized boulders in several places. Then, he would get himself into a position above them and make a strategic plan to take on all these men. He could go and fetch a posse, but that would take days not hours, and they might well be gone then. He had given his word to Scottie and shaken hands on it. To Joshua Strongheart, that was like engraving it in stone.

He rode along slowly, carefully for an hour and found a shadowed place among a large jumble of boulders that formed almost a cave with no roof. He let Eagle rest here and nibble on the grasses in the hideout, while he went out and looked down at the outlaw camp. He remained there watching until dusk, and saw they started preparing their cooking fire.

Strongheart retreated into the rocks himself, gathered some firewood, and made a smokeless fire. He made the fire and checked to make sure it would not reflect off the rocks where the men to his northeast and far below could see it or any smoke coming out of his rock formation. A plan was forming in his mind.

He gave Eagle a bait of oats from an oilskin bag in his saddlebags, then started his own dinner. He ate and bedded down early, not drinking any coffee, so he could go to sleep.

Strongheart awakened after midnight and went to his lookout spot in the rocks, glassing with his binoculars. As he figured, they were all sleeping in a circle around their campfire. There was one guard in front of the fire on a log drinking coffee.

Joshua went to his saddlebags and took out four leather horse boots. He slipped these over Eagle's hooves and tied them in place with the leather thongs laced through the tops of each. He saddled up without saddlebags. Eagle stood in anticipation of going on another great adventure with his master. He could not actually think that way, but he sensed something exciting was up.

Strongheart took off his boots and spurs and replaced them with his soft-soled porcupine-quilled Lakota moccasins. Mounting up, he rode slowly, quietly down the mountainside, noting that the guard was already dozing off by the fire and getting himself into a more comfortable position. Joshua left Eagle under some tall trees one hundred feet above the camp and started moving down on foot through the shadows. He spotted little Johnny Boy grazing with the remuda. He made his way as only a Lakota warrior could do, silently, to the horses. He tied a war bridle on Johnny Boy and led him away from the remuda and up to Eagle. The two sniffed each other, touching noses, and seemed to understand they had to be quiet and ignore normal herd seniority blustering like horses usually do. He let each eat a carrot-flavored horse biscuit he pulled from his pocket.

The Pinkerton agent then worked his way back to the camp and crawled on his belly from man to man with many snores piercing the silence of the forest night. It took an hour for Strongheart to accomplish his task and sneak away. So far, his plan was working. Not wanting to risk knocking a rock loose, he led both horses up the mountain and returned to his campsite. He did not want to risk sleeping too long, so he poured himself a cup of coffee while he put his boots and spurs back on. He checked his pistol and then retrieved his belly gun from his saddlebag. He made sure it was clean and loaded. He replaced his bedroll and saddlebags behind the seat on his roughout saddle, then sat and waited while he enjoyed more coffee and a few corn dodgers.

The birds were starting to sing and some crows started cawing overhead, but it was the blue jay screaming that awakened the first outlaw. He looked up and saw Strongheart astride Eagle grinning at him. Joshua nodded.

"Morning, boys!" he hollered.

Within seconds, they were all standing, blinking and rubbing their eyes. Several dropped into a gunfighter's stance.

Joshua said, "I wouldn't reach for those guns fellas. Might be a good way to get shot. You will be the Teamsters, right?"

One large one with red hair and twice the bulk of the others stepped forward.

"Who the hell are you?" he bellowed.

The Pinkerton said, "Joshua Strongheart," and he noticed several exchange nervous glances. He added, "I work for the Pinkerton Detective Agency, and I was hired by a young boy named Scottie Middleton to get this pony back you boys stole. I assume you are Crabs Hamrick?"

"Yeah, that's me. Ain't ya gonna ask me why I'm called that?" The big man fumed.

Strongheart said, "No, I don't really care."

"How could that little brat hire ya? What did he pay ya?" Hamrick roared.

Strongheart smiled and said, "One dollar."

"You come all this way to die over a dollar?" Crabs said.

"No, it was the price we agreed and shook on. I gave my word I would get him his pony back, and a man is only as good as his word," Strongheart said, and his steely stare into Crabs's eyes unnerved the man.

"Now, which one of you cowards shot that boy's father?" he added.

Crabs puffed his chest out and said, "I did, but it don't matter. That pony ain't going nowhere, and you are gonna die where ya stand."

His hand flashed first as he drew, which spurred all the others into drawing, and Strongheart cleared leather before any of them and just grinned as he heard gun after gun make a metallic clicking sound.

"Oh yeah," he said with a smile. "I forgot to tell you. I visited your camp last night while you were all sleeping and unloaded your weapons. The bullets are in my saddlebags here, but then again, you won't be needing them."

One of the other Teamsters stepped up and said, "Bullets or not, we all got knives. We can rush him boys, and he can't get all of us."

The gangster took one step and Joshua's left hand gun, his belly gun, fired and half the man's ear disappeared. The man grabbed what was left of his ear screaming in pain.

Strongheart said, "You are playing a rough game, mister. You can wrap it with your scarf. The rest of you, see if you can grab a handful of clouds. Except you, Crabs. Load your gun."

Crabs Hamrick felt like somebody had stepped on his grave. Shaking slightly, his loaded his gun and kept thinking about a snapshot but decided against it. He had heard about this man over and over. He holstered his gun.

Strongheart said, "You killed an unarmed hardworking man and left his little boy and little girl fatherless for the rest of their lives. You have six shots to kill me, Hamrick. You better make every one count. I am at least giving you a chance. Fill your hand, mongrel."

Crabs's eyes opened wide as he clawed frantically for his gun and had it almost halfway out of the holster when he looked into the two barrels of Strongheart's Colt Peacemakers and saw flame shoot out of them. They slammed into his chest, and he saw the trees and the sky as he folded backward and felt a weakness spreading through him. He was going to die and go to hell.

He heard the words of the outlaw next to him say, "Gee, two bullets right in the middle of the chest. Crabs is dead, boys."

He wanted to scream that he wasn't, but his mouth would not work, then everything went blank.

Strongheart said, "Drop the holsters and get ready to move. Fort Collins will have nice warm cells for you. You can order a late breakfast there."

Scottie was playing in front of the house with his sister. His uncle was at his new job at the territorial prison.

His aunt was beating a rug, and then with tears glistening in her eyes, she said, "Scottie, here comes Mr. Strongheart, and he's leading Johnny Boy!"

Looking at the tall handsome man leading his pony down River Drive, Scottie wanted to scream with joy, but he puffed his chest out, saying, "I knew he would, Auntie. A man is only as good as his word."

Now, over a year later, Scottie was bigger but riding Johnny Boy, making the pony look a little smaller with Scottie's growth. Scottie saw Joshua and rode forward quickly. He rode up next to him and reached up shaking hands.

Strongheart said, "Howdy, Scottie. You sure are getting tall. Have you been keeping your nose clean?"

Scottie beamed saying, "Yes, sir. I have been working at the sheriff's office some days cleaning and stuff."

Strongheart said, "I just wanted to see how you are doing."

Scottie beamed, "I'm fine, sir. My uncle is nice to me now and works at Old Max."

Strongheart fished in his pocket and pulled out a new pocketknife. He handed it to Scottie, who looked at it with great happiness.

Joshua said, "I picked you up a little gift in Denver that I thought you could use."

"Thank you, sir!" Scottie said. "Thank you, Mr. Strongheart."

"Keep it sharp, Scottie. See you around."

With that, he put the spurs to Eagle and lit out heading back across the river and then turning west.

19

THE FINAL BATTLE

Eagle trotted proudly as Joshua continued west, passing Old Max territorial prison and the Hot Springs Hotel. The road turned to the right and headed uphill toward Eight Mile Hill. A mile up the road, he came to the entrance of the wagon trail that ran along the crest of the Hogback, known by some as Razor Ride, which in 1908 in Cañon City would be renamed Skyline Drive. The Hogback was a long narrow ridge that bordered Cañon City on the west, rising eight hundred feet up in elevation above the town. The trail was created by some locals traveling the ridge of the Hogback overlooking the entire area.

A local rancher, D. E. Gibson, hitched a team of horses to a handmade plow and attempted to plow and cut a road up across the razor back ridge, but he was not successful. After that, Colonel Frederick E. Greydene-Smith suggested building a road there where the trail existed. In fact, many, many citizens of Fremont county suggested a road on the Hogback, as early as 1860. However, the road eventually called Skyline Drive would be built in 1908 using sixty prison inmates.

More importantly, Razor Ridge, or the Hogback, was the

vantage point where the giant murderer Blood Feather hid
despite his giant size and kept both Strongheart and his fiancée
under surveillance before murdering her when Strongheart
was away. Joshua would now camp out with Eagle and hide
on the eight-hundred-foot ridgeline to watch for Robert Hartwell or his henchmen, and then he would plan his strategy. No
matter where they went around Cañon City, Joshua could keep
them under his watchful eyes for miles in any direction.

   In Denver, Robert Hartwell had arrived and was assem-
bling his gang, or what was left of it. They met in the back
of the Cowboy Saloon, oddly enough, the place where
Strongheart had a run-in with several would-be toughs when
he was trying to get Scottie Middleton's pony back. By coincidence, Hartwell knew of the Cowboy Saloon and chose
to meet there, so no Pinkerton agents would be lurking at
the one he owned.

   Unbeknownst to him, Andy Vinnola and his brother
Antonio, both very good Pinkerton agents, had Hartwell
under surveillance from the time he first arrived at the railroad depot in Denver. Both men had Italian ancestry, so they
had olive skin, black hair, and dark eyes. Their parents came
over from Sicily, landed in New York, and worked hard for
many years to take care of their four children. Andy and
Antonio also labored for much of their youth, struggling at
various jobs trying to help keep the family together. However, when Andy and Antonio finally left the nest, they felt
like two caged birds who had been freed.

   Since they looked like they were related, they took seats
at a table nearby, where they could speak loudly, saying words
like "our sister" or "the family," knowing Hartwell would be
focusing on their voices, just in case. In the meantime, they
would eavesdrop on Hartwell's conversation with his gang
and then report their findings by telegram to both Strongheart

in Cañon City and Lucky in Chicago at Pinkerton headquarters. Joshua would come down off the Hogback each afternoon to check for telegrams about Lucky DeChamps.

Hartwell said, "I was going to send an advanced team to Cañon City before the rest of us, but that scoundrel killed two of our best men. Strongheart must be killed because he knows too much now about my business dealings. We will all go down there together, and we will hunt him down. If he tries to hide, we will find him, and we will fill him with holes like a sieve. Our train to Pueblo leaves at daybreak, then we will ride our horses from Pueblo to Cañon City, that's thirty-some miles, so we will arrive in Cañon City in two days. I will give a bonus of $1,000 in gold coin to the man who fires the bullet that kills that varmint. That stinking half-breed red nigger needs to be wiped off the face of the earth, and we're going to do it, boys."

Andy Vinnola wrote a telegraph to Strongheart and Pinkerton headquarters, which read, "RH leaves tomorrow am to Pueblo STOP then mounted to CC. STOP ETA in CC 2 days STOP 9 men total END."

Strongheart chuckled to himself and rode Eagle right to Schwinn's Saloon and Emporium at the east end of town because that was a center of gossip, and Joshua knew Robert Hartwell's men would want to stop there for a brew when they were done riding from Pueblo. Additionally, Hartwell would want to find out where Strongheart was, and saloons were the local news station in every town in the West.

Joshua left Eagle at the hitching rail by simply dropping his reins. When training the big pinto, he would cross his reins over the saddle or rig them to the saddlehorn, and he then would teach Eagle to walk behind him. After that, he had tied several lead lines to pieces of log he buried in the ground. He would ride up to each length of lead line, dismount, and drop his reins. However, he would first attach the lead line to the bottom of Eagle's bridle without letting Eagle look down at what he was doing. Then he would walk away. Eagle would try to follow and the lead line stopped him. It did not take too many times of dropping the reins and tying him for him to learn to stand still when he was ground reined.

He went into the noisy, smoky saloon and saw three Ute Indian cowboys at the bar. Seeing he was a half-breed, they nodded. Then he saw a variety of citizens, cowboys, and local ranch people that he recognized. He knew some of them knew who he was and did enjoy celebrity status in southern Colorado, so he knew as many as possible would try to listen in on his talk with the barkeep. He stepped up to the bar, and a muttonchopped gray-haired man with a friendly smile and garters on his sleeves came over and shook.

"Mr. Strongheart, ah heerd you never imbibe," the bartender said, "What'll ya' have, suh?"

Joshua smiled, saying, "You heard right. Give me a glass of that new drink, iced tea, if you have any."

"Shore 'nuff," the man replied. "Want sugar with it? Some folks love it that way."

"No, thanks. Just straight and icy please. I'm going to head up Grape Creek tomorrow and do some fishing, hunting, and relaxing for a few days," Joshua replied, making sure he was speaking loud enough for a few others to hear him.

He spent a few more minutes there talking, and positively knew that Robert Hartwell would know that Strongheart was headed up Grape Creek.

He left that saloon and repeated the same at McClure's Saloon downtown, then rode toward the Hot Springs Hotel.

Joshua had pursued the killer We Wiyake, Blood Feather, all the way up Grape Creek in the dead of winter, when the madman had kidnapped Belle's little niece. Strongheart saved the girl, and also became intimately familiar with the whole Grape Creek area. Grape Creek essentially carried most of the water from the Wet Mountain Valley up near Westcliffe, starting at an elevation of 8,100 feet and dropping to 6,000 feet north or northeast for about twenty-five miles until it poured into the powerful Arkansas River right across from the Hot Springs Hotel. It was very rugged rocky country with many rock formations along the way. Also, going south and southwest toward Westcliffe, from its mouth at the Arkansas he had many hiding places and ambush sites to choose from. If he went all the way to Westcliffe along Grape Creek, he would first pass by or through Temple Canyon, then going south, Volcano Gulch, Sawmill Gulch, Pine Gulch, Isinglass Gulch, Bear Gulch, East Mill Gulch, Democrat Creek and Gulch, Dead Mule Gulch, Four Mile Gulch, and finally its headwaters right near the town of Westcliffe, where the Deweese Reservoir would be erected in 1902.

Instead of staying up on the Hogback, he would wait a day and take a pack horse and some tools and head up the rugged rocky waterway. He had some surprises planned for the gang. Those surprises should help even his odds quite a bit.

In fact, he thought, he would ride out toward Pueblo because he knew that the gang would surely camp for the night at Beaver Creek and then have a relatively easy ride into Cañon City the next day. If he was wrong and they did not, he would travel fast and simply cut south and west through Florence to get to Grape Creek before them.

The next day, after riding across prairie all day, by late afternoon, the gang pulled into an area that suddenly dipped down into a small canyon through which Beaver Creek ran before meeting the Arkansas less than two miles away. There were

many tall cottonwoods along the clear cool stream and steep
rock cliffs that rose up out of the canyon. They rode to the
west of the wagon/coach road and found a private spot to make
camp and found circles of rocks, and even some firewood,
where numerous others had chosen this to camp before.
Strongheart was on the high ground watching and grinning.

When a bee or wasp stings, it will inject a venomous sting
in the skin of the victim. However, white with black stripes,
bald-faced hornets have a smooth stinger, so they can sting
a person or animal more than once. In fact, when they get
angry, they can sting many times.

Like most wasps, the bald-faced hornets have a caste system, in one nest, featuring the queen, a fertile female that
starts the colony and lays eggs; then workers, which are infer-
tile females that maintain the nest and young; then drones,
which are young males, with no stingers, and are born from
unfertilized eggs; and new queens—fertile females, each of
which may become a queen when fertilized and start a colony.
Finally, there are the males who fertilize queens and are the
ones that can really get angry and start stinging.

Their nest looks like it is made out of layers of paper. In
fact, it almost looks like papier-mâché. It is generally anywhere from one to four feet in size and oblong in shape.
From his uncles and late father's friends, he learned how to
easily transport a bald-faced hornet's nest without getting
stung. At night, all the hornets go into the nest in a hole in
the bottom. There are also a few other holes produced
because of them constructing their nest around branches
and twigs. Strongheart had seen a hornet's nest in the cottonwoods along Beaver Creek when he had camped there
previously. So, the night before, he got the nest, carefully
covering the main entrance-egress hole on the bottom, and
each smaller hole made around branches and twigs he broke

off. Now, he had all the hornets in one nest. He rode Eagle up on the high ground, looking over the campsite and waited, making his own dry camp.

The night passed and Joshua was up well before dawn. He watched as the men all awakened the next morning, making coffee, and one had made breakfast for all. Strongheart waited until they all had coffee and food and were looking forward to the rest of the day and maybe killing him. He chuckled to himself, shook the flimsy nest, pulled the plug out of the bottom, and tossed it over the cliff, with it landing an arm's length from the cooking fire. Joshua laughed and laughed watching the men down below yelling, running, swatting at hornets, except Hartwell, who immediately grabbed his slicker and draped himself like a mummy. One was allergic to the stings and died of shock an hour later, but by then Joshua and his pack horse were well on their way to Grape Creek, by way of Florence and then to Oak Creek Grade.

Hartwell was now finally afraid. This man had outfoxed him at every turn it seemed like, but the man was also too egomaniacal to even consider the fact that Joshua might beat him, let alone kill him. He only had two stings and one man had been stung dozens of times, and several had been stung at least a dozen times each. The whole gang was totally miserable and complained all the way into Cañon City, which was a three hour ride away if they walked the horses, which was the only wise way to handle them.

They immediately and easily found Schwinn's Saloon and Emporium when they rode into Cañon City, and every one of them was ready for a drink or more. They spent two hours there, and got advice from half the patrons on how to take care of their stings. They rode out with poultices made of chewed-up tobacco, bicarbonate of soda mixed with spit into a paste, and several other homespun remedies.

They also rode out with the information they needed about Strongheart heading up Grape Creek, and they went into town looking for a prospectors' supply store or general store where they might get a map of the area. They also got more supplies and bought extra ammunition.

They were directed to the Hot Springs Hotel, and it was suggested the hot mineral water would help their stinger wounds. Robert Hartwell sprang for several rooms, not because he was considerate, but because he wanted his hired guns healthy. They would soak in the water that night and leave the next morning up Grape Creek ready to kill.

This gave Strongheart even more time to prepare his surprises for them.

Cañon City was very snugly tucked into a bowl of rocks and hills. Surrounded on three sides by mountains, directly to the east, toward Pueblo was prairie, but with some small ridges and short rolling hills first. Protected by the mountains from the total assault of summer storms and the snowy carpeting of midwinter blizzards, it was also higher with cool mountain breezes making it cooler in the summer than Pueblo, but being protected, it was warmer than Pueblo in the winter. The next morning, the sun started baking distant Pueblo, and showed it was ready to blast its rays onto the hard rocks and towering rocky cliffs along both sides of Grape Creek. By noon, it was painfully obvious it was a very hot day, as the gang proceeded southwest along Grape Creek in the unforgiving hard rock funnel, which was channeling the heat onto the ten hard cases.

Riding in and along Grape Creek, they finally came to Pine Gulch. As they rode, they heard the echoes of their steel horseshoes clicking on the solid rock walls jutting straight up on their right for hundreds of feet, but out of the gulch off to their left they smelled the sweet odor of pine trees and felt a cooler breeze. Hartwell declared they would move into this gulch and make camp. Joshua Strongheart knew this would be the case, as it was the only place that made sense.

They made camp up Pine Gulch next to a spring and pick-eted their horses exactly where Joshua knew they would. It was well after dark. One guard sat in front of the fire drinking coffee, and another leaned against a rock to watch the horses, but was soon fast asleep, his head cocked off to the side. Joshua had been watching them from a rocky perch less than fifty feet above them while they prepared their camp. Wearing his moccasins, he slowly made his way through the path he had cleared of branches and sticks earlier. He then methodi-cally tied war bridles on each horse, then used their picket line as one giant lead line. He quietly led them out of the grove of trees, around a corner, and there mounted up on Eagle and led them at a fast trot several miles to Reed Gulch, which was full of rich grasses and flowing clear water. He then returned to the camp. Now, both sentries slept soundly.

Strongheart crawled into the campfire area, grabbed a cooled-down, ashen stick by the fire, and then crawled behind the one who was sentry for the fire and was now lying down sideways in front of the glowing embers. Slowly, carefully, he drew a big charcoal letter *X* on the back of the man's shirt. He barely stirred. Then, he crawled away to his hideout in the nearby overlooking rocks.

Strongheart earlier had prepared a passageway through the rocks and scrub oaks along the ridge that would totally mask his movements if he ran, crawled, or walked away along and over the ridge. He waited for dawn, taking a cat-nap himself.

Joshua enjoyed the smell of the evergreens wafting in along Pine Gulch and from Reed Gulch several miles away, where the horse remuda was grazing along toward Iron

Mountain. On his way back, he brushed their tracks away for the last mile toward the camp. He had already gone back covering their tracks in the trees where they were moved from the picket line.

Now, he grinned watching as Robert Hartwell and two of his top hands started yelling and screaming at the sentries. The men were complaining and grumbling and several started looking up into the rocks and off into the trees.

Strongheart hated back shooting, period, however these men had opened the ball in his mind and declared war on him, ten against one. He was going to punch their dance ticket for them, and do it on his terms. He carefully rose on one knee holding his Lakota bow in his left hand, a cedar arrow across his left hand, the nock of the arrow against the string, and the first three fingers of his right hand wrapped around the string, with the nock between his index and middle finger. He kept watching the guard by the fire, until he turned fully, exposing his back to him. When the man did turn, finally someone saw the X on his back, and started to say something. Before he could, though, Strongheart had drawn the arrow back, the heel of his thumb resting just under and in front of his ear. He took a breath, let half of it out, and held to the upper right of the man's chest. He concentrated on not snapping the string, and let the string slide smoothly off his fingertips, making sure he breathed through his nose and kept his mouth closed. Joshua knew that opening his mouth would lower the anchor point on his cheek and jaw and send the arrow over the target.

He watched it slice through the air and watched it enter the man's back right in the center of the large X. He took off crouching and running through the rocks and was almost over the ridge before the first of many bullets was fired at the ridgeline in his general direction in an attempt to find the hidden assassin by luck. The Pinkerton did not get to watch their reaction. Men were panicked, and Hartwell was furious. Nobody had to say anything. They knew that Strongheart had stolen their horses from under their noses, that he had done so while two armed guards were specifically watching the campfire and the horses, that he had placed a giant X on the back of the shirt of one of them, then in broad daylight put an arrow through the X, dead center, and hid or got away without even being seen. Several of the men present had been in the Midwest when he'd wreaked havoc on them.

Hartwell could not even speak he was so angry, and the man who was supposed to guard the horses said, "Mr. Hartwell, this Strongheart is more 'n a handful. We oughta scrap this . . ."

Boom! Boom! Hartwell had actually drawn his own pistol and shot the man in the stomach and chest, and he fell back over a log dying and screaming from the pain. Teeth bared, Hartwell faced all the rest of the gang,

He snarled, "Any other yellow curs here wanna tuck tail and run? Any takers?"

Men nervously shook their heads and waited to be told what to do next.

Seeing this, Hartwell pointed at three men together, and said, "You three, head up that gulch and see if you can pick up the trail of our remuda."

They looked at each other nervously, nodded, and took off carrying their carbines, with two drawing their pistols, too. It was easy, however, to hide tracks in this rocky sandy soil, and Joshua had already cut pine branches to blot out the tracks. Knowing the minds of outlaws, he figured that being lazy, they would give up in less than a mile. He was correct.

The three came back to the camp.

One said, "Mr. Hartwell, we checked for tracks way up the gulch, maybe a couple of miles. No sign."

Robert had sent another two out to search along Grape Creek in both directions. They came back in less than a half an hour.

"How did one man sneak in here, while we were all here, steal our horses with no one seeing, and make them disappear?" said Brandy Marks, his remaining top gun hand.

Hartwell said, "He thinks he has outsmarted us, but we are going to take care of him, Brandy. I am going to spit on his bloody body."

He sat drinking coffee, hoping his big black Thoroughbred might make it back to camp. The horse was smart, and it was the one thing he truly took good care of. That was because to him the horse was a tool that was superior to others. Also, because of its size, he felt much bigger riding that big horse.

His assumption was correct because the giant gelding was indeed coming back from Reed Gulch at a trot and a few others started to follow him. Pretty soon, they were all strung out, in a long spaced-out line.

The black rode by and then Eagle came galloping out of the trees behind him, and Strongheart waved his slicker at the others, yelling, and whooping. The black kept on toward its master, but the others were cut off, and ran the way they had come. He pursued them still waving the slicker and yelling louder.

Horses suffer from two afflictions. They are constant conditions. One is claustrophobia and the other is being prone to panic.

This small herd was now in the latter mode. Eyes opened wide, ears laid back, listening to the predator behind chasing them, getting more fearful with each wave of the slicker, they were running all out at full gallop back toward Reed Gulch. Once there they turned upstream, but Joshua ran around, cut them off, and sent them downstream well past the mouth of Pine Gulch. He knew they would start grazing and would be more likely to graze forward downhill on a slight angle, continuing to graze in that direction, as long as there was good grass and water.

By the time Joshua returned, he rode up on the ridge to the left, and watched the gang from the rocks with his telescope and started laughing. Robert Hartwell was up on his horse riding around the camp area barking out orders, and the whole scene was quite comical to the half-breed. The Indian Ring architect was watching his construction come unraveled, and he was becoming unraveled himself.

Strongheart thought about how appropriate this was that he, a man who walked back and forth between both worlds, might be taking down the leader and moving force behind the Indian Ring. He was a man of contradictions. He was a passionate Minniconjou Lakota warrior, but he was also a white lawman, a Pinkerton agent developing a national reputation, he was very adept with many weapons, yet he was very fond of quoting William Shakespeare.

In fact, looking down at the gang and knowing how important he felt it was to rid the world of them, he quoted Shakespeare aloud to himself, "'Tis best to weigh the enemy more mighty than he seems.'"

"Be careful, Josh. You finally have him where you want him," he went on.

Now, Robert Hartwell knew what direction the horses had been taken, because his gelding came from the direction of Reed Gulch. He sent the same three men back up the gulch and told them not to come back without the horses. Strongheart mounted up on the far side of the ridge to their right and rode off at a trot, planning to intercept them where they would be close enough for Hartwell and his men to hear gunshots but far enough that they could not walk or run and join in the gun battle.

The three men walked along in the gulch, carefully checking for tracks and signs and of course backtracking the very obvious tracks of the big Thoroughbred. Joshua checked from ahead several times, and could tell they were very nervous. He went on to intercept them.

It was getting closer to sundown when they came around a bend and one in the back found a trail with a couple hoof-prints in it passing through some trees.

He turned his head and said, "Y'all stand ready, boys! I got me some man tracks heah. Watch thet ground close but keep yer eyes on thet ridge!"

He followed the little trail and there were some seemingly windblown branches actually funneling him into the trail and into the grove of trees. It was a perfect place for Strongheart to have placed one of his surprises.

The eagle was a very sacred symbol of Native American culture and always has been. The plains tribes, such as Joshua's, never believed in killing eagles. In fact, the Plains tribes such as the Lakota believed in only taking feathers from a living eagle without hurting it. The way to accomplish this was by using an eagle trap. You had to be a select special warrior to even construct one or a net for catching eagles. Strongheart had carried a pick and shovel on his pack horse for just that such purpose. To construct one, the eagle trapper would make a large lid of small branches woven together, with a round cover bordered by bent branches. It was camouflaged and covered with leaves. He would dig a shallow grave-sized pit and lie on his back holding the lid over him. He would tie a captured rabbit to the lid by one leg, and wait. As the rabbit squealed and flailed around, eagles flying overhead would easily spot it, swoop down, and when it started to snatch it up, the brave would reach through the lid with one hand, grab the eagle's leg, and reach up with the other plucking several feathers. He would then release the leg.

The man tracking his carefully laid hoofprints was almost under the trees when gunfire erupted from the ground directly in front of him. He flew backward, the top of his head exploding. Strongheart stayed in his eagle trap listening and counting bullets as the other two, seeing their bloody friend die suddenly, fired wildly in the direction of the trees. They foolishly did not overlap fire and both ran out of bullets at around the same time and were trying to reload quickly when Joshua sat up, tossing the lid of the eagle trap to the side, and opened up with his carbine. He hit the one on the right dead center, killing him almost instantly, but he missed on the other one with his first shot, hit his left hip, spinning him with the second, and he carefully aimed the third shot and took the man in the head.

Down the gulch Hartwell and his men were completely unnerved hearing the shots, and each fearfully and correctly concluded that Strongheart had just had a shootout with those three men, and they were probably dead. Robert Hartwell's gang was now down to just a handful.

Not sure what to do, Hartwell saw that night would soon be upon them.

He said, "Men. Let's move our camp into those rocks where we have more cover, and we will make our camp smaller with no fire."

Brandy Marks, the only one with the courage to address Hartwell right now, said, "Boss, we are in the mountains and it will get cool tonight. He is watching us all, so no fire ain't going to fool him. Just make us cold. I need my gun hands warm, so they work right, boss."

Hartwell, scared out of his wits now, finally listened to someone and said, "That's a good point, Brandy."

Marks got several nods of approval from the other three. They made their fire and settled in. Dark closed in and the men sat around the fire drinking coffee and talking nervously.

Suddenly, the voice of Joshua Strongheart rang out from above them in the darkness, "You, men! My beef is with Hartwell! If any of you wants to walk out of here, just leave during the night, head down Grape Creek to Cañon City, and I will let you be! Anybody who is with Hartwell tomorrow morning is going to die! Make a sound decision!"

"I have always rode for the brand, boss," Brandy Marks said right away.

The others nodded like they agreed, but gave each other nervous looks.

Joshua knew they would stay in their camp until daybreak, so he headed back to the camp he'd made a mile away, where he left his pack horse. While Hartwell and his men sat in the rocks around a fire, most staying awake most of the night, listening for sounds, jumping over a rock that fell, Joshua had a nice fire in a grove of pines with scattered boulders, and he drank coffee and ate corn dodgers and a tin of peaches he had picked up in Cañon City. He knew if anybody came, Eagle would let him know. He slept soundly and woke up before dawn, well rested and ready to tackle the important challenge that lay before him this day.

By the time Joshua arrived at his overlook, it was dawn, and he pulled out his telescope just in time to see Brandy awaken and start yelling something that could not be heard. Hartwell jumped up drawing his six-shooter. They were alone. The other three had left an hour before dawn and were convinced that Brandy Marks and Robert Hartwell were dead men. Those three had no idea that the Vinnola brothers were waiting at the Hot Springs Hotel and watching for any that may come out of the Grape Creek canyon.

There was also another pair of eyes watching from the hotel. They had a twinkle in them. They belonged to Zachariah Banta, who always seemed to know where to go and knew everybody that should be known.

The three had left an hour before dawn and were fast-walking down Grape Creek as fast as they could move. Jumping at every shadow, they would walk fast, then jog a little while. Each felt like their mouths were filled with cotton, and two had severe pains in their lower abdomens. Their fear of what they had seen and had previously heard about Strongheart's actions in Indiana, had made them true believers that they would die if they stayed until daybreak. The three crawled away from the camp in their stockinged feet and then walked over rocks and even ran into cacti until they were well away from Robert Hartwell. Their feet were feeling it now.

Brandy Marks was not showing it at all. He had been through too much and was the classic hard case, but he was more frightened than he had ever been in his entire life. Two men had been killed under his guns for making fun of him for drinking brandy, his favorite drink. He always drank brandy simply because he liked the taste of it, but God help anybody who ever made jokes about it. Nonetheless, the nickname stuck with him. Brandy grew up in Akron, Ohio, in the area called North Hill, which was next to Cuyahoga Falls. He had a stepbrother who was two years older than him, and the stepbrother tried to sexually molest Brandy when Brandy was thirteen. The younger lad beat the stepbrother to death with a stout hickory club, then ran away from home knowing his mother would not even listen to his explanation and his stepfather would be out for blood. Moving out west, by the age of fourteen, Brandy was already riding the owl hoot trail.

Less than a decade earlier, people started referring to killers, bank robbers, bandits, and the likes as owl hoots. Then, the expression started that someone was *riding the owl hoot trail*, meaning he'd left a straight and narrow path for the life of a criminal. A cowboy in the Indian territory in 1870 explained that Indians used the sounds of hooting like owls to signal to each other when white men they were going to go into battle with were nearby. Some cowboys started calling them owl hoots, and because of so much being done in the shadows by criminals the nickname got transferred to them.

Robert Hartwell, on the other hand, was not frightened. He felt he was too superior to Joshua Strongheart. In his eyes, Joshua was impure, a half-breed. While it was a major source of pride for Strongheart to be that way, to a racist and elitist like Hartwell, it was disgusting. He often described Joshua Strongheart, not by his name, but as "that blanket nigger," or that "red nigger." However, Hartwell always thought he was superior to any man. The fact that he was very tiny and slight and plain-looking while Strongheart was very tall, muscular, and handsome, increased the hatred all the more.

As Joshua rode forward on his proud, prancing mount, Eagle, he understood this about Robert Hartwell. He knew this man was singularly responsible, probably even more than William W. Belknap, for building and strengthening the Indian Ring. The Indian Ring really was strengthened by the inaction or head-turning of some in the halls of power in Washington, D.C. Some invested money in the many larcenous Indian Ring trading posts operated by crooked handpicked sutlers. Belknap may have been the commanding general who got the credit or blame for the infamous Indian Ring, but Hartwell was his command sergeant major. He ran the operation, and he expanded the scope of the racist organization, which became an embarrassment, actually a disgrace and black mark on the U.S. government. Those who turned their heads in Congress and in the Grant administration were either investors, friends of investors, racists, or extremely selfish people in power who did not care about the decimation of the red man just so inroads could be made into their territory for westward expansion or mining exploration.

Joshua Strongheart rode that gulch toward a confrontation with pure evil times two. He found their tracks. Robert Hartwell had decided they should return to Cañon City, so he could recruit a new gang of toughs and then go after Strongheart again. They were exiting Pine Gulch, and Joshua assumed they would turn north toward Cañon City when they got back to Grape Creek.

He started galloping Eagle north, crossing over ridges at low points and saddles. His horse was half-Arabian and could go for hours in this heat without breaking a sweat. Often Eagle had walked other horses into the ground trying to keep up with him all day. On top of that, Hartwell and Marks could only travel as fast as Brandy's speed walking would allow. Joshua knew that Robert Hartwell would not even consider letting Brandy ride double with him. He was too haughty and above anybody else in his mind.

Strongheart would be waiting for them once again when they came northeast along Grape Creek and the showdown would happen. Joshua decided if he ever survived anything in his life, he must survive this fight. He was representing his mother's people. He was representing his father's people. He represented the country he loved. He knew there were horrible things perpetrated by people in America, such as broken treaties, slavery, and many types of discrimination. He also experienced discrimination and hurtful, hateful remarks toward him at times in his life, by not only white children and adults, but red ones as well. Why? Because those narrow-minded people saw him as a half-breed, a mongrel. He took great pride in the blood that coursed through his veins, and he knew that America became great because of the assimilation of many societies all poured into the one giant melting pot called America. He decided one of the factors that made America a great nation was because it was a nation of mongrels like him. He felt that his mother was one of the best examples white society could offer, and he also felt like the father he never met was one of the best examples that red society could offer. This tall, good-looking Pinkerton agent had a noble profession, and now he was on his most noble mission. He did not hate Robert Hartwell. He wondered what could possibly motivate a man to be so evil. However, he felt he was on a mission to strike down hatred. The gun hand with Hartwell, in Joshua's mind, was as guilty as Robert Hartwell because he enabled the hatred to continue instead of fighting against it.

Robert Hartwell and Brandy Marks came around a bend a few miles south of Cañon City. The sun was straight overhead, and a pair of breeding golden eagles sailed on the thermals high overhead. In lazy arcs, they swirled around watching the battle brewing down below. They saw Joshua Strongheart standing in the middle of the gulch. Eagle was ground-reined under some trees one hundred yards away. He wore his six-shooter, held his carbine in his left hand, and had another Colt .45 belly gun tucked into his gun belt in the front. So here it was. If Hartwell or Marks stopped now, they would be thought of as yellow, so, unspeaking, both kept moving forward, inching forward toward an appointment with destiny. They stopped at thirty feet.

Strongheart said, "You have a fine horse, Hartwell. I will hold fire, if you want to let him move away."

This actually made sense to the outlaw leader, and he dismounted and removed the bridle, hanging it over the saddle horn. Eagle gave a whinny and the big black horse trotted to him, and the two started sniffing each other. They soon were grazing side by side.

Strongheart said, "Hartwell, the one thing you have done good is take good care of that horse."

The little man thought that it was a correct statement and made sense. It was all he cared about.

Joshua said, "Did you notice that your horse is not pure white? It is pure black. You notice that mine is black and white, and you can look at them. They are getting along fine, grazing side by side. Too bad you never noticed things like that in your life before now. I will tell you this: When you are dead, I will see the horse goes to an owner that will care for it really well."

A shiver went down Hartwell's spine, and he did not know how to respond. He now suddenly felt fear, so he lashed out. Hartwell simply yelled, "You go to hell, Strongheart!"

Joshua said, "Nope, be too crowded in one minute with you two there."

That was their signal and all three seemed to start their draw simultaneously, and Joshua's gun boomed first. Then he fanned his and felt his left leg jerked backward as a bullet slammed into his shinbone. His leg really hurt, but he refused to go down and kept firing. He hit Brandy Marks in the stomach with the first shot, and the man was struggling and panicking trying to get his wind back. The pain was the worst he'd ever felt.

He looked at Hartwell, who had started tearing at his shirt, his eyes bugged out in panic and terror. He saw a bleeding bullet hole in his left chest and another in his lower abdomen above the groin. He could not breathe, but suddenly he could.

Looking at Strongheart he said, in shock and disbelief, "I'm going to die!"

Joshua said, "You wanted to hate. You're going to get plenty of hate where you're going. You deserve to die, Hartwell."

Robert Hartwell felt the worst fear he had ever felt in his life. His eyes rolled back in his head and his face slammed into a rock as he fell forward.

Brandy stared daggers at Joshua as he crumpled into a sitting position, holding his intestines in with both hands.

"You kilt me, Strongheart, damn you to hell," he said, with blood and some greenish liquid trickling out of his mouth. Then he looked over at Hartwell's body and added, "Well, I rode for the brand."

Strongheart said. "You picked the wrong brand to ride for, stupid."

Marks grinned, looked back at the victor, and nodded affirmatively, shrugged his shoulders, and fell forward on his face, dead.

It was late afternoon when Joshua Strongheart, bandage and splint on his lower left leg, rode across the Arkansas a little above the walking bridge. He led the big black Thoroughbred and his pack horse through the cooling rapid water, and over to the Hot Springs Hotel. There was a small crowd waiting to greet him.

His boss, Lucky DeChamps, was there with a cane, Andy Vinnola, Zach Banta, and several deputies and friends he had made. Joshua rode up to them, and they were grinning.

Andy spoke first saying, "Those three you let go were picked up by us as soon as they crossed the river. They are at the jail and have been singing like canaries. They told us about what you did."

Lucky said, "Another bullet?"

Strongheart looked down at his leg and chuckled, saying, "Another scar."

Lucky laughed.

He said, "Where is Hartwell's body? I assume you keeled him, too, *n'est-ce pas*?"

Strongheart grinned. "Sorry, boss, didn't want to load the body. I got a bullet in my shinbone, and besides I figured that buzzards, coyotes, and worms need to eat, too."

Another tall, handsome man stepped out from behind Lucky wearing a broad smile. It was Strongheart's friend, Chris Colt. He stepped forward and the two shook hands, nodding in mutual understanding that only two warriors could comprehend.

He said quietly, "The people want to know what you say, Joshua."

Strongheart grinned and said, "Tell the chiefs, it is done, my friend. Sorry for the friends you lost, Chris, but I'm glad that Crazy Horse sat on you."

Chris nodded and shook again, and walked away toward his horse. Soon, the leaders of several red nations would have the news that the leaders of the Indian Ring were no more.

Lucky said, "We need to get you to the doctor."

Joshua handed the lead line of the pack horse to his boss, and held the lead line now to the big black Thoroughbred.

He said, "I have to run an errand, Lucky. I'll meet you at the sheriff's office."

Strongheart said to Zach, "Zach, there's a good half dozen saddle horses grazing up in Reed Gulch just waiting for some rancher to take them in and give them a home. I'm sure you can find one for them."

Zach, grinning, said, "Wal, I reckon they might like livin' up yonder with them Black Mountain cowboys, if them horses don't mind not bein' chased by a durned posse every month. Ya know some horses get used to that excitement and die of boredom when they jest have to chase cows and such."

He winked at Strongheart.

Lucky took the line and rode away from the hotel.

Fifteen minutes later, Strongheart rode into Scottie Middleton's. The young man was digging holes for his aunt in her flower garden, when she and the boy looked up and saw Strongheart ride up leading the big black Thoroughbred.

Joshua said, "Mount up."

The horse was so tall Scottie had to grab the skirt above the stirrup, jump up, put his knee in the stirrup and pull himself up so he could grab the saddlehorn. Then, he quickly replaced his right knee with his left foot, swung his right leg up and over the saddle. His aunt had tears in her eyes.

Strongheart said, "A man needs a horse, not a pony. He's yours."

Scottie got tears in his eyes and said, "Thanks, Mr. Strongheart! Thank you. Thank you! What's his name?"

Joshua grinned, saying, "Whatever you want it to be."

Scottie smiled and said, "I'm going to name him after you!"

Joshua said, "Strongheart?"

"No," Scottie said, "I'm going to call him Hero."

Strongheart got a lump in his throat and winked at Scottie, tipped his hat to the woman, and rode away at a trot.

He really felt pain in his shin now, and wondered if he got into ragweed, too. His eyes were burning a little and watering a little bit.

He rode toward his meeting with his boss, where he would get his leg nursed and find out what his next adventure would be.

Joshua Strongheart knew one thing. He felt really good about himself.

AFTERWORD

All the items mentioned about William W. Belknap in this novel were true historical facts.

Additionally, Beautiful Woman's recounting of the Battle of the Little Big Horn was based on research I have done by checking into the true accounting of the battle. Instead of reading remarks from those wanting to fulfill presidential aspirations or rewriting military history, I read an accounting and statements by the Lakota, Cheyenne, and Arapaho who actually took part in the battle. They were there, and these were people who did not even have a word in their language for lying. They are Americans, too. Our government has sometimes forgotten that fact. Sitting Bull did, in fact, take part in a sun dance ceremony shortly before the battle, did cut fifty pieces of flesh, and did have the vision described where many soldiers appeared with their heads toward the inside of the circle of lodges, meaning they were killed by the red combatants.

Additionally, George Armstrong Custer did cut his hair

short before the battle because his wife had had a nightmare
seeing a Lakota warrior holding his scalp high in the air. He
carried the shorn locks in his pocket, and the Lakota did not
even know he was there until after the battle. Tom Custer's
body was found with his heart removed, and Rain-in-the-
Face did cut it out and eat it, as he promised he would.

Zachariah Banta in Cotopaxi was real, and many of his
descendants had that same quick wit, dry humor, and ran
cattle all around the Cotopaxi area for many decades before
finally moving the ranching operation to southwestern Texas
in the early twenty-first century via Zach's great-great-great-
grandson Byk Banta. Byk still runs his cattle ranching
operation from the back of a horse.

Sheriff Frank Begley was the sheriff of Fremont County,
Colorado territory in the 1870s, one of many in a long line
of fine lawmen in southern Colorado.

The Underground Railroad was real and enabled thousands of escaped slaves to be channeled into northern cities
and Canada.

Except for Brenna Alexander's home and other obvious
exceptions, all the locations and local histories mentioned
herein were actual places and many still exist today. I have
ridden my horse over almost every piece of land mentioned in
this book and in my other westerns, so you will know it is real
and not a Hollywood movie set. Please come along and join in
sharing with me the rest of the tales about Pinkerton agent
Joshua Strongheart in his future adventures also from Berkley,
a division of Penguin Random House. Strongheart's friend
Chris Colt was the hero of ten westerns I also wrote for Berkley's parent company, Penguin, and they have all been rere-
leased in eBook format by Speaking-Volumes.net. Chris Colt
will be featured in future Strongheart novels, too. Watch for
the fourth novel in the Strongheart series, *The Rider of*

Phantom Canyon, which will be coming along before you know it.

Family illnesses and the subsequent passing of my wife kept this sequel from being published closer to *Strongheart* and *Blood Feather*, but hopefully that is all behind us now and you will be seeing more from Strongheart very soon.

Until then, partner, keep your powder dry, an eye on the horizon, an occasional glance at your backtrail, and sit tall in the saddle. It does not matter if your saddle is a computer desk chair, La-Z-Boy, porch swing, or deck chair on a cruise ship. Many of us grew up with the spirit of the American cowboy and pioneer woman. It is good to keep a door to our past open, so we know where our strength, courage, and tenacity came from. It is the legacy of honor forged from the steel characters blessed by God, who created some of his mightiest warriors in the American west. It is indeed the backbone of America. To this day racism is still a problem in some quarters in America, and it is also a convenient excuse for those who want to stir up trouble for political gain.

If you need me, I will be on my horse up in the high lonesome coming up with more stories for you. That is where I get my tales. They are up there above timberline written on the clouds, and I swear that handwriting looks perfect.

ABOUT THE AUTHOR

Don Bendell is a bestselling author whose style has been likened to Louis L'Amour and Zane Grey; a disabled Green Beret Vietnam veteran; and a 1995 inductee into the International Karate and Kickboxing Hall of Fame. A widower, Don owns the Strongheart Ranch in southern Colorado, named for his number-one bestselling western, and is the author of the sequel *Blood Feather* (Berkley Books, August 2013), with more than three million copies of his twenty-seven books in print.

Don also wrote the Detachment Delta military thrillers from Berkley Books, as well as the Criminal Investigation Detachment trilogy. He has six grown children and eleven grandchildren. Bendell has dated John Wayne's oldest granddaughter, who remains a close friend, and has been likened to John Wayne in some ways regarding his personal code of the West, patriotic views, and love of the cowboy lifestyle.

Don has a masters degree in leadership from Grand Canyon University. Don married again in July 2015 and is also now pursuing a Ph.D. in general education at Walden University.